Walker

a parable

tom walsh

Living Life Fully™ Publications, U.S.A.

2

Published by Living Life Fully™ Publications
United States of America
http://www.livinglifefully.com

To the many people I've known and loved throughout my own walk in life; may the road rise up to greet you and ever give you new and beautiful experiences. And may your eyes and hearts be open to learning all the road has to teach you.

The end is nothing; the road is all.

Willa Cather

Chapter 1

He stepped onto the road in the bright early early morning, just as the sun had finished climbing over the flat western horizon, before it had gained the power to warm the world with its light. He wore no shoes and the pebbles of the road dug into his feet, but he paid them no mind. He stood silently in the road, looking first to his left, then to the right, thinking about which way to go. In both directions the dirt path stretched far beyond his vision, and both ways looked to be about the same.

He stood there for a long time, undecided, and the sun continued to climb. It soon reached that miraculous point at which its rays began to give heat, that point for which people and animals have given thanks forever, and as he felt the first touch of warmth on his right cheek, he felt which way was right, and turned towards the sun and began to walk.

The morning all about him was alive. Birds were all about, singing their beautiful songs and showing off their gift of flight as they went from tree to tree. He watched them in amazement as he walked slowly by. They were of all colors—black and yellow and red and green and blue—and their songs were the most beautiful sounds he had ever heard. He constantly looked about himself, admiring without reservation or limit the world that surrounded him. The sky was a clear, deep blue, and the green of the leaves of the trees rose strongly and gracefully before it. Behind the trees to his left stretched long fields of deep, lush grass that ended only where the sky touched the earth. The trees to his right didn't end—the forest stretched as far as his eyes could see.

He watched the birds fly, he watched the squirrels climb and jump from tree to tree, he watched the rabbits feed on the grasses that sprang from the ground. He saw several turtles making their way laboriously across the packed dirt upon which he walked and upon which nothing grew. He watched bees lumber from flower to flower, and he watched a red fox come from somewhere inside the trees to his right, run along in front of them, and disappear back into them. He watched it all with a growing sense of awe and wonder, and within him was a feeling that he had no words to describe, a feeling like none that he could remember. But that was fine by him, for he didn't feel the need to put into words anything that he saw.

About mid-day, the road became a little bridge, but only for a few moments. It crossed over a stream that flowed softly and smoothly and surely between its low, grassy banks. He left the road for the first time since he had stepped onto it and walked down the bank to look at this new wonder. The water was pure, clear, and cold, as he found out when he stuck his hand into it. He smiled at the feeling of the water flowing against his skin; it was very pleasant, much like the feeling of the breeze against the skin of his body. He watched the sunlight glisten on the moving water, jumping from here to there and back again on the surface, dancing to the sound of the current in the silence of the unspoiled countryside. An occasional small fish swam lazily by, allowing its course to be determined by the gentle flow of the current. Sometimes they would even turn and swim against the current for a moment or two, though he knew not why.

After a long while of watching the stream, he stood and climbed the bank back to the road. He was confused for a moment, for though he faced the same direction as he had that morning, the sun now shone on his other cheek. But he knew the direction in which he had been traveling, so he shrugged his shoulders and began to walk once more. He crossed the bridge and continued on his way, and in his mind were the memories of the water, the fish, the magic of what he had seen and felt. He reveled in the feeling of the sun on his naked shoulders, and saw with no small surprise that he was now preceded by his shadow, which had been following him all morning. Now it slid along the ground beneath him and before him, much smaller than it had been when he had started his journey.

* * * * *

The road kept on and on, always straight, always true. The scenery about him changed slowly and silently, but often. Far to his left, just above the horizon, a mountain range stood still and silent, watching him walk along. He looked at the range often, for the sight of it gave him a feeling of elation, of freedom, though he wouldn't have been able to explain that feeling at all.

Later in the afternoon, the traveler began to notice that his shadow was growing ever longer, and he felt the warmth of the sun diminishing ever so slightly. He stopped and stood still. He had wanted to walk towards the warmth, not away from it. But he had chosen his course, and it seemed that his course was now leading him in a way he had not foreseen, even though it continued in the same direction. The realization was disconcerting, but he didn't let it bother him for long. He had made a decision, he had chosen the direction, and he would stay true to his way. Things were as they were, and he felt no need to change them. He started on his way, smiling at his shadow, which seemed to like his decision for it still led the way. His shadow seemed not to be a big friend of the sun, for it used his body as a shield from it, molding its form to match his, gaining the most protection possible. His shadow was quite intelligent, it seemed.

Soon the day became dusk and a hush fell over the land, the hush of the countryside preparing itself for the oncoming night. The traveler walked on, feeling the first chill in the air and liking the way it felt. The colors left the earth slowly, gradually replaced by shades of grey or black. A light breeze kicked up, brushing tenderly through the leaves of the trees with a soft rustle that brought a feeling of peace with it. A few birds were singing their farewell to the day, and somewhere in the fading light frogs and insects began to fill the evening with their own songs. The music in his ears was wonderful, and he felt happy. And he kept on walking as the first stars appeared in the darkened sky before him, tiny points of light that couldn't be touched. He stopped for several long moments and looked behind him at the last remnants of the day's sun, an orange-red glow that sat softly upon the silhouetted horizon.

It didn't take long before many more stars appeared, and he could see and feel them all as he walked. He felt as if each star were an eye, a friendly eye, looking down upon him to take care of him. He walked a bit more slowly, taking more care because the road was nothing more than a shadow in the starlight. He also wanted to hear all that he could of the sounds of the night, the chirrups of the crickets, the croaks of the frogs, the howling of some far-away something. Several times he heard the flutter of wings as some creature flew above him in the darkness.

Then, several hours after the night had fallen, the sky ahead of him began to glow again. Not as it has done that morning, but somehow brighter, more focused—the light didn't spread all over, as it had before. In a matter of minutes, the moon began to peek over the edge of the world he could see, and soon he was face-to-face with the most wonderful star in the sky. It was huge and round, and it hung just above the horizon, rising very slowly. The countryside around him became brighter, but the colors did not return; he wondered how such a thing could be.

He walked and walked, on and on through the cool, noise-filled night. He had plenty of company. There were rabbits running all about, and he could barely see their forms as they flashed across the road ahead of him. The owls were awake, and their calls flew through the pure night air like the call of a friend, letting him know that he wasn't alone. The moon rose higher and higher, and he waited in vain for the warmth he had felt from the sun. It somehow grew smaller as it climbed the sky and followed the course of the sun, but what the traveler liked best were the stars that shot from time to time across the picture before him, leaving their trails hanging for long moments across the heavens.

When the morning had grown its coldest and the moon was falling in the sky behind him, the sky before him began to glow again. This time, the glow was familiar. He hadn't had any idea of what would follow the moon, but he knew inside that this was the return of the sun he had seen before. The birds began to sing again in expectation of the coming day, and he felt the elation that they must be feeling inside himself. He knew that daylight and warmth would soon be with him, and he found a feeling inside himself that he had never before known—a feeling of hope, of expectation, of anxious waiting, with just a little bit of impatience. The day was coming, and he was joyful. The glow grew brighter, and his smile grew wider as he watched the sky. The colors returned to the world, and he began to notice once more the minute details that had been lost to his sight while the sky had been dark. A forest was there, far off to his right, and the mountains that had watched him all the previous day were gone, left far behind. The grass shone with wetness, and he stopped to examine a blade of grass, now covered with tiny, perfect drops of dew. From where had it come? He smiled as he realized that the important thing was not from where it had come, but simply that it was there for him to look at and admire and enjoy.

He could see the birds once more as well as he could hear them, and having their company made him feel good. The sky once again became a clean, clear, fresh blue, and one small fluffy cloud hung in the air to his right. He watched it as it changed color from grey to orange to white, just as the sky before him changed.

At some time during that morning, the traveler looked behind himself and saw what looked to be a tiny black dot, far, far away on the road where he had been not much earlier. He continued walking, occasionally looking back and seeing that the dot had each time grown bigger since the last time he had looked. After a long time had passed, he could finally make out some details, for the dot had come much closer to him and had become a horse, a cart, and a man. The traveler wondered at the change—what didn't change in the world?—and he stood still at the side of the road, watching the three approach together.

The horse, the cart, and the man all looked to be old and tired, the traveler saw as they came closer. He was amazed that the horse had four legs upon which to walk, while the cart had wheels to roll upon. As for the man, he had legs but he didn't seem to use them at all; instead, he sat on the cart while the horse pulled the two of them.

"Whoa!" the old man said to the horse, pulling gently on the ropes that were in his hands and tied to some metal in the horse's mouth, and that was the first word that the traveler heard. The old man sat on the cart, looking at the traveler; the traveler stood on the roadside, looking at the old man. The man's skin was darker than his own was, and looked to be much tougher than his. He wore grey clothing—a simple shirt, pants, and even shoes, and his eyes were bright and friendly as they regarded the man on the roadside.

"Lovely day, ain't it," the old man asked with not a hint of any inflection that might have made the statement a question. He looked up at the sky with love and took a deep breath of the clean, fresh air, then exhaled slowly, smiling. The traveler smiled back. He didn't understand the words, but he knew what the man had said.

"Looks like you could use some clothes," the old man continued, reaching into the back of the cart and pulling out a small bundle. "You're in luck. These are my son's things, and he's just about your size." He threw the bundle to the ground before the traveler, who kneeled down to pick it up.

He untied the string that held everything together, and the clothes fell out upon the ground. Before him lay a pair of pants, a pair of underpants, a pair of socks, a pair of shoes, and a shirt. All were about the same grey tint as the clothes the old man was wearing.

He looked at the man on the cart to see how he was dressed, then looked down at the clothes that lay before him. They were simple clothes, both on the man and on the ground. He picked up the pants and put them on, then did the same with the shirt, dressing himself as the old man was dressed. When he finished, he was left holding a pair of underpants, and he didn't know what to do with them. The old man roared with laughter—friendly laughter—and he reached down to his own pants and pulled the waistline down at the hip.

"Here's where they go, my friend," he said, and the traveler immediately liked the sound of that word, though he didn't know why. He pulled off his shoes and socks and pants, put the underwear on, then put the pants, socks, and shoes back on.

"A lot more work than you needed," the man said, amused, "but the same result, I suppose. Now you're all set. You ain't going to shock any poor woman out of her teeth now. You want to ride to wherever it is you're going?" he asked, patting the seat beside him. The traveler shook his head instinctively—he would continue walking. He approached the horse, rubbing his hands gently over it flanks, its neck, its back. He felt its power, its age, its dignity—the dignity of a being who had worked hard all its life and earned everything it had gained. He saw the same dignity in the old man, he saw a lot of life and power, but he also saw something in the man that the horse did not have—he saw the smile, the laughter, the spark in the eye, the love of life, the enjoyment of being alive.

"Well, then," said the old man, "I'll be on my way." He slapped the reins softly against the horse's back, and the animal began to move forward. "It was nice talkin' to you," he said, and laughed again. "Not that you did a whole lot of talkin' yourself! It's a nice day for walkin', though—enjoy yourself!" The traveler stood where he was and watched the first person he had met ride slowly away on the road in the direction the traveler himself was going. After a couple of minutes, the old man turned around and waved. The traveler copied his action and waved back.

When the three had once again merged into a single dot, the traveler started walking again, following them, following the road. He walked slowly at first, trying to get used to the clothing he now wore. The shoes on his feet fit well, but they hadn't yet been broken in and his feet began to hurt as he walked. It was the first pain that he felt, and he didn't like it. After some time of suffering, he stopped, took the shoes off, and laid them down at the edge of the road. After several moments of consideration, he took the socks off, also, and put them atop the shoes. Then he continued onwards, leaving them behind.

Chapter 2

The day turned again to night, and night once more became day. The traveler walked on, reveling in the changes, in the songs of the birds, in the clear blue sky and the trees and the flowers and the rivers that he walked past. He became excited at the glances that he caught of animals that he didn't know such as deer and foxes and squirrels and snakes. Time went ever on at its same, unhurried pace, and the world and the traveler followed its lead.

The next day, when the sun was once again at his back and dropping towards the horizon behind him, the traveler saw another spot on the road ahead of him. His interest grew, but he didn't change his pace; he would reach it when he reached it.

It didn't take him long to catch up to it, for the figure he had seen was that of an old woman who walked slowly along the road in the same direction as he. He reached her side just as the sky behind them displayed its first colors of sunset. The woman looked at him, and though she did not smile in greeting, he could see that she was pleased to have met up with someone.

"Good evening," she said to him. Her voice was rough from the use of many years, but still strong and firm.

"Good evening," the traveler repeated as best he could, wondering what the words meant and hoping that he was giving an appropriate reply. They walked on in silence for several minutes, and he looked at her closely as they walked. Her skin was much like that of the man he had met, much rougher than his own and much darker than the other man's had been. Her skin reminded him of the nighttime and the peace and quiet that he felt when the sun was gone.

"Where, may I ask, are you going to?" the woman finally asked, looking at her new walking companion. The traveler understood her meaning, if not the words themselves, but he didn't know how to reply.

"It's a nice day for walkin'," he said, and the woman regarded him closely.

"Yes, it was," she answered cautiously. "Where will you sleep tonight?"

"Sleep?" the traveler repeated, sensing that it was the main idea of her sentence.

"And what about dinner?" she asked, confusing him thoroughly. "When was the last time you ate anything? You look pretty skinny to me—looks like you could stand to get some food inside of you." She looked him up and down as a worried mother would look. "Aren't you hungry?"

"Hungry?" He didn't know what she was talking about, and he didn't know how to ask what she meant. But the entire conversation left his mind as they came to the crest of a hill and could see what lay beyond. That's when the traveler saw the most extraordinary thing he had ever seen, and he stopped in his tracks, his mouth open in surprise and awe. The woman stopped as he did, quite surprised at his reaction.

"It's not such a special village," she said, almost apologetically, "but it's a nice place to call home."

"Home?" the traveler asked, his eyes not leaving the village, liking the sound of this word, too. In the full glow of twilight, the little houses that made up the village stood out dimly against the hills that stood behind them. There were very few of the houses, fewer than thirty, and they were all rather small as far as houses go. They were all white, and each was built in the same style as the others. Each one had one small window in the wall that the traveler could see. In some of the tiny windows the traveler saw light shining, like stars that were almost within his reach. He could see that the houses weren't natural, that they hadn't been created at the same time or in the same way as the hills and the trees and even the road upon which he stood. He watched them, amazed at their strangeness and beauty, as he and the woman came closer to and then entered the village. For the first time, he saw another road leading off the road he knew.

But he didn't have much time to think about the houses or the other road, for very soon they arrived at the woman's house. In the last glow of twilight he couldn't see much of it—just enough to know that it was very small. In a moment, they were indoors. He found it strange to see that the woman closed the door to keep the beautiful night out. Then she lit a candle, and there was light in the room—a much softer light then that of the sun. She lit another, and there was more light. The traveler breathed deeply of the air in the room. It was different from the air he was used to outside. There was a heaviness to it, a mustiness that he never before had felt. There were many odors in the room that he had never smelled, and they all mixed together so that it was impossible for him to identify the source of any of them from where he stood.

He watched the flame rise from one of the candles, and he wondered if that was what stars looked like when one got close to them. The flame was sure and steady, rising up to stand against the darkness.

"Sit down," the woman said kindly, pointing to a chair. He approached it slowly, thinking of the man he had seen before, thinking of how that man had sat on the cart. He sat down. It was an interesting feeling, somewhat pleasant, even. His feet and legs felt different now that his weight was off of them. He looked about the room. It was simple—at one end of it an old wood stove sat against the wall; at the other end was a fireplace. Apart from the chair upon which he sat, there was only another chair and a table in the room, and all were made simply from unfinished wood that had aged many years since being cut. The woman lit a match and started a fire in the stove.

"You must be very hungry," she said. "I don't have a lot, but what I have should fill you up."

The traveler examined the table that stood next to his chair, running his hand over the old, scarred wood. It was smooth to the touch, but there were many wounds on its surface. A cupboard was built on the wall next to the stove, out of the same kind of wood, it seemed, and there was a pile of straw on the floor in one corner. A second door was in the wall opposite the one through which they had entered; it was closed, and he had no idea where it could lead. The woman stood at the stove, stirring something in a large pot, humming softly to herself as she concentrated on her task. He liked the sound of her humming. Suddenly, the flames on the candles flickered slightly, and he watched the shadows in the room rise and fall, twist and squirm, jump from right to left. The only sound he heard was the woman at her work, as she stirred and hummed and threw new things into the pot. He was sure that the humming was a necessary part of the work she was doing.

The inside of the house was cooler than it had been outside, and the woman soon went to the fireplace and started a modest fire. The flames fascinated the traveler—flames in the fireplace, flames in the stove, flames on the candles. Those in the fireplace moved around more, changing places with one another, never standing still, moving around together but individually. On the candles, the dance of the flames was different, completely alone, and every so often the flames stood completely rigid, pulsating with life but not using it a bit.

Soon the woman put two bowls on the table, and a spoon beside each bowl. She then took one of the bowls to the pot on the stove and filled it up; she brought it back and set it on the table, and repeated her actions with the other bowl. She looked at him as she sat down, the first time she had looked him in the eye, and she smiled. He relaxed a bit, not knowing why, but feeling some tension leave his body. He smiled back at her, then looked at the vapor that was rising out of the bowls, dissipating as it rose in the air.

"I do hope you like it," she said, picking up her spoon, her voice comforting to him. "If I'd have know I'd have a guest, I would have brought some fruit for you. But this should fill your stomach up just fine." She put her spoon into the bowl, then lifted it to her mouth and blew on the soup the spoon was carrying. The traveler did as she did. The hot liquid touched his lips, and the pain from the heat caused him to drop the spoon back into the bowl. The woman smiled, again, saying "You have to be careful—it's very hot. Do it like this." She put another spoonful to her mouth and blew even longer, then put it into her mouth.

He was confused. He had never felt anything like the pain of the burn, and he wondered why the woman would do such a thing to herself. For some reason, he started to think of the shoes he had left at the side of the road. But he did as she suggested he do, and found that the taste of the soup in his mouth was pleasant and interesting. There was no pain after he blew longer, and the warmth seemed to be an important part of the taste. He swallowed the soup instinctively and felt its warmth go all the way past his throat and into his stomach. A tingling spread over his whole body, and he liked the way it felt. He repeated the action, again and again, just as the woman did, until the bowl was empty.

"You work up an appetite when you do a lot of walking, don't you?" the woman asked, smiling, as she refilled his bowl. He liked her smile, though out on the road he somehow wouldn't have been able to imagine her smiling. She had seemed too serious, too stern, too weary to be able to do so. But a change had come over her when she arrived at the little house, and she seemed to be almost a different person. Was that what "home" meant? He continued eating, and she continued eating, and soon the pot was empty.

"I guess we were hungry," the woman said. "Did you like it?"

The traveler smiled and nodded and put his hands on his stomach, which was now full—another new, another nice feeling.

"It's not that often that I have the honor of having a guest for dinner," the old woman said. "People don't seem to want to be with you when you're old. People like youth, people like to feel young, to be around young things, young people. Nobody likes to be reminded of death, and we old people are a bit too near death for people to feel comfortable around us. It's always following us around, and others can feel it." Her eyes glazed over, and the traveler was surprised to see moisture well up before her eyes. He also saw that she somehow was no longer with him.

"But I was young once, too," she continued, a smile playing on her lips. In the candlelight, the wrinkles on her face weren't well defined, and the traveler was able to see the beauty of her features that age had hidden— she had once been a pretty young woman, though the only traces of that beauty that remained were in her eyes and in her smile. "It wasn't so long ago, either. Almost like yesterday, in fact. It was wonderful to be young, but I didn't take advantage of it nearly as much as I could have. I never felt the joy of my youth, never loved the youth that I had. I never thought of growing old, of losing my youth. Then it slipped away, before I even knew what was happening. By the time I realized what I was losing, it was gone. And then I spent many years being angry at myself for having wasted it, and I spent those years driving away those I loved." She stopped, and they both sat in silence for quite a long time. Then she closed her eyes and shook her head slowly. When she opened her eyes, the traveler saw that she was once again with him. She sighed a heavy sigh, and the silence in the room grew stronger.

"I guess it's about time I was off to bed," she said, and stood. "You can sleep over here," she told him, pointing to the straw piled in the corner. She opened the second door and left the room, coming back in a moment carrying two blankets. She spread one of them over the straw, then spread the other over the first. "It's not the most comfortable thing in the world, but I suppose it will do. I'm not really so well prepared for guests."

The traveler stood and walked over to the bed, wondering what he was supposed to do. He sat down on it, looking up at the woman, who had turned away. She walked over to a candle, and with a quick puff of air from her mouth extinguished its flame. She walked over to the other candle and did the same thing, and instantly there was only the orange-red glow of the small fire in the fireplace.

"I hope you sleep well," she told him in her rough but gentle voice, stopping at the door and looking back. "Good night." Then she disappeared through the door, leaving the traveler alone.

He sat still for a long time, staring at the coals in the fireplace as they grew dimmer and dimmer. He missed the stars that he had grown used to, missed the sounds of the night as he walked over the road, missed the moon that had accompanied him for so long. He didn't know what the bed was for, and he didn't know why he had stopped.

But he did know inside himself, somehow, that things were as they were, and that he could learn from everything.

Much time had passed when a strange noise began to come from the room where the woman had gone to. It was a strong, low, repetitive noise, and he had no idea what it was. He stood and went to the door, pushing it open the slightest bit. There in the moonlight that came through a small window in the wall the traveler saw the woman lying on her back, a blanket spread over her body, her mouth wide open, snoring very loudly. Her torso moved up and down slightly under the blanket, in rhythm with the sound coming from her mouth. The sound filled the whole room, which the traveler saw at a glance was even more sparsely furnished than the other— it contained only the bed upon which the woman slept and a small table next to it, upon which sat an unlighted candle. He saw nothing else there. He watched the woman, entranced, for several long minutes, then he suddenly understood. He went back to the straw pile, lay down on his back, and pulled the upper blanket over his body to his shoulders. Then he closed his eyes and opened his mouth and imitated as well as he could the sound that the woman made, doing his best to coordinate the sound with his breathing.

Time passed quickly and before he knew it, he heard the sounds of the woman getting up and entering the room. He opened his eyes and stopped snoring, and in the first light of the morning he saw the woman standing in the middle of the room, looking over at him.

"My, you snore loudly," was all she said, and then she started to prepare breakfast. The traveler noticed that her movements were much different than they had been the night before—a bit sharper, fresher, with more energy behind them. In just a few minutes breakfast was prepared and eaten, though this time there was nothing warm, as he had expected and even half-hoped. What he liked about breakfast was the sweet taste of the jam and the smooth taste of the milk that they drank. She had opened her door to find a bottle there, even though he was quite sure there had been nothing there the evening before. He felt that his stomach was once again full, and when everything on the table was gone, he looked at the empty plates and said, "I guess we were hungry."

The woman regarded him rather strangely. "Yes," she said. "I guess we were."

He smiled at her, feeling inside that he wanted to thank her, but not knowing the words for it. He knew that he needed to be out on the road again, for this place wasn't for him even if it did have its good sides. The road was waiting for him, and he missed the nighttime and the feel of the air on his skin. He stood.

The woman looked to the door. "I suppose you'll be going now," she said. "It was nice to have someone to talk to, even if you didn't do much talking back."

He nodded to her, trying to express his gratitude with the look in his eyes.

"You be careful on that road," she said. "You never know who you're going to run into out there."

Chapter 3

As he went out of the village, he studied the houses he walked by. They were made of stone, just like the rocks that he had seen beside the road and on the road and almost everywhere, only these were large and they were piled one on top of the other. The doors were all closed to the world, yet some of the windows were open to let in the morning's cool, fresh air. Through some of the windows he saw people—a woman looked out at him from one of them and smiled a greeting; he smiled back. An old man did some sort of work at a table much like the one at which he had eaten; the man's back was to him, so he didn't see what kind of work he did, nor did the man see him. Through other windows he saw nothing but more walls and other doors inside.

Then he was back on the road, and he knew that was where he belonged. The sun already was up high enough to warm him, and he closed his eyes and lifted his face to it. The heat brought a smile to him, and he once more started to walk towards the sun.

The sky once again was wearing a deep radiant blue, and a soft breeze blew in his face, caressing his skin as it made its way past him. It spoke to him with a soft murmur in his ears, but he didn't understand what it was saying.

As he walked, he had something to think about. He remembered the old man in the cart, the way he had talked, the smile and the laughter he had given freely along with the clothing. Of all the sounds the traveler had heard, the man's laughter was among the most pleasing in his memories. He was sure the old man must be far ahead of him on the road by then, and he was also sure that he would never catch up with him, for he had no cart with an animal to pull it. He thought he would never see the old man again.

His thoughts of the old man led him to thoughts of the old woman, and the seriousness that she showed towards life. He wondered what she was doing as he walked along, and he imagined that she once again must have been preparing something to eat. She seemed to do a lot of that. Or perhaps she was out walking on the road as she had been when he first met her. He didn't know if he ever would eat again, but he knew that he always would have a pleasant memory of how it felt to do so.

The ground on the road hadn't changed at all since he had started, and the feel of it on his feet was comforting. The dirt was packed hard and the pebbles and small stones were scattered all about. He felt the stones only when he stepped on them, and sometimes they gave him a sharp pain that made him realize how nice all the other steps without pain were. Each stone that he stepped on seemed to have its own form, its own personality.

Many, many steps after he started that morning, he saw the first black cloud to his left, poking its head over the horizon. It was beautiful, and he stopped to regard it for many long moments. Before that, he had seen only the white, fluffy clouds that fit so well in the blue blue sky, but this cloud was different. He felt its power, felt the force behind it and within it. It was a thing of beauty with a strength he had never before seen or felt. After he began to walk again, his attention often to his left, he felt the air about him slowly change. The breeze picked up strength and became a wind, and it now came from his left, also. The air grew very damp and heavy, and though he could see no water on himself, he felt that he was wet. His ears now roared with the song of the wind, but he had just as little luck in understanding it as he had had with the murmur of the breeze or the brook.

He could feel the hair on his head blowing about just like the long grass on the side of the road.

The cloud was lonely for a very short time—almost before the traveler noticed what was happening, the entire sky to his left had turned dark dark shades of grey, while the sky to his right remained the vibrant blue of the morning. He was sure, though, that the darkness would soon take over that part of the sky, too, and he looked forward to seeing the world with a new covering. He stopped and watched as the clouds approached the sun, then covered it up completely.

The animals that he happened to see all were running to the holes in which they lived, but he had never seen anything like what was happening. He didn't think of looking for shelter—he saw no need to do so. The clouds were very powerful, and very beautiful.

Then fell the rains. They came with a roar, on the heels of a thunderclap that shook the very land and trees about him. He watched as a sheet of water fell from the sky and enveloped him and everything else. The drops were large, and they were many; in a matter of moments, he was soaked. The drops tried to jump back up towards the sky as they hit the ground, but they were immediately knocked back down by those that followed.

The traveler stepped into the middle of the road, staring up at the sky. The raindrops pummeled him as he stood there in the now-dark world, soaking his clothes and his hair even more, and he loved the way it felt. A bolt of lightning suddenly lit up the world, showing him for a moment that all that surrounded him was now wet, now dancing in the wind, bearing the onslaught of the tempest. The wind whipped through the trees and bushes and grass, driving the rain through them all. A burst of thunder ripped through the black skies, and he wondered just what it was that the sky was trying to say. Whatever the message was, it was being given quite forcefully.

As his eyes readjusted to the darkness of the day, he saw, far ahead of him on the right of the road, a light. He saw it for only a moment, for just then another lightning bolt filled the sky with its brilliance; when it faded, his eyes once again needed to adjust. When they did, he saw the light again. Since it was shining in the direction in which he had been walking, he decided to find out what it was.

Walking now felt very different to him. The road was covered with water, and his feet splashed playfully as he went. In some places, the dirt of the road had already turned to mud, and his feet sank the slightest bit into the road. He found that he had to lean into the wind to avoid being pushed to the side, and the rain constantly beat against him in the gale. It was all new to him, exciting to him, and he liked very much how it felt.

The light that he had seen came through the window of a house. It was a large house, and it stood right beside the road. The traveler stood before it, watching the light in the window, examining the building. He could see very little in the dark, but the flashes of lightning that came from time to time showed him that the house was made of stone at the bottom and something he didn't recognize above the stone. Even the stones were different—they weren't like the ones on the road or those of the houses of the woman's village, but these were all the same shape and fit together perfectly. They were stacked evenly to form a flat wall. There were several windows in the wall, but the light came from only two of them—those which were much lower than the other two. He could see that through both windows the same room was visible. A door stood between the windows, and above the door was written a single word which the traveler could neither read nor comprehend. It was written in black letters that stood out strongly with each flash of lightning: "Welcome."

Suddenly a form appeared in one of the windows, then almost as quickly disappeared; in moments, the door opened and much more light poured out of the room into the darkness, but the traveler couldn't see where it went. A man stood in the doorway, motioning for the traveler to come nearer. "Come in! Come in!" the man yelled over the gale. The traveler started forward, walking on the smallest road he had seen, the road that led from the road he had been on to the door of the house.   This road was made of the same stones that much of the house was made of, and the surface was very hard beneath his feet.

The man touched him on the shoulder and led him into the house. The warmth inside the room was pleasant and comforting after the wetness of the storm. He hadn't noticed just how cold it had become outside. The man quickly closed the door behind them.

"My, my!" he exclaimed, looking the traveler up and down. "Aren't you a sight! Quite a storm we're having, isn't it?"

The traveler smiled and nodded.

"Of course, the man continued, "I personally like storms. They make things much more interesting. My wife hates them—says they're horrible. I disagree. But we've got to get you out of those wet clothes, don't we? You wait here just a minute. I'll be right back." He left through a door that stood open in a corner of the room, and he was back quickly, carrying a bunch of clothes in his hands. He handed them to the traveler.

"Put these on," he said, pointing to another door. "You can go in there." The traveler went through the door into a room that was very dark; the man followed him into the room and reached up and touched something that was sticking out of the wall. A light suddenly appeared in the air above the traveler's head, just like the one that he had seen in the other room, just like the moon at night, only brighter. The traveler looked at the light in amazement; even more than it looked like the moon, it looked just like a small sun, only it was inside. He looked behind himself and saw that he even had a shadow.

The man noticed his astonishment and shrugged. "It's just a light," he said. "When you get the wet stuff off and the dry stuff on, come on out—I'll have a cup of hot tea ready for you." He closed the door, and the traveler was alone.

He took off his wet clothes slowly, looking at them. They were so different from the clothes that he had put on—they looked nothing like they had before. They were much heavier, and water dripped from them onto the floor. They had no shape anymore, but just hung in a soggy mass until he dropped each piece to the floor.

He picked up the towel from the top of the pile the man had left on a table. He unfolded it, only to discover a puzzle. How was he supposed to put it on? It wasn't like any of the other clothes he had worn or seen before. He held it up to his chest, letting it fall lengthwise to the floor. That was fine for the front, but what about the back? And how did the other clothes fit? He pulled the towel away from his body, then noticed how dry his chest was. He held the towel to his shoulder for a moment, then pulled it away to find the shoulder also dry.

In a minute he was completely dry, and the towel was very wet. He dropped it onto the pile of wet clothes and quickly dressed himself. These clothes were softer than the others had been, more comfortable. They felt very pleasant as they rubbed against his skin. He stood there, fully dressed, and looked about the room he was in.

The walls and the ceiling of the room were white and smooth, whereas the floor was a deep brown, made of long strips of something that looked familiar to him, somehow reminding him of the trees. The strips were laid down next to each other, forming a smooth and shiny surface that reflected the light from above him. There were three chairs in the room, but they were nothing like the chairs in the old woman's home. These were made of the same material that the floor was made of, but on the chairs the material was carved into ornate designs, and the chairs were beautiful to look at. Two of the chairs stood on either side of a large box made of the same stuff as the chairs and the floor, but of a much lighter hue. The other chair stood next to a small bed that looked similar to that on which the old woman had slept, so he knew what it was for. Lying on top of the bed was a beautiful cover of many colors, which were arranged to look like the flowers he had seen so many of on the road. He reached out to touch it and found that the cover was just as soft as the clothes he was wearing.

Just then he heard three soft knocks coming from the other side of the closed door. As he slowly approached the door, the knocks were repeated. He reached up, and knocked softly three times on his side of the door. After a moment of silence, the door slowly opened and his host stuck his head and shoulder and one arm inside the room.

"Are you alright in here?" he asked, sounding concerned. The traveler nodded his head. "I thought you'd fallen asleep or something," the man said as he came into the room and picked up the wet clothing. "Come on out in the living room—I've got the tea all ready." The traveler followed him into the other room and sat down in the chair the man motioned to.

The chair was soft and comfortable, very pleasant to sit in, and he immediately thought back to the old woman's house and the rickety old chair he had sat in there. He wondered why she hadn't had a chair such as this new one, since it was such a nice feeling to sit in it. It was covered with a soft red cloth, though he could feel something hard beneath the softness. The part on which he sat was even softer than the parts on which his arms rested, and he had sunk in several inches when he sat down.

"You're quite a strange one, aren't you?" the man asked as he brought in a tray laden with many things. He set the tray on a small table that stood between the traveler's chair and another just like it. "You seem to understand what I'm saying, but you don't talk. I'd say you were somewhat slow, but I can see in your eyes that you're not." He paused and stared at the traveler, who stared him back straight in the eye.

"Can you talk at all?" the man asked finally.

The traveler broke eye contact with the man and stared into the fire in the fireplace, deep in thought. In a moment, his face brightened and he looked back at the man. "Quite a storm we're having, isn't it?" he asked.

The man stared at him for a moment, then his face brightened with a smile. "I see," he said, nodding his head. "I see. You're just learning, aren't you?" The traveler nodded. "But you understand what I'm saying, don't you?" Another nod. The man sat back in his chair, still regarding his guest.

"Well, son, my name is Kennison. Do you have a name?" The perplexed look on the traveler's face gave him all the answer he needed. "Kennison," he repeated, pointing to himself. "I am Kennison. Do you understand?" The traveler smiled and nodded.

"Kennison," he said, pointing at the man.

"Good!" Kennison exclaimed, and reached out to pour tea from the pot that sat on the tray into two cups that also sat on it. "Now we've got to come up with a name for you, I guess—supposing, of course, that you don't have one already. Do you have any preference?" The traveler shrugged. "Well, what is it you do?" Kennison asked. "Many of us get our names from our professions." The traveler shrugged again. "We could call you something like 'stranger' or 'traveler,' but neither of those words sound like names at all." His brow wrinkled as he though, and he looked down at the floor. About half a minute passed, then he looked up.

"I've got it!" he said, looking at the traveler. "Do you walk everywhere you go?" When the traveler nodded, Kennison reached down and picked up both cups of tea, handing one to the traveler. "Then we'll call you 'Walker.' Doesn't sound like much of a name—most people have two or three, you know—but that's okay. It'll do just fine. No, no—hold it by the handle, like this," he said as he noticed the pain register on Walker's face. "Sip it very slowly, too, so you don't burn your tongue. And blow a lot." He demonstrated how to do so, slurping loudly as he did.

Walker raised his cup to his mouth and copied the slurping sound that Kennison had made.

"Come now, my friend!" Kennison exclaimed, smiling. "You've got to drink some of it, too. The slurping's only half the fun!" He demonstrated again, and Walker copied.

They sat in silence for a while, listening to the music of the rain pounding on the roof of the house, slurping at their tea, staring into the flames in the fireplace that were keeping the room warm. As he set down his empty teacup, Walker finally broke the silence.

"I guess we were hungry," he said.

Kennison's eyes grew wide in amazement. "You do talk!" he said happily. "It looks like you've got a ways to go to learn *what* to say, but it's a start." He put down his teacup. "Now you see, we were drinking. You drink when you're thirsty. You should have said, 'I guess we were *thirsty*.' Had we eaten something, of course, then you would have said what you did."

"I guess we were thirsty," Walker said, smiling. He was enjoying the lesson. He had never heard so much speech before, and he was soaking it up eagerly. Kennison seemed to be a good teacher, for he was patient and kind, so Walker listened attentively as he spoke, repeated when he was told to repeat, spoke when he felt he should.

Time passed quickly thus, and before they knew it the rain stopped. Looking out the window, Kennison noticed the sunshine on the leaves of the tree in the front yard.

"Oh, come quickly, Walker!" he exclaimed, jumping up from his chair. "If we're lucky, we're going to have us quite a treat right about now." He rushed over to the door, threw it wide open and ran outside, not even looking to see if Walker was following him. He stopped in the middle of the road, looking up at the sky with eyes that reflected a great sense of awe. He turned back to the traveler as he caught up with him, and Walker saw tears in his eyes. Kennison lifted his arms and pointed, turning his face back to the sky.

"Look," he said quietly, and Walker looked.

Walker discovered what it was to lose his breath. Up in the sky, stretching almost from one end of the horizon to another behind Kennison's home, hung a huge double rainbow, completely unbroken. For several seconds he forgot to breathe, then his breath escaped him in a sigh of wonder. The sky behind the arcs was black and strong and angry, but the rainbow formed a fence that shielded them from its ferocity. Before them the birds flew through the air, which felt much fresher, much cleaner than it had before. Their songs filled the sky, and a light breeze wafted against Walker's face. Up above, spots of blue shone through the clouds, and the sun felt warm and comforting on his skin.

They stood in silence for many minutes. Neither of them wished to move. The rainbow began to fade slowly, its colors losing their sharp edges, its outline becoming indistinguishable. Soon it was gone, and Kennison and Walker looked at each other and shared a smile.

"You know something, Walker?" Kennison said, and Walker felt a trace of sadness in his voice. "Everybody in the world is one of those, even more beautiful than the one we just saw. Unfortunately, most people don't allow that part of themselves to shine through because the storms inside of them overpower the beauty. How beautiful the world would be if we all could learn to let the rainbow shine through."

He turned and walked slowly back to the house. He stopped at the porch, turned, and breathed deeply of the storm-cleansed air. Then he went inside. Walker looked down the road upon which he now stood once more, in the direction he had been heading when he stopped because of the storm, then followed Kennison inside, stopping on the porch and breathing deeply before he entered the home.

"Now that the storm's over," Kennison said, sitting down once more in his chair, "I reckon my wife will be home soon. She'll be pleased as punch to meet you, and she can cook us up a wonderful dinner. I'd do it myself, but she doesn't allow me in her kitchen. Can't say that I blame her—prevention is always the best cure for bad food."

They continued talking, and Walker continued to learn to speak. Very quickly and eagerly he learned, and Kennison taught just as eagerly. Soon Kennison's monologue became a dialogue and they were talking to each other, though not without a great deal of effort on Walker's part to form thoughts into words and Kennison's part to understand his guest's meaning and correct him when necessary.

Before they knew it, they heard steps approaching the door and voices outside. Kennison jumped up.

"They're here, Walker!" he cried out. "They're finally here!"

Walker stood, regarding Kennison with a questioning gaze. "They?" he asked. "Who are 'they'?"

"Why, my wife Gloria, of course!" Kennison replied, hurrying to the door. "And since I heard two sets of footsteps and voices, that means she brought my little granddaughter with her!" He threw open the door, and a very little person yelled "Grandpa" and rushed through the doorway, jumping at Kennison, who reached down and caught her, lifting her high above the floor, high above himself. The face on the little person was softer than those on the adults Walker had seen, and it was full of life and excitement. The child's eyes sparkled brightly as she looked down at Kennison, and the sound of her giggling filled the room in a very pleasant way, reminding Walker somehow of the many brooks and streams he had passed by.

"Hello, sweetheart!" Kennison said, and Walker was surprised to note that he spoke to the smaller person in a voice much different from that he had spoken to Walker with. "How's my little princess doing?"

"I was scared, Grandpa," she said, her expression growing serious. "The storm was so strong, and I thought it would never go away."

Kennison set her down on the floor and kneeled before her. He seemed to have grown younger since the little one had entered the room, and Walker wondered if Sweetheart was somehow able to give her energy to others.

"Don't you worry, little lady," Kennison told her. "You just always keep in mind that storms always pass. They may be long and frightening and hard to get through, but the sunshine will always come around again." He put his face to hers, and touched his lips to her forehead; then, with a light smacking sound, he pulled them away. Sweetheart smiled, then looked up at the woman behind her.

So enthralled had Walker been by the child that he hadn't noticed the woman who had walked in after her. She was standing behind the girl now, regarding Walker with questions in her eyes. She was shorter than Kennison, but taller than the old woman he had seen the day before. Her features were not as hard as the old woman's had been, and the traveler felt an openness with this woman that he hadn't felt before. Her clear green eyes and her expression calmed him, and he knew immediately that he liked her just as he liked Kennison.

Kennison looked up just then and followed her gaze to Walker.

"Well, I'll be!" he cried, standing, still holding on to Sweetheart's hand. "I almost forgot that I had a surprise for you ladies. This is Walker—at least, that's what I call him. He was out walking in the storm, and I invited him in. He doesn't talk too much, but he's learning. I think you'll find, honey, that he's quite an enjoyable enigma." He took a step closer to his wife and put his lips to her cheek. "How was the walk home, honey?"

"Muddy," she said, glancing at him, "but beautiful. Did you see the rainbow?"

"Rainbow? 'Did we see the rainbow,' she asks. Tell her about the rainbow, Walker."

"Nothing else in the world like that," Walker said, slowly and carefully. "It was beautiful."

"You see!" Kennison exclaimed. "You see how well he talks now? Didn't say a word the whole first hour he was here. But give him some time with me, and he'll be bending your ears before you know it."

"That I don't doubt one little bit," Honey said to him, then approached Walker with her right hand extended. "I'm very pleased to meet you, Walker. I'm Gloria. Welcome to our home."

"Thank you," Walker replied, confused. If Gloria was her name, then why did Kennison call her "honey"? "I'm very pleased to meet you, too. . . . Gloria." He said her name in the form of a question, almost, though nobody seemed to notice his confusion.

"Well said, my boy!" Kennison said. "You'll be a walker *and* a talker here pretty soon. And this here's Tricia, my granddaughter."

"Hello, Mr. Walker," Tricia said, and Walker noticed a great change in her—she was no longer the cheerful bright little person she had been, but she spoke to him in a much more subdued manner. Walker was concerned for the first time, afraid that he might somehow have caused the change in her. Kennison noticed his concern, though.

"She's a bit shy around strangers," he said softly to Walker. "You just have to give her a bit of time to warm up to you."

Walker extended his hand to Tricia. "I'm very pleased to meet you, Tricia," he said quietly, and Tricia shook his hand and gave him a small smile.

"Now that introductions are out of the way," Gloria said, clapping her hands together, "is anyone interested in something for dinner?"

"Absolutely!" Kennison said. "And if you need any help, you just let me know!"

Gloria smiled. "There'll be none of that, now. You'll help us best by staying in here and keeping Walker company." She took Tricia by the hand. "We can take care of dinner on our own!"

Kennison winked at Walker. "Didn't I tell you?" he asked with a chuckle.

Chapter 4

The meal that Gloria served was much different from the one he had eaten the night before with the old woman. This one was served on a plate, and there were several different things on the plate, not just soup in a bowl. There was also bread that they all shared and different utensils and glasses full of a white liquid that they called "milk." Walker watched the others eat and learned quickly from them.

Tricia warmed up to Walker almost as soon as they started eating, and in no time her exuberance was back. She began asking Walker question after question, and soon became quite frustrated when she realized that Walker had few answers for her.

"What do you mean, you don't know where you're from?" she asked indignantly. "Everyone knows where they're from. Don't they, Grandpa?"

Kennison, who had been listening intently to his granddaughter's interrogation, shrugged his shoulders.

"I would have said so myself, a few hours ago," he replied, "but I'd say we ought to believe our guest when he says he doesn't know."

Tricia thought that over for a moment, then turned to Walker. "Then you don't have any parents or grandparents?"

Walker shook his head and shrugged simultaneously. He had no answer.

"And no brothers or sisters?"

Again a shrug.

"What about friends? You have to have friends somewhere, don't you?"

Walker looked to Kennison with a helpless look on his face, and Kennison chuckled. "It looks, Trish, like we may be the first friends this man has." Walker smiled when he heard that, and Tricia looked from her grandfather to Walker and then to Gloria in amazement.

"You mean that you don't have anyone else in the whole world?" she asked. "What would have happened if you hadn't met us?"

Walker wasn't sure what the "whole world" was, but to him it sounded vast. "I don't know," he said in answer to her question, still pondering the concept of a whole world.

"That's one of those things that are kind of useless to wonder," Gloria told Tricia gently. "You see, he *did* meet us, and he is here now, and we are his friends now, and there's no way of ever knowing what might have happened if he had just walked right by our house because he wasn't meant to do so. So many different things could have happened that almost any guess you make could be right."

"But now you're here and now you're our friend," Tricia told Walker, who smiled broadly back at her.

"Thank you," he said.

"You're welcome," she replied matter-of-factly, and then stood up and started clearing the dishes from the table, as everyone had finished eating.

"Thank you, dear," Gloria said, putting her plate on top of the ones that Tricia was holding.

"You're welcome," Tricia said again, and took the plates into the kitchen.

Gloria turned to Walker. "Why don't I show you where you'll be sleeping," she said, and stood. Walker did the same, and he followed her as she led him to the room where he had changed clothes before.

"We don't often have guests these days, but the guest room is still made up and ready for you. I hope that you'll find the bed to be comfortable—most people who sleep there do. Here are a couple of towels that you can use when you take a bath. The bathroom's the next door over." She slid past him and went back into the hallway to the other door, which she pushed open. "I think you'll find everything you need in here—there's soap and shampoo." She stopped speaking and regarded Walker curiously. "You are familiar with baths, aren't you?" she asked.

Walker shook his head. "No, I'm not. What's a bath?"

Gloria smiled. "I had a suspicion. This here is a bathtub, and you fill it with warm water like this," she said, reaching and turning the knobs. "This one is hot water, and this one is cold. When you turn them both on, you can make the water as warm as you'd like. When the tub is full, you take off all your clothes and get in it. The water helps you to clean yourself, and the soap there helps, too. Make sure you rinse all the soap off of you, or it's very uncomfortable. Do you understand so far?"

Walker nodded. "Yes. It looks very—interesting."

"I guess you could call it that. Now, after you feel that you're clean, you get out, dry yourself with one of the towels, and you put your clothes back on. Then you're finished." She thought for a moment in case she had forgotten something. "Oh, yes—always have the door closed when you do anything that you have to take your clothes off for. I'm not sure why, but that's just the way it's done. Do you understand?"

"Yes, I do. What's this for?" he asked, pointing to the toilet.

Gloria's eyes widened, and she seemed to be at a loss for words. She looked closely at Walker. "You're serious, aren't you?" she asked.

Walker nodded.

"Dear!" she called aloud to Kennison. "Could you come here a moment?" Then she spoke to Walker. "I think this is something that my husband could explain to you much better than I."

Kennison came into the bathroom. "What's up?" he asked.

"Walker isn't familiar with a toilet or what it's for," Gloria said. "I think I'll leave you men to discuss this one amongst yourselves."

"Oh, my," Kennison said in surprise. "Oh, my! Now how do I go about this one?"

Walker shrugged again, surprised at Kennison's awkwardness. He smiled, trying to put Kennison at ease. Kennison laughed, at a loss for words.

"Well, I guess we've gotta do what we've gotta do," he said.

A few days later, Trish invited Walker to see her secret place, her favorite place in the world. Walker was intrigued, for she had been telling him about the place for two days, but between going to school and doing her chores, she hadn't had time to take him there. Walker wanted to find out how someone could keep a place secret from other people. Trish's explanation of what the word "secret" meant left him a bit confused, but early one morning she and Walker set off to visit the spot.

They started out through the field behind the house, and Walker saw that they quickly left the road behind them—it was the first time that he couldn't see the road when he wanted to. He felt something new, but he didn't know what it was. He wanted to see the road again, he wanted to know it was still there, waiting for him, ready for him.

Tricia saw that there was something on his mind, and she saw that he glanced backward from time to time. "What's wrong?" she asked, stopping where she was and looking Walker in the eye. But he had no words for it. Something inside of him was making him uneasy; something was making him restless, and restlessness was a feeling with which he was entirely unfamiliar. He didn't yet have the words to explain to Trish just how he felt, even if he were able to figure it out. He felt even worse because he saw the concern in her eyes, saw the feeling inside of her that she wanted to help him, that she wanted to do something to ease the confusion she saw in his eyes.

He shook his head and smiled. At least he could do his best to make her feel better. "Nothing's wrong," he said quietly as he followed her across the field. "It's just a strange feeling inside, I guess."

She smiled back at him, and he could see that she wasn't completely convinced that there was nothing wrong. She changed the subject.

"My secret place isn't really a secret, you know. I know that lots of other people go there and sit and enjoy it. But I like to go there and just be quiet and listen to everything that's going on inside my head. Grandpa says that we all have storms going on in our minds, but that almost none of us ever take the time to slow down and listen to what's going on in there. I think that's why he's such a nice man, and I think that's why he's always happy—he listens. He listens to me whenever I need him to, and I love that about him. It's interesting, though, because Grandma doesn't listen the way that Grandpa does, but she's just as happy as he is."

"They're different," Walker said.

"Yeah—you're right," Tricia replied. "They're different people and different things make them happy. They're such nice people to be around, though—I couldn't imagine my life without them, to be honest with you."

They walked on in silence for a long while. The field soon gave way to thin forest, and Walker reached out and touched the trees as he walked past them. Touching them was much different than just looking at them, he noticed, and he wondered why that was.

Tricia stopped next to a small tree, no more than a foot tall.

"You see?" she asked, kneeling down beside it. "This is what trees look like when they're tiny, when they're very young. They come from seeds"— she reached out and picked up a small acorn from the ground—"like this, and when the seeds are planted, they send roots into the ground and trunks and branches and leaves up towards the sky. The roots seem to do most of the work, and they get stuck underground while everything else gets the sunshine and wind, but I guess when a storm comes along, the roots are pretty protected, while the top of the trees may get blown over or hit by lightning or something. It's a strange relationship, Grandpa says."

She looked up a Walker. "I'm not sure why I'm explaining this to you," she said, "but you seem to know even less about stuff than I do."

"I don't know why," Walker replied thoughtfully, "but I think I know less about everything than everyone else knows. I think that will change, though. I'm learning very quickly."

"That's sure true," Trish agreed enthusiastically. "Just a few days ago, you couldn't even talk. "Now look at you!"

Walker looked down at himself, perplexed. Tricia laughed.

"It's just a saying," she giggled. "It means 'look how far you've come.'"

"I think I've come very far. But I think I still have very far to go." With those words, he felt the pull inside of himself again, and his mind went back to the road.

"It's that feeling again, isn't it?" Tricia asked. "That feeling that you don't know what it is?"

Walker nodded.

"Then come on—we have to go see my spot, and you have to do what Grandpa says—you have to listen to it." She started off quickly through the trees that grew thicker and taller the further they went. Walker watched in amazement as the sunlight grew dimmer as it fought to make its way through the leaves and branches of the trees that towered above him; where the light did hit the ground, it shone even brighter than it did outside the forest, in sharp contrast to the dimness that surrounded it. The colors in the forest were beautifully muted, not as bright as the colors outside, but with their own elegance, their own vitality, their own life. The sounds in the forest were trapped—they couldn't fly off into the empty space of the fields and roads, so they sounded more intense, somehow closer and more personal. Walker found that the songs of the birds meant even more when they were shared with him in this more intimate setting, this beautiful place that was full of life and energy and oxygen—as he breathed, he could feel the strength enter his lungs and course through the rest of his body.

Tricia walked on for five more minutes, not saying a word, but sometimes she looked back to make sure her companion was still with her. Then she stopped, turned around, and put a finger to her lips.

"It's right over this rise," she said quietly. "Don't make any noise, because sometimes there are deer at the pond, or some other animals. They're really pretty."

She took his hand in hers and led him forward, over the rise, towards the sound of falling water. Walker felt the air become wetter, cooler, and the ground changed as they walked—it was covered with moss, and more and more mushrooms grew near the water. As they crested the rise, he saw a beautiful small waterfall that poured into a pool of dark water. The pool was surrounded by bushes and trees that thrived in the humid air, and Walker felt a great sense of peacefulness come upon him and Tricia as they approached the water. Tricia let go of his hand and walked slowly to the water's edge, seemingly entranced by the place.

She turned to Walker and smiled. "Grandpa says this place is holy," she said quietly, "because this is a place that's full of God."

"God?" Walker asked.

"Uh-huh," Trish said. "God likes places like this because they're peaceful and beautiful. You see, he gave us a world that's peaceful and beautiful, but we've turned it into a noisy and ugly place, so it's harder for us to get to know God. So we have to find places like this where we can talk to God and get to know him better."

Tricia stopped and examined Walker's face. "You don't know who God is, do you?" she asked. He shook his head and shrugged. "Well, then, you'd better sit down, because Grandpa told me all about him, and I'll tell you what he told me. But it's not just what Grandpa told me—a lot of it's what I know myself, inside. Grandpa says we have to trust the feelings we have inside more, because then we'll know more about the world and we'll trust life more."

Walker sat down on a large rock, and Tricia sat down on a rock next to his. They sat quietly for a few moments, listening to the music of the water, watching the sunlight that filtered through the leaves and danced upon the ground and the tree trunks and the rocks and the water.

"Grandpa says that God made the world," Tricia started, "and I think he did a pretty good job. Everything's so pretty, and there are so many nice people in the world that it's a great place to live. One of my friends says that her dad says that the world's a terrible place, full of evil and bad things and bad people, but I think it's sad to look at the world that way. He doesn't sound very happy, and I think he makes himself that way. Grandma says that bad people choose to be bad, and that there's plenty of bad in the world, but that doesn't mean the world's a bad place. She says that the bad people are here to help us to learn and to grow. If we didn't have any obstacles to get over, we wouldn't change as people, she says, so we have to have bad people."

She looked over at Walker and saw the confused look on his face. She thought a moment, then laughed. "Oh, yeah—I started talking about God, didn't I? I guess I didn't say much about him, though.

"You see, God isn't a person, like you or me. I'm not sure what he is—he's just God. But he's the one who made you and me, so that we could live here on this world and learn what he's put here for us to learn. I don't know what that is, yet. You see, God wants us to be happy here, so he gave us all these beautiful things. But I think the thing he wants us to learn the most is trust, and that's why we have to trust God, even though we can't see him or talk to him or anything. Grandpa calls it faith, and he says that the whole point is to learn to have faith in someone who's there, but who we can't see.

"When we talk to God, that's called praying, and we pray to him to thank him for everything and to ask him to help us, to protect us. I pray every night when I go to bed, and I think I pray when I come here, but I'm not really sure—I just kind of talk to God, you know? Kind of like I'm talking to you right now, except we can't see him.

"Grandma and Grandpa say that there are people who believe there's no God, but for me, I know he's there. I feel it inside, and I have to trust that feeling. I think life would be very empty without having God there with me. If I just come here, it's just a place. But when I come here and talk to God, it's like I'm sharing something beautiful with a friend. Life's so much better when we share it." She stopped and sighed loudly, putting her chin on her knee.

"Do you have someone to share things with?" she asked Walker.

He shook his head, still thinking about what Tricia had said about God.

"No," he said quietly.

"Is it lonely, not having anyone?"

He shook his head. "No," he said. "The world is still beautiful. And right now, I have you."

Tricia smiled. "That's true." She looked up at the trees above them. "Can't you just feel how quiet it is here?" she asked, and Walker smiled. They sat quietly, enjoying.

They passed half an hour that way, not saying anything to each other. After a few minutes, Walker realized that he could hear Trish breathing, that he could hear his own heart beating in his chest. The silence was incredible, and the birds that sang closely and at a distance didn't seem to interrupt the silence at all—they complemented it, strengthened it in a way he didn't understand. The water kept on falling, but that sound also did nothing to interrupt the stillness. Walker didn't understand it, but he enjoyed thinking about it.

"Grandpa calls it 'harmony,'" Tricia said, "when things work together so well that you almost don't even notice the separate parts, you just see it or hear it all as one thing. That's harmony."

Walker nodded. He almost asked Tricia how she had known what he was thinking, but he realized it wasn't important.

"He says that's what God is, too—harmony. And that people who can't see or feel God can't see or feel harmony—they only see all the separate parts, and they can't see how everything works together.

"He says that as I grow up, people will teach me to see all the separate parts, and I'll see less and less of the harmony as I grow older."

"Why?" Walker asked.

"I don't know," Trish replied. "But he says I have to try to keep seeing the harmony as much as I can and not see the world like most of the adults do. I'm going to try to keep seeing it."

"I think you should," Walker responded, watching the water fall from the edge of the rock into the pool below it. "It's beautiful this way."

The next morning at breakfast, Walker had news for Trish and her grandparents.

"I must leave," he said quietly, looking Trish in the eyes as he spoke. Then he looked to Kennison and Gloria, feeling a sense of sadness inside with the realization that he wouldn't be seeing them any more.

"You can't go!" Tricia protested. "You just got here!"

"I must," Walker repeated. "Yesterday, you taught me about God and about harmony. And you taught me that I have to listen to the feelings inside of me. I feel inside that I must go and follow the path before me—I just have to go. I don't know how to explain it."

"You have to be walking," Kennison volunteered, "just as you were when we met you."

"Yes."

"I understand," Tricia said quietly and sadly. "I had a feeling yesterday, when you looked back when we were in the middle of the field. You don't want to get too far from the road, do you?"

Walker shook his head. "I have to be on the road. I don't know why. I don't have any memories, like you have like you've told me about. Just the road, and an old woman, and an old man who gave me clothes. And now you. And beauty. A lot of beauty."

"Will you remember us?" Tricia asked.

"You will always be with me," Walker told her with a smile, "and I will always be with you. And we will see each other again. I'm sure."

Gloria stood. "I'll make you a bag, then, of things you'll need. Food, and a blanket at least."

"Thank you," Walker said.

Chapter 5

Walker left after breakfast. The sun's light filled the sky, but the horizon still hid the sun from his view for the time being. The air was chilly, and there was something different about the way he felt—the way the air felt. It wasn't the same early-morning air he had felt in the morning before arriving at the family's house, but he couldn't figure out just what the difference was. He also knew that he wasn't the same person who had arrived at the family's house; he wasn't sure, either, of just what the differences in him were.

All he knew for sure was that the morning was beautiful, as all mornings were. The air was fresh and he could breathe deeply of its aromas as he walked.

The first difference in himself that he noticed was that he was carrying something new with him—he had many more memories in his mind, and as he walked these memories played themselves over and over in his head. Memories of the family, memories of the old woman and the way she ate and talked and snored, memories of the friendly man on the cart who had given him clothing. He remembered falling asleep for the first time at Kennison's house, and he remembered the feeling of waking up in the morning. He remembered how hunger had started to visit him once he began to eat, and how it felt to satisfy that hunger. He also remembered learning how to speak and how to understand when he was spoken to, though it didn't seem to be learning as much as it was remembering something that had been there inside him already.

He was amazed at how real the memories felt, how close he felt to the people who were in his mind. The pictures that he imagined were crisp and clear and perfectly detailed, and the sounds he heard from the past were true in every way. He understood a bit better the way that Kennison had felt when he sat in his favorite chair, reminiscing as he stared into the embers of the fire. He understood why the man had such a wistful smile when he did so—the joy of memory coupled with the inability to bring times back was a bittersweet sensation, indeed.

He also knew why Tricia's eyes had always been so wide—she was storing up memories of her own, refuge from the trials of tomorrow, saving them up in a place in her mind where nothing could get to them to break them or take them away. She had much time ahead of her, he knew, and he was sure that she would have many wonderful memories saved up by the time she got to be her grandparents' age.

He also knew that there were many more memories that would take their own places in his mind, and he looked forward to making them a part of himself, whatever kind of memories they might be.

By the time the sun began to warm his skin, the house was nothing more than a memory itself—though he strained his eyes as much as he could to see it when he turned around, there was no house there to be seen. Another memory, and he was surprised to find that even though he held the memory of the house and the people quite clearly in his mind, he still had a desire to see his friends again, to speak with them again, to touch them again. He felt something inside urging him to go back, to leave the road and spend more time with them—but it was a feeling that hadn't been there when he had taken leave of the old woman or when he had watched the cart disappear into the distance. Tricia had said "I'll miss you," and he realized that the feeling inside of himself was the same one he had seen reflected in her eyes as she had uttered those words. He sighed deeply, turned and forged ahead on the road.

For the road was all he had then, and it stretched ahead of him just as it had before he had stopped and spent time with the family. Now that he had left them, he knew that he needed to focus on where he was and what he was doing, or he might miss something very important—something might be there for him to see or hear or feel, and he didn't want to miss any of it.

All around him, the world was alive, from the grass that grew next to the road to the birds that flew above him and sang as they sat on the branches of the trees. Now he had names for most things, names that he shared with many other people, it seemed. It seemed strange to him that everyone would call a certain animal a certain name, for certainly someone could think of other names to call things.

He shifted his pack to his other shoulder. He carried with him food and water now, and he wondered why he hadn't needed them before. He hadn't known hunger until he had eaten with the old woman; he hadn't known thirst until he had drunk. For every new experience he learned of he seemed to learn a consequence of that same experience, no matter how pleasant the experience was. When he learned to sleep, he learned that he sometimes grew tired in the middle of the day, something that hadn't happened before, or he felt that he needed to go to bed rather than stay up and continue an enjoyable conversation.

Several hours into the day, he noticed that the road ahead of him seemed to end—it climbed a hill, then ended in the middle of the air. He knew that it probably kept going down the other side of the hill, of course, but how could he be sure? He smiled as he thought about it—what would he do if the road didn't continue? Where would he go then? What would he do? He was pretty sure he didn't have to worry about it, but it was interesting to think of.

Then it struck him—the language he had learned had given him another way of thinking, another way of looking at things. He remembered very few thoughts from the time before he had language—he had had many impressions, reactions, and feelings, but the language he had learned had given him the ability to think of things that he couldn't see, that he couldn't hear, that didn't even exist. Just a few days earlier, he would have just looked at the road; he would have just seen it and followed where it led. Now, though, he was thinking about what would happen if the road stopped existing.

Did the words give him this power of thought?

He continued walking; he had nothing else to do, and he knew it was right to do so. So he walked, and he thought. And as he thought, he noticed that his preoccupation with the thoughts was turning him inwards; he wasn't seeing nearly as much as he had seen on the road before. During his first few days, he had seen everything, had felt the aliveness of the world around him, had felt as if he were a vital part of it. Now, his eyes often fixed themselves to the dirt of the road before him as he walked, and at times he would walk a considerable distance without seeing anything except the dirt. He stopped as the thought came to him, and he turned around.

That tree—the magnificent tree that stretched so gracefully and powerfully into the sky, surrounded at its base by a field of colorful and playful wildflowers—how had he missed that? How had he walked right past it without seeing it?

And what else had he missed that he never again would have the chance to see?

Tricia's words came back to him, about her grandfather's warning that she would see less and less of the harmony as she grew up.

Was he growing up? he asked himself with dread.

And if this was growing up, did he want to do so?

The thoughts perplexed him—he felt a certain power in them, a certain sense of wholeness, but he also saw how they isolated him from the world around him.

He tried to stop them, but now that he had the thoughts, he couldn't stop thinking. He found that he just started thinking about not thinking.

He turned back around and started walking once more. It was all so confusing.

A few minutes later, all the thoughts were thrust from his mind as he came to the top of the hill he had seen. Almost from one step to the next, his perception of the world changed, for suddenly he saw stretched before him a mountain range much nearer to him than the other one he had seen, and all words and thoughts of words left him. Even his breath left him for a few moments as the sheer magnificence of the sight made him stop walking and stop thinking. The mountains stood far in the distance, but they stood gloriously, watching over all the world around them. As Walker gazed upon them, letting his eyes move from one end of the range to the other, he felt something stir inside of him, a feeling that he could find no words for, a feeling of insignificance at the sight of the range, but a feeling of belonging as he realized that the mountains were just as much a part of the world as he was, and that he was just as much a part of the world as the mountains were. He was sharing the air and the sunlight and the breeze with the most beautiful sight he could imagine, and his view of the world had changed forever.

The land before the mountains was flat; he could see that he had much more walking to do before he reached the base of the mountains, so he would have a lot of time to look at them, to think of them. The sky behind them was pure blue, with not a single cloud to be seen.

Walker looked back at the hill he had just climbed. It had been rather steep, but it hadn't been difficult to climb. The mountains, though, looked different. There was much more "up" to the mountains, and he wondered if he would find a road leading to the top of the mountains so that he could go down the other side.

He realized, though, that the question meant nothing at the moment— he would find out the answer when he got there. Instead of thinking about it, he sat down on the grass next to the road and watched the mountains.

"Pretty magnificent, isn't it?"

Walker started—he must have been sitting there longer than he thought, because he hadn't seen anyone approaching. He turned to see a man, much younger than Kennison, standing on the road and staring at the mountains.

"Every time I come to this hilltop," the man continued without waiting for a response, "I feel as if I've been born all over again, like I'm looking at the world through a completely new set of eyes."

"Yes, it's beautiful," agreed Walker.

The man turned to him and extended a hand. "My name's Amar," he said, quietly but confidently. Walker took his hand and shook it, looking closely into the man's eyes.

"I am Walker," he said.

This man's body was different than those of Kennison and Gloria and Tricia and the old woman and the man on the cart—his skin was deep black, and he was much thinner overall, and his face was rounder than their faces had been. But looking into his eyes, Walker saw that there was no difference there at all, other than the difference of distinct personality. Amar's clothing was simple and colorful—a bright red shirt hung down below the top of a bright blue pair of pants. His shoes were brown, and Walker could see his feet through holes in the front ends of them—he never before had seen sandals. His hair was short and very curly, very close to the skin on his head, and his smile was wide and bright and full of energy and life and laughter.

Amar looked back into Walker's eyes. "I see you are a friend," he said. "Shall we walk on together?"

Walker looked about himself, then nodded. He picked up his bag, and he and Amar began walking towards the mountains.

"What do you mean when you say that you see I am a friend?" Walker asked after a few minutes.

Amar regarded him. "Do you mean to ask what I mean by 'friend,' or do you want to know how I know you are a friend?"

"Both," Walker replied.

"That's a part of life that's easier to know than to say," Amar said, "but I will try. I will start with 'friend.' I believe that my definition is not much different than that of other people. A friend is a person who will help you, who will be there when you wish them to, simply because they know that you are a fellow human being who needs help from time to time. A friend is a person who loves others, and who loves you for who you are rather than for what they can get from you.

"I find that many people make the mistake of thinking that we have only a few friends in our lifetimes, but those are the friends with whom we share a special closeness. In truth, the world is full of our friends. Our friends are all those people who want the best for the world and other people. All those people who want bad, who want to hurt others, those people are friends of nobody, least of all themselves."

"Bad?" Walker asked. "Hurt?"

Amar looked surprised. "You are unfamiliar with these terms? Then either you haven't been in this world long, or you're unfamiliar with the language." He laughed. "Though I see that neither of these possibilities can pertain to you." He looked back at Walker. "Although now that I think about it, who's to say? Appearances rarely tell a person's history."

Walker looked perplexed. "Then how is it possible to see in my eyes that I'm a friend?" he asked.

"Because the eyes are where one sees the spirit of another person. If a person is full of anger and hatred and suspicion, then that person's eyes show those things, and I will know that this person cannot become a friend until he lets go of those emotions that keep him from becoming the person that he was meant to be."

"I don't understand," Walker said. "Aren't we made the way we were supposed to be?"

"I believe that we were all made with the potential to be the people we're supposed to be. We all have souls and we all have minds and we all have wills. Many people look at the world and see a beautiful place full of potential and love and beauty—those are the people you want as friends. But many people look at the world and see a place that hurts, that causes pain, that destroys and corrupts. Those are the people you don't want to have as friends, for those are the people who will pull you down with them, who will fill your mind with similar thoughts, who will turn you from a positive person to a negative person. Unfortunately, these are the people who most need friends, but it takes a very special kind of person to befriend them. God made us all with the potential to be positive people, contributing to the growth of this world, but many people choose to be negative, diminishing the light of those who wish to do good."

"Why?" Walker asked.

Amar sighed. "Because, my friend, it's easier. It's unfortunate, but it is true. It's much easier for a person to think that the world will not let her advance, because then that person will not have many expectations of herself, and it's easier to fulfill low expectations."

"Expectations?"

Amar looked closely at Walker, then thought for several minutes before he spoke again.

"My friend, it seems that I was mistaken when I said that you were familiar with the world and the language. An expectation is quite simply the way you see your future. If you see a future for yourself that is rich in expectation, then you see a future for which you must work, for which you must put forth a great deal of effort. If you expect little in your life, though, you will have to do a minimum amount of work, and it will be much easier for you to reach any goals or ideals that you've adopted as your own. For example, I am a teacher, and I've wanted to be a teacher for as long as I can remember. When I was a child, I expected to become a teacher, even though I knew that I would have to spend many years studying in order to reach that goal. Studying has never come easy to me, so I have had many rough years, memorizing things that did not want to stay in my mind and being tested on material that was difficult for me to understand. But I was fortunate—my parents and I had high expectations for me, and I was willing to do the work to meet those expectations.

"On the other hand, one of my friends when I was younger was very lazy, and he tried always to do everything with as little effort as possible. His parents tried to encourage him, but they were unable to do so. He has accomplished nothing in life, for he has never had the desire to accomplish anything. He has always been a nice man, but he is very dissatisfied with his life. And he is dissatisfied because of his own actions and decisions—he had few or no expectations of himself, so he has accomplished nothing.

"A third type of person feels that the world owes them, and feels that they are entitled to the best the world has to offer, without any sort of effort on their part. These people often accomplish many things through the effort of others, and when they finally decide to look inside themselves to see what they've done with their lives, they often find that they haven't done much of anything at all.

"None of these people are bad, though, and any of these people may make good friends. The bad people are the ones who hurt others for their own gain or to compensate for their own hurts or fears. They are the people who cause pain in others, who discourage others, who use and abuse others. These are the people who most need love and friendship, but their very actions cause people to avoid them, for people know that being around this type of person can cause them much misery in their own lives. Often these people are angry at the world or at other people, and they want to make others suffer to make up for the suffering that they've gone through themselves. Somehow, they believe that this gives them satisfaction and power, but the truth is that any time they hurt another person, they are adding to their own dissatisfaction, and thus to their own pain."

"But if God created us all with the possibility of loving, why don't we all love?"

"That, my friend, is the question of the ages. I believe we all don't love because we are each free to work towards our potential, or work away from it. We know in our hearts what is right for us, but we often ignore that, instead looking for success as other people define it. Many people blame God for their circumstances, but they're like the child who is in a room full of toys who cries because there's nothing to play with. The world is full of possibilities, not limitations, yet we have to decide if we're going to look at the potential or the limits. This freedom that we have can be beautiful, allowing us to live life fully, or it can be a terrible sword, cutting us off from our true selves."

"Possibilities . . . not limitations," Walker repeated to himself.

"Yes, my friend—if you can remember that, your view of the world will never cause you sorrow or pain. Remember, though, that not all possibilities are for all people, so one should not become discouraged when one tries to do something, but fails. One must merely look elsewhere to find another possibility that may fit better."

Amar stopped suddenly, stretched his arms above his head, and looked around. "Are you hungry, my friend? It's mid-day, and we still have much walking to do. We have a stream here for water, I have some food my wife packed for me, and we have a beautiful mountain range and some friendly trees to keep us company. This is about as perfect a spot as we'll ever find."

"Yes, I'm very hungry," Walker said. "And you're right—this spot is perfect."

Amar walked over to the stream, then knelt and pulled a cup from his pack, filling it up with stream water. Then he knelt next to the stream and splashed the water on his face, wetting his hair, then on his arms and chest.

Walker went to a spot near him and stuck his hands in the water—its coldness shocked him, but he tried to ignore it, and he splashed water on his face, as Amar had done. The act shocked him so much that he lost his breath for a few moments. Amar laughed as he watched him try to catch his breath.

"You must be careful—cold water shocks your body. This water comes from those mountains, from very high up, where it used to be snow. It moves very quickly, so it doesn't have time to warm up before it gets down here."

"Snow?"

Amar gazed at Walker with a kindly expression on his face. "Ah, my friend, you seem to be quite the enigma." He walked back to a flat spot and sat down, holding his pack in his lap. "Where are you from?" he asked Walker.

Walker remembered the question, but he still had no answer. He shrugged his shoulders.

"You don't know. Do you realize how unique that is, that a man does not know where he is from? I know nobody who does not know his or her origin. But let me take that back—I now know only one person in my entire life who does not know where he is from. You are very unique."

"Everybody is unique," Walker said. "We are all different."

"Yes, but you are blessed to be a bit more different than the rest of us." He pulled some food from his pack, unwrapping a large sandwich and splitting it in two, handing the larger half to Walker. Walker was surprised, but only for a moment. He reached into his bag and pulled out a block of cheese that Gloria had packed for him. He split it in two and gave the larger half to Amar. They both smiled, and they thanked each other, then ate in silence, gazing at the mountains.

Soon they got up and began to walk again, and Amar taught Walker the names of many of the plants and trees and animals they saw as they walked. Walker noticed that he saw things a bit differently after he had learned their names—they had a new aspect to them, something they hadn't had before. Or was the change in him? It made little sense to him, for he knew that the sparrow that he saw before he learned its name and the sparrow he saw after he learned its name were the same creatures, but the way he saw them was different. The daisies he had seen earlier were the same flowers as those he saw after Amar taught him their name, and they hadn't changed in essence, yet they had changed in some indefinable way. He asked Amar if he knew what was changing.

"You are putting the world in order—you are learning some control over the things you see by naming them. Be careful with this, Walker—it's not always such a good thing."

They walked together for several hours more until another road branched off perpendicular to Walker's road. At the intersection, Amar stopped.

"This is where we must part ways, my friend," he said, extending his hand to Walker once more. "I live down this road, and I see that your future lies upon the road before you. I thank you for your company, and for the pleasant time we've been able to spend together."

"I thank you," Walker said. "Good-bye, my friend." And as he looked into Amar's eyes, he knew what Amar had meant, for he saw that he was, indeed, a friend.

"You will always be in my heart," Amar said, then turned and started up the road.

Walker continued on. As he walked, the sun started going down behind him, and the light about him began to change in tone and texture. It softened, and everything the light touched also seemed to soften, to mellow, to deepen. Even the mountains before him changed in the new light, and they looked to be completely different from the mountains he had been watching for hours. The sky turned pink in places, orange on some of the clouds closer to the horizon, and the sun turned red behind him as it started to hide below the flat land that he had just walked over. As he looked back at it, he thought of Tricia and Kennison and Gloria, and he wondered what they might be doing at that moment. He wished that he could share the sunset with them, for he knew that they would truly appreciate it, but that was no longer possible.

After the sun was gone, he found that the chill in the air was deeper than it had been before he had spent the nights indoors. It was his first evening outside since he had stayed in the old woman's home, and though the temperature seemed to be about the same, the air felt much colder on his skin. With food had come hunger, with sleep had come tiredness, with language had come introspection, with shelter and comfort and warmth now came discomfort and coldness. He pulled a blanket from his pack and put it about his shoulders, then he yawned as the first touch of sleepiness came upon him.

Within an hour he was lying in a small crevice between rocks in front of a small fire, wrapped in the two blankets that Gloria had packed for him. He looked up at the sky, marveling at the beauty of the stars that made the darkness much less dark.

Chapter 6

He awoke with the sunlight the next morning, the chill in the air reaching through the blankets to his skin and even further inside of him. It wasn't an uncomfortable chill, but it was enough to make him wonder what it would be like if the air were to be any colder. He thought back to the nights when he had walked all night long, and he smiled at the memories of the beauty that he had seen in the moonlight. With that thought, he jumped up in surprise, scanning the sky above him—there had been no moon that night—he hadn't seen it at all before he had fallen asleep.

What had happened to it?

But the sky was already light, and there was no moon to be seen—he would have to wait until nightfall, then look for it once more. Perhaps he had gone to sleep too early, and his friend had appeared after he had closed his eyes for good. He couldn't know.

He ate a piece of the bread and cheese that Gloria had packed for him, and drank some of the water from the bottle she had also put in the pack. He stood and looked back at the road that had brought him to that place—it was a very long road, and he knew that he couldn't see all of it. He had walked an entire day's journey since leaving Tricia and her family behind, and he knew that if he wanted to go back, it would take another entire day's journey to get there. He was surprised at the idea of going back—it was the first time he actually had thought about turning around and retracing his steps, about going the opposite way on the road. Somehow, the idea didn't seem right, and he didn't know why.

As the sun began to emerge from behind the mountains, Walker started out. He walked towards the sun, towards the mountains, which were quite a bit nearer than they had been when he had first seen them.

The air of the morning was fresh and chilly, and he was glad for the heavy shirt that Kennison had given him. The world around him was still very flat, as if nothing dared come out of the ground in sight of the majestic mountains that watched over their domain. There were very few trees, but there were still plenty of birds around to keep him company. Their songs were thrilling, bold and alive and celebratory, and Walker was grateful that they were willing to share their songs with him. Once he saw a herd of small animals not too far off, and when he saw them start to move he was surprised at the way that they jumped into the air as they ran, almost as if they were playing, celebrating the energy and aliveness that they had inside of them. He wondered what it would be like to feel that kind of excitement, that kind of energy, and he wondered why he didn't seem to feel it.

About an hour after he started, when the sun was starting to warm up the world, he came across a trio of people walking in the opposite direction. He saw them much earlier than he met them, and he watched them as they came closer to him. He was sure that they must be watching him in the same way as he came closer to them.

Walker was surprised when they met. There were two men and a woman, and he hadn't seen anyone as dirty as those three people were. Their clothes were dirty, their hair was dirty, and when they got close to Walker he could smell an unpleasant odor that he had never smelled before.

"Good morning," Walker said with a smile, but they didn't respond. They merely looked at Walker with expressions in their eyes and on their faces that Walker had never seen before.

Suddenly, he knew just what Amar had meant when he had said that one could tell one's friends by what one saw in their eyes. Walker didn't want to be with these people—he wasn't judging them, but he didn't feel comfortable in their presence, didn't see anything in their eyes that could make him want to be around them. In fact, something inside of himself was telling him that he needed to stay away from them.

Physically, they looked much more like Kennison and Gloria than like Amar. Their skin was light, and they weren't as thin as Amar, and their hair fell to their shoulders instead of being close to the skin. The two men were about Walker's height, while the woman was as tall as the men's shoulders. Their clothing was dark and heavy, and it looked as if it had been grey at one time but now was much darker because of the dirt that covered it.

Their eyes, though, made the strongest impression on Walker. Their eyes were clear and bright and blue and their gazes were piercing, and for the first time, Walker felt nervous in the presence of other human beings. He didn't know what caused the feeling inside of him, and he couldn't put a name to it, but he knew that he wanted to get away from them.

Instead of stopping, as they had done, Walker kept on, picking up his pace as he walked by them.

"Wait," he heard one of the men say. "You shouldn't pass by us so rudely!"

Rudely? Walker wondered what the word meant, wondered why they thought he should stay with them if he felt so strongly that he should leave.

"Do you have any money for us?" the other man called out as Walker continued to walk, moving further and further away. "Do you have any food?"

Walker kept going, and he heard the three of them start laughing as he continued on his way, not looking back at all.

But the eyes of the three stayed with him. How could such a simple thing—other people's gazes—make him feel so torn inside? How could an encounter that lasted only a few seconds leave him feeling so cold, so lost inside? It made no sense.

Why hadn't he wanted to talk with those people? They were human beings, just like the old woman and Kennison and Gloria and Tricia and Amar, but somehow, they weren't like the other people he had met. He wished that Amar or Kennison were there with him, for he knew that one of them could explain to him what had happened. He thought of what Amar had told him about seeing a friend in the eyes, and the different kinds of people that one runs into. He especially thought about what Amar had told him about people who were full of anger and hatred and suspicion, and people who tried to hurt others for their own gain, and while he really had no idea what the terms that Amar had used actually meant, he was sure that he had just witnessed that very thing on the road in those three people.

After several minutes, he turned to look behind himself, and he saw that the three had continued in the same direction they had been heading. He felt relieved to know that they were getting further and further away from him.

By late afternoon he was much closer to the mountains. He had started to walk by many houses like Kennison's. Each one was different, though. He saw that they had many similarities—doors and windows and walls and chimneys—but they also had many differences. Some were very wide, while others were thinner; some had large windows, some had small; some had brown doors, some had green, some had blue; some were tall, with windows above windows.

Before he knew it, he was in the middle of a small town that seemed to envelop the road. Many, many roads led off to the right and left, and Walker had to pay attention to make sure that he stayed on the road he was supposed to be on. At one point he stood in a small square, surrounded by buildings, and two roads lay before him, stretching out into the other side of the town, both of them leading more or less in the direction he wanted to take. Walker felt the heaviness of a new decision upon him.

But his decision was put off when a man standing in a shop doorway noticed him standing there.

"Good afternoon!" the man said enthusiastically. "You look like you have a choice to make." He left the doorway and approached Walker, his hand extended. Walker took his hand, and shook. He didn't know why, but it seemed the thing to do. He liked it.

"Yes," Walker said quietly. "I must choose a road to take."

"Ha!" the man said with a smile. "Welcome to life! We all have that choice, almost every day." The man was a bit shorter than Walker, with thinning brown hair atop his head. His face was strong and friendly, with deep furrows on his cheeks when he smiled. His teeth were white and strong, and his green eyes held a sparkle that made Walker think of Tricia. His body was stout and strong, and Walker thought that he might have been the strongest man he had seen.

Walker thought the statement over for a moment. "I don't understand," he said.

"It's easy," the man said, obviously glad to share his ideas. "Roads are metaphors. I mean, they exist, of course, but they're always a means to an end for most of us. We just use them to get where we're going. One day we'll die, which is our ultimate destination, and all our lives up until the point when we die can be seen as a road through time.

"Unfortunately, most people see the destination as the most important part of any journey, and they neglect to see all the beautiful things that surround them while they're on their journey."

"I didn't see a tree yesterday," Walker replied thoughtfully. "It was beautiful—it rose into the sky as if it were trying to touch it, and the light from the sky made its colors and shadows very strong. I walked by it—I didn't see it until I turned around."

"You were probably so caught up in thinking that you didn't even see the world around you."

Walker's face showed the surprise that filled him. "How did you know that?"

The man smiled. "Because that's how we are," he said simply. "I do it all the time, myself. We think too much and see too little. We speak too much and listen too little. But that's our choice. Unfortunately, most people don't realize that they're making the choice until it's too late to go back and change anything. It's quite a shame, though. Think about it—if you missed that tree, there are many other beautiful things that you probably missed also. But you'll never know about them because you didn't turn around like you did with the tree."

Walker looked at the man as if he had just been told terrible news. He had thought about that before, but hearing the same idea come from someone else made the idea stronger, and he turned and looked back at the hills he had just come through outside the town. He stared back, thinking about all he had seen, wondering about all he hadn't seen. Then he turned back to the man.

"It's sad," he said quietly.

"Yes, it is," the man agreed. "But it's past. And now you still have your future. You can try not to do it again. Have you been traveling long?"

Walker shrugged his shoulders. "A while," he said vaguely, not because he wanted to be vague, but because he wasn't at all sure of the answer.

"Are you traveling right now?" the man asked.

"Yes," Walker replied, turning towards the fork in the road. "I'm—"

"No!" the man interrupted emphatically. "The answer to that question is 'no!' Don't make that mistake my friend. Right now, you're talking to me. And even though I may not be the wisest man in the world or the best company around, you must try to get all you can out of every 'right now' in your life."

Walker felt that he wanted to argue, to tell the man that he hadn't meant it that way, but he realized that the man was right. He wasn't traveling at that moment.

"I see," he said.

"Yes, you do!" the man cried. "I can see that you do. That's pretty rare, you know—most of us take much longer to see the sense behind ideas like that. You look like an honest man, with a great deal of integrity. How would you like to work for me for a while? I own this bakery, and I've been looking for some good help for quite a while. You won't get rich, but you'll have a place to stay, and you can earn some money to take with you when you travel again."

"Money?" Walker asked, his mind immediately going back to the three people he had seen earlier on the road. He could see in his mind the looks in their eyes that had disturbed him so much.

"You seem startled. What is it about money that makes you react so?"

Walker told him about the trio, about the look in their eyes, about the feelings he had.

"Yes, I see," the man said when he was done. "You were right not to stop. People like that aren't the kind of people you want to spend time with. They'd be just as content to kill you as to walk five miles with you. And they look at money as a tool, as a manipulative tool, as power, as a way to control people. Most of us look at money as something functional, something that helps us to trade our talents and abilities for the goods we need in a very simple way. But I'll tell you what—why don't you come in for a sweet roll and a cup of tea, and we can talk about work. What do you say?"

Walker looked at the roads he might take, then looked at the man's shop, then back at the man. He realized that he trusted this man who reminded him very much of Kennison and Amar.

"Yes," he said. "I will work."

"Good to hear!" the man said. He took Walker's hand and shook it again. "By the way, I'm Ehrlich—Gustav Ehrlich, and it's very nice to meet you, Mr. . . ."

"Walker," Walker replied. "My name is Walker—I have only one name."

"Well, Walker, I think you'll enjoy the job. It's a lot of work at times, but baking is God's work, you know—feeding the people who need food to live."

"God's work?" Walker asked, and Ehrlich smiled.

"Well, no more than farming is God's work. Or medicine, or dentistry, or motherhood, or any of the other jobs that people do. We'll talk about it—I think you and I will have many good talks. But come—let's have that tea and sweet roll, and we'll talk about the job and pay."

"Very well," Walker consented, then followed Gustav into the bakery, wondering what kinds of memories he was about to make to take with him when he went on. As he stepped through the door and smelled the wonder of the baked goods, he already knew he had made the right choice.

Chapter 7

The job with Gustav Ehrlich turned out to be rather simple—Walker had to follow directions and do what he was told. He became fascinated with the work very quickly, as he mixed the flour and the sugar and the salt, as he learned the different types of bread and the different ingredients that went into them. Why did this bread take eggs, while this other took no eggs, but needed milk? Why did they include yeast in the recipe for this bread, but not in another? More than anything, he loved smelling and tasting the results of their work. The taste of hot fresh bread was one of the nicest sensations he had experienced, and it never lost its beauty. Getting up as early as they needed to was no problem for Walker, for he loved to see the sunrise each morning through the window of the bakery.

He was also amazed at how the flour stuck to his arms—the first few times he worked with it, he wasn't quite sure that his arms hadn't become completely white for good, that he hadn't changed himself by working with the flour. When he worked with it for a long time, it got in the air and floated all about him, and he loved to look at himself in the mirror at those times to see how the flour had gently settled on his hair and face and shoulders. It always brought a smile to him when he saw his reflection then.

The most wonderful thing about the bakery, though, had to be the oven. It was immense, and it took an entire hour to heat up in the morning. That was one of Walker's most important jobs, filling the bottom level of the oven with wood and getting a healthy fire going as soon as he woke up. He loved to watch the fire catch, usually very slowly, creeping along a piece of wood until it covered it fully, then turning the wood to black as the wood spent its energy. The heat was beautiful, too, especially early in the morning when there was a chill in the air.

Ehrlich noticed Walker's fascination with the flames.

"It's beautiful, isn't it?" he asked Walker one morning. He picked up a piece of wood. "Fire isn't quite clear to me, but I think I have a pretty good idea of how it works. You see this piece of wood?" He handed it to Walker, who examined it closely. "It's nothing. It's dead, for all practical purposes. But it's full of potential, just like you and me.

"You see, the flame is nothing more than a catalyst that allows the wood to expand to its potential, that allows it to release its energy in the form of heat. When the wood is lying on the ground, it expends no energy, but it is full of potential. That potential is converted either by animals and insects that eat of the wood, and thus turn the potential into energy that drives their bodies, or by flame, something that allows the energy actually to be energy, as opposed to potential. Anything that burns is the same way—full of potential, yet until the flame is applied, it can be nothing helpful, nothing worthwhile. Potential does nothing to help anyone—it's the fulfillment of that potential that becomes helpful to the whole world.

"You and I are very similar—every person on this planet is full of potential, yet unfortunately, few people ever reach their full potential. Do you know why?"

"Because they have no fire?"

Ehrlich smiled. "Precisely. Most people sit around, doing the same things over and over, waiting for some sort of catalyst to come along and turn them into fulfillment of their potential. They don't understand that the catalyst rarely just comes to them—they must go out in search of it, and they must actively try to find it.

"And many people, as soon as they find that catalyst, they try very hard to put out the flame, because they're afraid of what's going to happen when the flame engulfs them completely. They have the opportunity to reach fulfillment of their potential, yet they shy away from allowing that potential to break free. They want complete control over the fulfillment of their potential, not realizing that it's only in the letting go of the control that they can ever find the fulfillment.

"Still others, sadly, spend their entire lives running from the flame, never letting it touch them, for their fear is so strong that they cannot live fully. They spend their lives in darkness, fearing the illumination of the flame that would allow them to see through the darkness that they choose for themselves."

Walker stared at the wood in his hands. His eyes ran over every curve, every split, every grain, every aspect of the thing. It did, indeed, seem dead in his hands, but he knew what would happen if he were to put it into the fire—it would catch along with the other pieces, and add its heat to the heat of the rest of the wood, adding to the energy that filled the oven and turned the mixtures of flour and water and egg and salt and whatever else was in there into something edible, something that was a necessary part of the community.

"But when the energy is gone," Walker asked, "what then? The wood is gone."

"Then we find more wood," Ehrlich replied. "But that, my friend, is the most beautiful part—we humans are like wood in that we have potential that may or may not be reached, but we have the extraordinary ability to replenish our energy. On the purely physical level, we can eat, and we can sleep, and our bodies can continue on, with just as much energy as before, perhaps with even more.

"Our spirits, though, are renewed every time we feel satisfaction with an accomplishment, every time we hear the words 'thank you,' every time we see the positive results caused by something that we've done. Our spirits are a wonderful gift, yet we spend very little time trying to make our spirits grow, trying to develop them, trying to help them reach their potential. People will spend years learning information or processes or knowledge, but very few learn about the higher part of ourselves."

Walker was thoughtful. "This spirit," he asked, "do I have one?"

"Of course you do, Walker. And yours is strong—as strong as a child's, I would say. Somehow, you haven't allowed it to weaken, as most of us adults have. I work very hard to keep my spirit healthy, to keep it as healthy as a child's spirit. It takes a lot of work, though—I have to think all the time about ideas that I wish to accept or reject, about actions I wish to take or not take, about people I wish to spend time with or avoid—there are so many ways that we can hurt our spirits, and for some reason, it seems that most people search out the ways that most harm them. Usually, it seems to come down to fear."

"Fear must be very strong, if people can make themselves unhappy because of it."

"Well, the relationship between people and fear is much trickier than that. It may be simply a difference in words, but people don't make themselves unhappy because of fear—fear enters them and causes them to make themselves unhappy. But you're right, my friend—fear is probably the strongest element on this planet, for it controls a great number of people."

"Can you tell me more about fear?" Walker asked.

Ehrlich smiled. "You'll learn more about fear than you want to. Right now, we have bread to make."

Walker smiled. He couldn't imagine learning more about anything than he wanted to—every little bit of information that he learned opened up an entirely new realm of knowledge of which he knew nothing. He loved it.

He also loved working with the customers and working with money. He quickly learned the principles of multiplication and addition and subtraction and division, and he was astonished at the perfection of numbers and the perfection of the principles that governed numbers. He respected the money because Gustav taught him to respect it, but he found that he wasn't quite sure whether he liked it or not—something about it made him feel a bit uncomfortable, something about the way some people looked at it and watched it as he counted change.

He met all kinds of people. He met housewives doing their daily shopping, and he met men and women who worked all day long, who came in for lunch or breakfast or something to take away the strength of their hunger until they were to eat a full meal. At first, he was a bit unsure around the customers, for he wasn't completely sure how he should act around them, but he watched Mr. Ehrlich—as his customers called him—and saw that he was as comfortable around his customers as he was around anyone else. Walker soon found himself feeling a connection to all of the customers.

"They're all human beings," Gustav told him, "just as you and I are, and they deserve to be treated as such—with all the dignity and respect and courtesy that we're able to give them. They may not all act nicely all the time, but those who don't are the ones who are hurting the most."

Walker saw that people treated Gustav Ehrlich very well—with much love and respect—because Gustav Ehrlich treated them with love and respect.

One of his favorite people was a woman he met on his first day there. He was sweeping up the front of the store early in the morning, and the woman came in to buy bread for breakfast. She was different than Gustav and Kennison and Gloria—her skin was smoother, her body somehow stronger—she seemed to have more energy than the other people he had met, other than Tricia, but she wasn't as small as Trish. Kennison had called Walker a young man, and when this woman walked into the store, Gustav greeted her with a hearty "Good morning, young lady!"

"Good morning, Gustav," she said, then turned to Walker. "Good morning," she said in a voice as kind as any he had ever heard. "It's very nice to see a new face in our village. Welcome. I'm Marie." She held out her hand to Walker, who took it and shook. Marie was just as tall as Walker, and she was heavier than most of the women he saw in the village, but she looked to be very healthy, not fat. Her black hair fell straight to the small of her back, and her blue eyes were almost challenging, but welcoming at the same time. Her smile put him immediately at ease, and he was impressed by the way it seemed to brighten up the room. Shaking her hand was different than shaking the men's hands had been—she put very little strength into her grip, and Walker let go almost immediately, afraid to hurt her hand.

"I'm Walker," he said quietly, drawn deeply into her eyes as she gazed at him. Suddenly, he was sure of what Amar had told him—this was a friend, someone he could trust with anything. And not because of any special connection between them, but because of who she was. He had seen something similar in Gustav's eyes, but not this strong.

"Where are you from, Walker?" she asked, "and what brings you to our village?"

"I was going through," he said, "towards the mountains. Gustav stopped me and asked me to work for him. I needed money, so I agreed to work."

"A good thing, too," Marie said. "The mountains are going to be impassable within the next week or two. Winter's on its way, and it's very fierce in the high country."

Walker looked at Ehrlich, not sure of what she had just said. Gustav smiled, and looked at Marie.

"Walker speaks our language perfectly," he said, "but there are some words and concepts that he just doesn't get. Sometimes I think it's because he's never been exposed to ideas like winter, but of course, that's ridiculous. He would have had to be raised in a cave somewhere for that to be true."

Marie turned back to Walker. "You never did answer the first part of the question," she said. "Where are you from?"

Walker shrugged. "I don't know."

Marie smiled. "Well, there's a straightforward answer. Do you mean that you don't know in a metaphysical sense, or that you don't know where you were born? In which country?"

Walker smiled, then shrugged again. "I don't know," he repeated.

Marie gazed at him for several long moments, and Walker saw something in her eyes change—they were suddenly piercing, as if she were trying to decide whether or not to believe him. It wasn't an unpleasant change, for as Walker looked back into her eyes, he knew that she had to end up believing him. One must believe the truth.

"I'm sorry," she said with another smile. "I don't mean to pry. It's not very polite of me to ask so many questions, is it?"

"It's not impolite," Walker said.

"You're quite an enigma, Mr. Walker. It's just that I'm not sure if you're a philosopher, a poet, or a child, or a wonderful mixture of all three."

"I'd say there's more than those three, Marie," Ehrlich said. "Just as in all of us, if we let them come out. The difference is that Walker here lets them come out, quite naturally."

"I often wish that I could do it so easily. I'm like everyone else, I guess—I stifle the parts of me that don't seem to be useful at any given time."

"Would you like the usual, Marie?" Ehrlich asked.

She smiled. "Since you've already put 'the usual' into that bag while we were talking," she said, "the usual will be fine. Jacob has to go to his parents' village for a few days, so you may be seeing more of me than you want to." She addressed Walker, "When my husband leaves town and I'd like someone to talk to, it's always a great comfort to know that Gustav has a table to sit at, tea to drink, and something warm and sweet to eat. Not to mention great conversation."

She gave her money to Ehrlich and took the bag as he handed it to her.

"But for now," she said, "I must be going. It's been a pleasure to meet you, Mr. Walker. I'm sure we'll see each other again. Good day, Gustav."

"See you soon, Marie!" Ehrlich called after her. He turned to Walker. "There goes a wonderful woman. Wise beyond her years, somehow, and as kind as any human being I've ever met."

"She is very nice," Walker agreed, beginning to sweep again. "She's very friendly."

"That she is, my friend—that she is."

As the morning wore on, Walker met many more people from the village, but as he looked into everyone's eyes as he greeted them, he rarely saw the same spark that he had seen in Marie's eyes, or that he saw in Gustav's. It was the same spark that he had seen in Amar's eyes, and in Kennison's and Gloria's and especially Tricia's, but not everyone seemed to share it. Many people were very friendly, some were indifferent, some seemed very sad, and some made no eye contact at all. He worried that he might see the same thing in someone's eyes that he had seen in the eyes of the three people on the road, but no one with such eyes came into the shop.

Late in the morning, he saw Gustav relax a bit.

"Now comes our slow time," he told Walker. "We have a chance to relax and have a bite to eat ourselves. Would you like some tea?"

"Yes, please." Walker remembered Gloria's tea with fondness, and he looked forward to tasting it again.

When they were seated and had begun eating, Gustav noticed that Walker seemed to be preoccupied.

"What are you thinking about, Walker?" he asked.

Walker looked at him, then looked out the window. "Where are you from?" he asked Gustav.

"I'm from right here," Gustav said with a shrug. "My parents lived here, and their parents before them. In fact, this bakery used to belong to my father, and I learned the trade from him as I grew up. I've done some traveling, but I've always lived right here—this has been my home. Why do you ask?"

"Because I do not know where I am 'from.' I don't remember anything of being a child, of being young, of having parents. I remember only a very small amount of time. I remember walking and knowing nothing of language and seeing the entire world and seeing how beautiful everything is. I remember meeting people and learning language and starting to think of things that I hadn't thought of before, to think of things that distracted me so that I did not see as many beautiful things any more. When I meet people, they all seem to have a past, to have memories that they love to think about, that bring them comfort and smiles."

"And often pain," Ehrlich added.

"But I have no such memories," Walker replied. "Where am I 'from'?"

Ehrlich thought for several long moments.

"I don't know," he finally replied. "I can't answer that question for you. But you remember yesterday, don't you?"

"Yes, I do."

"And you remember the day before that?"

"Yes."

"Then you're definitely in the process of making memories. For some reason or another, you've started much later than the rest of us. Maybe something happened to you that made you forget everything before a little while ago. There was a man here in the village who got hit in the head by a falling brick while he was working on a house. He almost died, and when he returned to consciousness, he remembered nothing of his past—he didn't even recognize his wife or his own children. It took him many months of piecing things back together before the memories started returning to him. Maybe something like that happened to you."

Walker thought about that for a few moments. "I suppose that's possible. If it happened to me, I wouldn't remember it happening to me, would I?"

"Not at all. This man didn't remember the brick falling on his head."

"But I still would like to know where I am 'from.' What do I tell people when they ask me that question?"

"I don't know. Maybe you could say that you're from very far away. Maybe you could make up the name of a village. That wouldn't be the truth, but it would stop people from asking many questions."

"But the truth is very important, is it not? You speak of truth as a very important thing. So did Kennison, and Tricia."

"There you go—you see, you do have some memories. Just keep in mind that you don't have as many as other people, and that they don't go as far back. As far as the truth is concerned, yes, you're right—it's very important. Possibly the most important part of life. But whenever you say 'I don't know' when someone asks you where you're from, expect to have many questions following your answer, because that's a question that almost no one in the world answers with those particular words."

"But it would be the truth."

"Yes, it would be the truth."

"And if I made up the name of a town, it would not be the truth."

"No, it would not be the truth. But would you be trying to deceive anyone?"

"What do you mean?"

"Would you be trying to cheat anyone by telling them the name of this town? Would you be trying to hide something that would hurt someone else or yourself? Would you be trying to gain something personally at the expense of someone else by telling the name of the town? Or would you simply be trying to get past an awkward part of a conversation that would always be the same, and would always leave everyone dissatisfied with any answer you could possibly give them?"

"It's very complex."

Ehrlich smiled. "Welcome to life, my friend. For example, if someone comes into the shop and asks me what I think the weather will be like tomorrow, but I don't have time to have a conversation about the weather, especially if I know it's someone who likes to have long conversations about everything, I may simply say 'I don't know,' even if I'm sure that tomorrow will be sunny and bright or rainy and cold. I find it hard to condemn myself for being dishonest when I know that any other answer would cause me to get behind in my work and cause many of my customers to have to wait a very long time to get what they need."

Walker stared at Ehrlich, perplexed. He saw the sense in what Gustav had just said, but he found it very difficult to reconcile the concept of honesty with the idea of not telling the truth.

"It's very complex," he finally repeated.

"It's very complex," Ehrlich agreed. "Have another sweet roll."

Chapter 8

Walker learned much as he stayed on with Gustav Ehrlich. He learned of baking, and he learned about and from the other people he met. He loved to work, but he also liked the time he spent not working, for then he went for long walks by himself. He found that it was pleasant to have a place to come back to after a walk.

The days grew much cooler very quickly, and he was fascinated to see that the colors of the leaves on the trees were changing. The days also were growing shorter—he soon had much less time after he finished working to go for his walks before darkness came. The changes of the world were all new to him, and Gustav and Marie were more than willing to explain to him all of the changes.

One brilliant fall day, Walker went for a walk with Marie. He had met her husband, Jacob, and he liked him a great deal—he was very much like Marie. Marie came in often to have a cup of tea with Gustav, and Walker usually took part in the conversations. But he had never spoken alone with Marie until they took the walk.

They walked slowly out of town, with the afternoon sun to their right. The air was very cool, and Walker wore the coat that Gustav had bought him with his first pay. The coat was comfortable, and he liked how the material kept in the warmth so much more than his shirts did. Gustav had shown him a piece of cotton and explained to him the process that was necessary to make material out of it. He had also shown him some sheep and explained to him the way that wool was spun in much the same way as cotton to make cloth.

To Walker, it seemed that the world was full of miracles. That a plant from the ground or the coat of an animal could be made into clothing for people was nothing short of a miracle in itself, and he didn't understand how nobody seemed to recognize that fact—that it was, indeed, a miracle. Gustav told him often that he appreciated Walker's perspective, that he found it helpful to be around someone who was so amazed by so many things, but Walker couldn't understand how or why so few people saw things in the same way he did—as miraculous parts of a beautiful world.

Marie came close to seeing things that way, and Walker was sure that her perspective had a lot to do with the fact that she seemed to be a friend to him immediately.

As they walked, Walker asked Marie about her marriage.

"You and Jacob are married," he said, looking at a huge tree that had turned to brilliant red and orange hues.

"Yes, we are," Marie replied, following his gaze. "It's a beautiful tree, isn't it? It's one of my favorites—every year, it's the most beautiful of all. It's a maple."

"Every year?" Walker asked, his mind now filled with another question. He pushed the new question back in his mind, though, for he wanted to continue with his first line of thought.

"What does it mean?" he asked. "To be married?"

"Do you want the simple answer, or the full, much more complicated answer?" Marie asked him. He looked at her and smiled; she knew better than to ask. She laughed. "I guess we'll be taking a rather long walk this afternoon. But give me a few minutes to gather my thoughts—I haven't ever considered giving an answer to that particular question."

They walked on in silence, listening to the breeze, watching the sunlight on the trees and the hills and the grass that was all around them. Walker looked to the mountains that already had changed considerably—the upper portions of the mountains were now white, covered in snow, Gustav told him. The whiteness gave them an even more majestic appearance that they had had before.

Finally, Marie spoke.

"I can't pretend to speak for everyone—many people are in miserable marriages, mostly because they married more to avoid being alone than because of any love that they felt for the other person. Many people are afraid to be alone, to spend time on their own, for they feel that if they're alone, they're somehow bad or wrong or undesirable. They need company, and the first person who comes along who treats them well is a potential husband or wife. Unfortunately, often the other person also is marrying to avoid being alone, and to have someone with whom they can face this cold, cruel world of ours."

"Cold and cruel?" Walker asked, surprised. "I don't understand."

Marie sighed. "Nor do I, to be honest. But many people see the world that way. Those are the words that they use to describe the world. It's very sad, mostly for them, but also for the other people who never get the chance to see what kind of people these people could be if they were in a more positive relationship."

"Because they never reach their potential?"

"Precisely. But I say all that because you asked me what it means to be married, and I have to answer you based on my ideal, the way I see things. You see, to me it means that two people are willing to give each other everything of themselves, the good and the bad, and both people must be willing to accept everything of the other, the good and the bad. By bad I don't mean bad like evil, just the things that might get on our nerves or that might not be what we see as ideal. We can't go into marriage with the hopes of changing the other person, for if we do so, we set ourselves up for disappointment. Each of us must be who we are, and not someone that somebody else wants us to be."

Marie laughed. "Maybe it would be easier if you were to ask me what marriage *isn't*, Walker. I can certainly answer that question much more easily, it seems.

"So maybe I should just tell you how Jacob and I approach our marriage. These generalities are always dangerous, anyway—they end up being untrue or exaggerated in most cases. I'm very fortunate to have met Jacob, for we get along very well and we treat each other with a great deal of respect. Because of that respect, we have very few real problems in our relationship. We still have misunderstandings from time to time, and we still hurt each other's feelings now and then, but Jacob knows that I'm a human being who needs to be treated with love and respect, and I know that he's the same thing, so we do our best to treat each other with love and respect.

"You see, marriage is a step, a part of the process most of us go through in order to lose our selfishness. When we get married, we change our focus from self to other—and in return, we have a partner who is willing to make the same shift, who is willing to focus on us rather than on him or her self. That other person supports us, helps us, teaches us, tries us, tests us—all of the things that are necessary for learning. That's the ideal, of course. If that other person isn't willing to make that shift, the marriage is doomed to be miserable, and one or both of the people in the marriage is doomed to be dissatisfied and unfulfilled.

"Of course, the selfish people—the ones unwilling to make the shift in focus—are usually quite content, for not only do they look after their own best interests, but now they have someone else to look after those same interests. Sadly, they often never even see that there's a problem, for everything's going fine for them."

"So both you and Jacob focus on each other, rather than yourselves?"

"More or less. I mean, we still have to look after ourselves—we have to stay healthy, we have to keep learning, we have to do our work, we have to keep ourselves clean. But we have to learn to lose our focus on self if we're going to be good parents when we have children, which we fully intend to do. Children, for the first few years of their lives especially, are purely self-centered, and if we expect them to help us out, we're going to be disappointed. The whole purpose of parenthood is to help our children grow, and we have to keep our focus on that ideal, while still looking after our spouses and our selves. And we never can do that if we haven't learned how to shift our focus from our selves."

"Then what is love?"

Marie stopped in her tracks, then laughed. "I've spent all this time talking about marriage, and I haven't once mentioned the word 'love,' have I? That's so interesting." She began to walk again; Walker kept up with her.

"Love is probably the most misused word that we have in our language. Ideally, we should love everyone equally, because God put everyone on this planet, and we're all the same in heart and soul. But much of the problem comes with the idea of 'romantic' love, which is what many people use as an excuse to be abused. They feel that they've 'fallen in love,' and they basically become addicted to the person they're in love with. That's what I was talking about before, the people that just need someone else there for them.

"But most people aren't able to love truly at all—sadly, it's usually because they don't love themselves."

"I don't understand what you mean by that."

"When we love people, we respect them, we recognize their uniqueness and their natural state of being. We love them simply for what they are, not because of anything they've done. That's the ideal, anyway—if it's true love, there are no conditions on that love. We don't say, 'I love you as long as you act a certain way,' we say, 'I love you, period.' But many people put more conditions on themselves than they do on others, and they don't allow themselves to make normal mistakes without judging themselves very harshly, without making themselves feel that they're somehow not deserving of their own love.

"So when these people get into relationships, they don't know how to love unconditionally—they expect so much out of their partners that their relationships are doomed to have many problems because their partners can't live up to those expectations."

"How do we learn to love our selves?"

"Simple—we accept ourselves, flaws and all. If we see a fault in ourselves, we do our best to change it, but we don't get angry with ourselves for having faults. We allow ourselves to make mistakes without condemning ourselves for them. We see everything we do as learning experiences, whether we succeed at everything we do or not. We allow ourselves to be human, to be fallible, and we give ourselves credit when we succeed or when we do well or when we accomplish something. We keep ourselves healthy, mentally and physically. We make sure we surround ourselves with people who are kind and loving. We allow ourselves to rest, we eat nourishing foods, we go for long walks to relieve stress.

"It's really odd, but most people are much more willing to try to love other people than they are to try to love themselves."

"And how is it part of marriage?"

"I can only tell you how I feel with Jacob. With him, I feel many of the same feelings that I do with Gustav, for example, only greatly intensified. I feel that I want to be with Jacob as much as I can. When we're together, I don't really feel that we're two separate people—we're enough alike that we think alike and react to things alike. I can anticipate him, and he can anticipate me. I like spending time with Gustav or with other friends, but it's not nearly the same as when I'm with Jacob. We can sit together for hours without saying a word, and that's fine. I feel a physical attraction to him—I want to hold him, to make love to him. But the physical aspect of our relationship supplements our emotional relationship—it's a bonus, if you will. One must be very careful not to mistake physical attraction for love. The two concepts do not necessarily go together."

The sun was already behind the mountains, and Marie and Walker were nearing the village in the last few minutes of twilight.

"Everything is very complex," Walker said quietly, "and there's so much to learn. It's very difficult to keep it all straight. I think, though, that I'm very fortunate to have very good teachers like you and Gustav and Amar and Tricia and Kennison. I'm starting to think that I may be here to learn all these things, though I don't know why I never learned it before. Maybe I did, but I forgot it all."

"That would be very strange, to forget everything. I couldn't even conceive of not having a memory of anything more than a few weeks ago."

"But I'm lucky to have very good teachers. You're teaching me all of the important things of life, I think."

"Why, thank you, Walker. Just remember that the best teaching is useless if the students do no learning. There are plenty of people who wouldn't listen to a word I have to say. The important part of learning is choosing to listen."

"Why would we not listen?"

"You'd be surprised—some of our most effective teachers are those people who do things that we never would do, and we learn from their bad examples what we should not do. We certainly shouldn't listen to them when they give us advice."

"I think I've met people like that," Walker said, thinking back to the three people on the road. "But I didn't talk to them."

"You will," Marie assured him. "You'll meet people like that and you'll talk to them. You may even spend time with them. It's inevitable. But do you want to know that greatest irony of all about love? Those are the people who are the hardest of all to love, yet they're the very ones who need love more than anyone else. They just don't want to accept it, or don't know how to—they push it away, they ridicule it, they pretend they don't need it, so they never get it, and things get worse and worse for them."

"So we should love them more than we love others?" Walker asked.

"Absolutely not. We should love all people equally. Some people just need it to be shown more strongly."

Walker sighed. "I have much to think of," he said quietly. "Thank you."

"No, Walker, thank you," Marie replied. "You've made me think of many things that I otherwise wouldn't have thought of, much less tried to put into words. I think I've learned just as much as you have. Good night, friend." She reached out and took Walker's hand, giving it a short squeeze.

"Good night, friend," he repeated, and she took the left path of the fork they had reached; Walker continued down the right path, wondering how often he would find that people's paths would not lead down the same road.

When he got to the bakery, Gustav was sitting at a table, drinking tea and reading a book.

"Good evening," Walker said, sitting at the table with him.

"Hello, Walker!" Gustav said, holding up a hand. "Just one moment." His eyes never left the book, and Walker watched them move back and forth, looking at something on the pages before him. In about a minute, Gustav closed the book and looked at his friend.

"I hate to leave a book in the middle of an idea, especially when it's a good book. How was your walk?"

"My walk was beautiful," Walker replied, wanting to ask about the book, but also wanting to ask Gustav a question. Sometimes he didn't want to have so many questions, but the thirst for knowledge inside him was unending, and he wanted to know about everything.

"Will you tell me about the book later," he asked, "in case I forget to ask you?"

Gustav smiled. "Absolutely. But right now, you have something else to ask me, something to do with your conversation with Marie, I'd wager."

"Yes," Walker said with a smile. He was always amazed at Gustav's insight. "Marie and I talked about being married. Why aren't you married?"

Gustav's expression changed immediately, but Walker couldn't tell exactly how. The smile never left his face, and his eyes still had the sparkle that they always had, but suddenly he went from being bright and cheerful to being something else.

"I was married for a very long time, Walker—almost thirty years—to a precious, loving woman who was the greatest light that ever shined in my life. Her name was Elissa, and she lived here with me, helping me with the bakery."

"Did she sleep where I sleep now?" Walker asked, and Gustav chuckled.

"No, she slept where I sleep. We slept together. We ate meals together. She was a wonderful woman who would do anything for anyone who needed her help, and who made my life much fuller just by being here with me. I loved her very much, and she loved me, I know. When we were together, everything in the world was a bit brighter, a bit calmer, a bit more beautiful. We didn't even have to be together physically—I always knew she was there behind me, no matter where I was and no matter where she was, and that was more than enough for me."

"What did it mean, to be married?"

"It meant that we had committed ourselves to each other, to doing our best to help each other whenever we could, by whatever means we could. It meant that we shared the joy and the sorrow and the love and the laughter and the pain. It meant that we were there for each other."

"To make each other happy?"

"No." Gustav thought for a moment. "We could help each other to reach happiness, but we couldn't make each other happy. We can only make ourselves happy. Others can help, but true happiness is something that we all must strive for in ourselves."

"Where is she, though?"

"She died, Walker. A little less than a year ago. She was fortunate, for she didn't suffer long—she had a short illness, and she died."

Walker looked confused. "Died?"

"Don't tell me you know nothing of death?" Gustav asked, amazed. "My goodness—death is the only constant of life. It's the only thing in life on which we all can depend. Right now, Walker, we're all alive—our hearts are beating, we're breathing, we're thinking, we go to sleep at night and wake up in the morning—the process goes on and on. But one day, that process will cease—we'll no longer breathe, no longer think or eat or sleep. We'll die."

"And then what?"

"Well, other people will put your body into a box, then bury it in the ground. Or they'll burn your body and scatter the ashes. But your soul— now, that's quite a different story. But to tell you the truth, it's getting very late, and we have to get up very early. Maybe we could put this discussion off until tomorrow?"

"Of course," Walker replied. "I'm beginning to think too much right now, anyway. There is so much to learn."

"And just think—you really haven't even started yet." Gustav laughed, then got up and cleared the table. "Sleep well, Walker," he said, then walked back into his home, which was attached to the bakery.

"Good night," Walker called after him. He put out the lights and climbed the stairs to his room in the loft above the bakery, where he lay down and thought about all he had learned.

Chapter 9

Soon came the first snow to the village, and it came with a fury that startled Walker. He had heard the winds the night before in the moments when he was half awake, but he had heard wind before. Even after he woke up, he had no real idea of what was going on outside, as it was still very dark and there was no way he could see the snow on the ground. He was a bit surprised when Gustav entered the room more agitated than Walker had ever seen him.

"Everything's all set?" he asked Walker, looking in at the flames that would heat the oven. "Good, good. We have a lot of work to do today. I wasn't at all ready for this storm—I don't think anyone saw it coming, or they would have told me yesterday. It's a bad one, though, so we have our work cut out for us. With this kind of snow, most of our older customers won't be able to get here for their bread, so we'll have to take it to them. Do you think you can handle that?"

Walker shrugged and nodded. "Yes, of course," he said.

Ehrlich stopped and looked at Walker. "You've never seen a snow like this, have you?" he asked. Walker shook his head. "In fact, I'd bet that you've never seen any kind of snow, have you?" Walker shook his head again.

Ehrlich laughed and put a hand on Walker's shoulder. "Son, you're in for quite an education today. It looks like everything's all set in here for now, so why don't you take that shovel over there in the corner and go outside and clear some of the snow from the sidewalk."

"Sure," Walker said. He put on the heavy coat that Ehrlich had given him, put on his shoes, and took the shovel, ready to go.

"You're not ready yet," Ehrlich told him. "Take these." He handed Walker a pair of gloves and a scarf—Walker could see what the gloves were for, but Gustav had to wrap the scarf around his neck for him. "And you'll have to borrow my heavy boots for now, until we can get you some."

Walker changed into the boots, wondering at so much preparation.

Ehrlich smiled. "Have fun," he said, with a mischievous gleam in his eye.

Walker nodded, went to the door, and opened it.

The fierceness of the biting cold that swept into the room shocked him, and he slammed the door shut again before he realized what he was doing. He turned to Gustav, who was watching him. Walker's eyes were open as wide as they possibly could be, and they held a hundred unspoken, unanswered questions.

Gustav laughed—a kind laugh, the type of laugh a father laughs when his son discovers how cold the water in the lake is when he's about to go swimming.

"Snow," he told Walker. "Blizzard, actually, but I think you get the point, no?"

Walker said nothing. He smiled faintly, then turned and opened the door again, then forced his way out into the morning, shovel in hand.

Gustav walked to the door and opened it. "Put the extra snow in the space between the buildings, there!" he yelled, pointing. Walker nodded in reply, and Gustav closed the door.

Once the initial shock of the cold and wind and wet wore off, Walker stood still, listening to the wind force its way through the openings between the buildings, and he even heard the snow itself landing on the snow that had fallen before it. The morning was beautiful in its fierce darkness—it was like nothing he had ever seen before. He could see the snow falling, being blown almost sideways, in the light that came through the window of the bakery—he and Gustav were the only people up that early in the village, so there were no other lights.

The snow was already up to his knees, and he watched it as he walked, watched it part before the strength of his legs, watched it cover his foot and lower leg as soon as he put a foot down. He took off one glove and picked up a handful of snow. It amazed him how cold it was and how quickly he felt the need to put the glove back on. Even after he pulled it back over his fingers and hand, the cold stayed on, and he decided that he wouldn't take his gloves off again unless he needed to.

He started to shovel, to lift a load of snow and toss it into the space between the buildings where Gustav had told him to put it. When he tried to lift it, though, he was surprised at just how heavy it was—he could lift it, but it took a lot of effort for him to do so. Once he threw the snow into the space, he reached down for another load, and then another and another.

Walker worked quickly, and he was surprised when he finished with the small area right in front of the door. He watched as the falling snow quickly covered the area he had just cleared, though not nearly as deeply. He thought about clearing the spot again, but he knew that Gustav needed his help. He went back inside to work.

"You work very quickly, my friend," Gustav told him when Walker entered the shop. "Here—I've taken the liberty of preparing you a small breakfast to warm you up. I don't know if you've ever tasted hot chocolate, but I think you'll find that it's a wonderful way to take off the chill."

Walker hung up his coat and took off his boots. "It's beautiful, the snow. It comes from the sky, but it's not like rain."

"Oh, but it is!" Gustav exclaimed. "It is rain. It's just that it's too cold to be water—it freezes in the air, and when it hits the ground it's in the form of snow or ice. And yes, you're right—it is beautiful. Just wait until the storm passes and you can go for a walk in the newly fallen snow—it's one of the most beautiful experiences in the world. The air is crisp and cold, the snow is smooth and untouched, the sky is blue and clear—there's really nothing at all like it."

"It sounds wonderful," Walker said, drinking more of his hot chocolate. "This chocolate, too—it tastes very nice. You were right—it's perfect."

"You know what I like about you, Walker?" Gustav asked, then went on to answer his question. "You like things. You appreciate things. You look at something and you see the beauty in it. You don't look for flaws or imperfections or shortcomings or mistakes. Those are always there, always. But what point in focusing on them, when they're right there with beauty? That's the essence of love, my friend—seeing the beauty in everything. I think that's why I like Marie and Jacob so much, too—they're very much like that. Jesus said that we all had to be like children in order to get to heaven, and I think that's what he meant—we have to see the world through the eyes of children, looking for the beautiful and miraculous and the love and the hope. I thank you for that—it does my heart good to see someone else who appreciates without reservation, without condition."

"You're welcome," Walker said, finishing up his pastry, then taking his last drink of hot chocolate. "Who is Jesus?"

Gustav looked surprised. "That's right," he said. "You don't read, do you? Well, there's a lot to be said about Jesus and religions and God and all that, and not a whole lot of time this morning. We can talk about it sometime when we have time in front of us, okay?"

"That sounds good. It should be interesting."

"Oh, that it is, no matter which side of the fence you're looking from. But come—we have a lot of work to do, and people will be depending on us today more than on any other day."

"Because of the snow?"

"Because of the snow."

The day was filled with work, but not all of Walker's time was spent in the bakery. On that day, Gustav needed him to deliver bread to the people he knew wouldn't be able to make it to the bakery on their own. Walker had to take double the normal amount of bread to each household, for Gustav didn't know how long the storm would last, or just how bad it would get—there was always the chance that they wouldn't be able to deliver at all on the next day, he said.

Walker trudged through snow higher than his knees, and by the end of the day, it was almost halfway up his thighs. The snow was, indeed, beautiful, but Walker could also see how destructive it was, and how much it changed the world into a much less inviting place, a much less hospitable place. He was glad each time that he stepped into the bakery that he had such a place to step into, a place that was warm and dry. He imagined himself on the road in such a storm, with nowhere to go for shelter, and he wondered what would happen if he were to be stuck outdoors on such a day. He certainly would be cold.

"You would probably die," Gustav replied when Walker told him what he was thinking. "You would freeze to death."

"And the process of life would stop?"

"Exactly." He handed Walker another three bags. "These three people live very near—take these, then you'll take a rest and dry off and warm up."

"That will be very good," Walker said, taking the bags and heading out the door into a village that looked so much different than it had the day before. And he knew it didn't just look different—it *was* different. People were spending their day differently than they had the day before, and even the possibilities of what they could do were greatly limited by the weather.

Some of the houses were much prettier in the snow—they had much more personality when they were covered in a blanket of white than they did otherwise, though some things were just completely covered up. Walker's favorite bushes in front of Marie and Jacob's home were gone, just memories on that particular day. All of the stones and decorations and other small things that he remembered from walking about the village were gone, also. The world was different.

He didn't have much time to look, though, for something inside told him not to stay out too long. He was surprised at the way his eyes stopped working the way that he was used to them working—he couldn't focus on things as he normally did, and he couldn't see any colors at all after a while, until he got back in the bakery and let his eyes readjust.

When he was back inside for a rest, Walker asked Gustav, "If a rock is covered up with snow and I can't see it, is it still there?"

Gustav looked at him in surprise. Then he smiled. "My goodness—you're turning into a philosopher already. That's one of the more common philosophical questions, that of existence. You've seen the rooms I live in, right?" Walker nodded. "And you've seen the kitchen where I cook my food. But that's in another room right now, a room that we can't see. But is that kitchen table there, at this moment? Or does our knowledge of, our memory of that table create it for us each time we walk into that room?"

Walker thought the question over for a few moments. "I don't know," he said.

"Exactly. And you shall not know. Theories are wonderful to think about—you can theorize about existence apart from experience all you want, but the most important theories are those that can be applied practically to our lives, like the theories that govern heating and lighting and our relationships with other people. All the rest is interesting to us, but very impractical. Some people make their livings thinking about such things, but when all is said and done, for the rest of us, talking about such things is an interesting diversion—no more, no less.

"I read a book once by a man who said that with the power of our minds we could swim through solid earth, make it become liquid simply through the power of our own thought, and swim through it. Fascinating to think of, but I've never known of anyone, the author of the book included, who actually could make such a thing happen. It becomes a problem when people present theories as facts, for then the people who are reading or listening see something wrong with themselves when they aren't able to apply the theories in their own lives."

Gustav stopped and smiled. "What is it about you, Walker? You always make me go on and on about things that I normally don't even think about that much. It's kind of nice, though. I should think like this much more often, to tell you the truth."

"It is very interesting to listen to you," Walker said quietly, "even if I'm not sure that I understand everything that you say."

"Just let it all sink in, Walker. Give it time. You don't have to understand everything immediately. Give it time. Right now, I'd like to eat, though. Are you hungry?"

"Yes, I am," Walker replied. "I am very hungry."

"So am I. Let's fix up something to eat."

Late that night, Walker woke up and listened for the wind, but it had ceased. He rolled over in his warm bed and smiled—now he would see what Gustav had been talking about when he spoke of the world after a snowstorm.

Morning came quickly, as it always did at the bakery. Walker started the fire, then dressed and went outside to clear up what was left of the snow on the sidewalk in front of the bakery. The silence was almost overwhelming, and it was somehow muted, somehow different. The moon shone brightly in the sky, so he could see just how much the world had changed, but he still couldn't wait for the sun to come up.

Later, after they had done all the morning work and the sun had arrived, he went for his first walk in the snow. It wasn't like the deliveries had been the day before, for those had been stressful and somewhat frantic in the driving storm. Gustav made him wear a special pair of shoes that were much longer and wider than his feet so that he wouldn't sink down into the snow, and Walker walked along on top of the snow, out to the edge of the village where the plains began.

As far as he could see, the world was under a thick carpet of white—nothing looked the same as it had just days earlier; everything was full of wonder and magic. The branches of the trees were coated in the snow, most of them sagging down closer to the ground under the weight of their new load. The trunks of the trees, for the most part, were covered with snow on one side and still clear of snow on the other. The air was clear and cold, with no breeze at all, and the blue of the sky made the snow much more brilliant than it would have been otherwise. The ice crystals in the snow shone brightly in the morning sun, gleaming here and there in many different colors—the fields and trees sparkled before him, holding him captive with their beauty.

In fact, the only reason he moved at all was the cold. After he had stood there soaking in the scene for many long minutes, he felt his body start to react to the cold, and he was surprised at just how unpleasant the feeling of the cold was—he longed to be indoors again, longed to have shelter and heat.

Once he started walking again, though, the feeling diminished. As his body heated itself up through his exertions, he became more comfortable, and his desire for shelter and heat was no longer as strong as it had been just moments before. In just a few moments, he once more felt that he could stay out there for a very long time, as long as he kept walking.

He knew, though, that Gustav would need his help soon, so he slowly started back to the bakery.

Before he got there, though, he saw Gustav walking towards him, wearing another pair of the snow shoes.

"Come on, Walker," Gustav called out, turning down the street that was right before Walker. "We have someone to see."

"Who?" Walker asked as he caught up with him.

"Mrs. Goodson, the woman who comes to the bakery every morning and tells you that you look just like her son. She's dying."

Walker hurried along with Gustav. He liked Mrs. Goodson, for she always was kind to him and she always seemed to go out of her way to talk to him. He didn't know why, except that she always said that Walker reminded her of her son. He didn't care why, either, for he always found that talking with her was pleasant.

She lived in the third house on the street, and there was a young woman at the door, waiting for them.

"Good morning, Gustav," she said kindly. "It's been a very long time, hasn't it?"

"Yes, it has, Laura. A very long time. It's wonderful to see you again." He gave her a long hug, then stepped back a step. Laura wore a simple dress, and her hair was put up atop her head. Walker could tell it was blond, but he had no idea how long it might have been. She looked very tired—her face was drawn, and her movements seemed not to have the sharpness that Walker saw in most people's movements. In her eyes he saw a pain that he hadn't seen before, but he also saw caring and gratefulness for their presence there.

"I just came back the day before yesterday," Laura explained, "when I found out that mother had worsened. I was going to come to see you, but the storm caught me by surprise."

"As it did all of us. I thought it might storm soon, but not as badly or as soon as it did. How is your mother?"

"She's near the end, I believe. She keeps asking for you, and for someone named Walker."

"This is Walker," Gustav said, introducing the two. "Walker, this is Laura, Mrs. Goodson's daughter. She now lives in the next village over, with her husband and two children."

"Three now," Laura corrected him.

"Three? My goodness—how time does take us by surprise sometimes."

"Yes, it does," Laura agreed. "But you should see her now—she's been asking for you both."

They walked into a back room, where the woman that Walker remembered as an energetic, enthusiastic person lay quietly and calmly on a bed, seemingly without any energy at all. She turned her head towards them when they walked in, and Walker could see at a glance that her eyes hadn't lost a bit of their fire or their caring. She was still the same woman, even if her body wasn't acting the same.

"Gustav. Walker," she said quietly. "Thank you for coming. I'll be going soon—I can feel it. I won't keep you long. But I wanted to thank you, Gustav, for all that you've done for me and my family over the years. I'd like to say that I'll miss you, but somehow I don't think that's a feeling I'll have in heaven—there will be so much to get used to. Besides, you'll be there soon enough. God's time and heaven's time aren't like our time, anyway."

Gustav reached out and took her hand. "Nevertheless, I will miss you, Eva. I could never count the number of smiles you've brought to me when you've come into the store. And I appreciate every one of them." He smiled. "And though it will seem a very short time to you, there in heaven, I trust I still have a few more years of baking bread left in this world."

"I'm sure you do," she said quietly, then looked at Walker. She let go of Gustav's hand and reached for Walker's. He took her hand and sat on the edge of her bed, looking into her eyes.

"And you, my dear Mr. Walker," she said, squeezing his hand a bit. "I'd like to thank you for the light you've brought into my life these past few weeks. I admire your innocence, your desire to learn, your great appreciation for everything you see in this world. Talking with you has been like talking to an adult child—one who knows and accepts the responsibilities, yet who hasn't lost that ability to see the wonder in everything that surrounds us on this beautiful planet. Thank you for reminding me just how wonderful this life is, and just how many miracles surround us every single day we live here. You couldn't have come at a better time—my last few days have been so much richer for the way you've helped me to change my perspective.

"Never lose that innocence," she implored. "Please, promise that no matter what happens to you in the future, you'll hold on to that innocence. I ask you for your own sake, as well as for the sake of anyone else you may meet—I can only pray that you may help someone else as much as you've helped me."

"But how have I helped you?" Walker asked, confused. "I've done nothing for you that was special."

"Come, child—your modesty is a big part of who you are. But you've done plenty for me. You've taken the time to talk to me when I wanted to talk, and you've actually listened when I spoke. You've shown me the beauty in the simplicity of a loaf of bread. You've told me of the wonder you've felt when you've gone for long walks in the evenings, and you've shared with me the beauty of all that you saw during your walks. To you, you were just telling me what you saw, but to me, you were opening my eyes to the beauty that I had stored up inside of me, but didn't realize. All of my memories have stayed inside of me for years, and I've had a great treasure in those memories, but I never realized just how rich I was until you started to share with me just how fantastic this world is.

"And now I feel that I can move on, that I can go to God and with a clear conscience tell him, 'Yes, I have lived the life that you've given me as fully as I've been able to, and yes, I have appreciated the beautiful world that you gave us to live in. My memory is full of treasures, and I recognize them as treasures, and I hold them as treasures.'

"And I can tell him that, Walker, only because you've opened my eyes—and opened my mind—to these things. Thank you."

"You're welcome," Walker said quietly, still unsure of how he had helped her. He really had no time to think of it, for Eva died just then. Walker was still holding her hand, and he felt the life slip from it, felt it become weight in his hand, saw Eva's body sink ever so slightly into the bed. He put the hand upon the other hand on her chest, then turned to Gustav and Laura.

"She's gone," Gustav said quietly. Laura had tears on her face.

"I feel like crying," Laura said, "but she lived such a full life that I don't see her passing as sad. I'll miss her, but I'm grateful that she was a part of my life." She looked to Gustav and Walker. "Thank you both for coming."

"Thank you for calling us," Gustav said, giving her another hug. He turned and looked at Walker.

"It seems that the student is quickly becoming the teacher," he said with a slight smile. "Let's go, Walker." He turned back to Laura. "If there's anything that we can do, please let us know. In any case, we'd be honored if you could come by for dinner this evening."

"Thank you very much—I think I'll take you up on that."

"We'll eat at six o'clock, then. We'll see you then."

Chapter 10

Soon winter was fully upon them, and over the next few weeks the weather turned very cold, so Gustav and Marie had plenty of time to teach Walker to read, a task that they both undertook with enthusiasm. Walker picked up the skill quickly, and he soon was reading whatever he could find, though there weren't too many books in the village to choose from. That fact didn't daunt him, though, and he enjoyed reading the good and the bad, the exciting and the boring, as he developed his ability to interpret the written word.

"This is fascinating," Walker told Gustav late one evening. "When I pick up a book, all of a sudden it's like I'm in another world, a world created just by words. The characters really have lives, even though they don't exist at all. It's like the writers are creating an entire reality through the words that they use, and I can watch the characters live their lives."

"It is a fascinating process, isn't it?" Gustav agreed. "I love to let my imagination run free and enjoy the worlds in the books—while you're reading them, they truly do seem to exist."

"It seems that words are very powerful. If they can create worlds, what else can they do?"

"As you've told me before, your life wasn't nearly as complicated until you learned language. And when you had words, you started to miss many of the beautiful things in life because you were thinking so much. I suppose that we have to ask ourselves if the power of words is all positive, because words can be used to destroy as surely as they can be used to create and build."

Walker pondered that idea for several moments. "So they also can be used to create negative worlds and negative people."

"Absolutely. I remember reading a play once in which the characters actually did exist simply because the writer had thought them up and put them in words. And in a way, it makes sense. Think about it: You remember Kennison, don't you?"

"Of course I do."

"So you would say that he does exist."

"Yes, I would. I remember him. I remember the things he said."

"And do you remember the main character of the last novel you read?"

"Yes, I do."

"And that character is there in your memory just as Kennison is. And you remember things that he said."

"Yes," Walker said quietly. "So in my memory, there's no difference between Kennison and the character."

"Well, I wouldn't say that there's no difference. With Kennison, you remember certain smells and sounds also, and you don't have those from the novel, unless the author was very good at making you feel those things. But the character, the type of person he was, the things he did, the things he said—those things all are in your memory, almost indistinguishable from so many other memories."

"So someone who can use words can be very powerful."

"If they use words well, absolutely."

Walker sat still for several long minutes, thinking about what Gustav had said.

"If a writer can give us new memories, then, how can we trust our memories of things that we've lived through? How do we know that they are our actual memories, and not something put in there by someone else?"

Gustav stopped kneading the dough he had been working on. He stared at Walker for several long moments, not sure how to answer. "My goodness, Walker," he replied slowly, "I honestly don't know the answer to that question. My only guess would be that our memories are safely locked within our brains, where other people can't get to them. Our brains are a tremendous mystery, and they are uniquely ours. It's not possible for people to get inside of them. You can't read my memories of Elissa, for example—I have to tell you about her, tell you about the memories that I have of her. But if someone were to find a way into our brains, I imagine that they'd be able to read our memories. I don't see how they would put memories in there, though—that's just impossible. It's a frightening thought."

Walker sat quietly again. "I feel sometimes that I'd like to make up a past," he said finally, "just like the writers do, so I wouldn't be the only one without a history, without the memories that everyone else has."

Gustav stopped his work and came and sat down at the table with Walker.

"I know that this is hard for you my friend," he said, "and nothing that I can say can help to change that. But you must believe that if you don't know your past, there's a reason for it, and a very good reason. You are a man who is searching—for a past, and for yourself—and I truly believe that the search will bring you to what you need to know. You must trust life to give you what you need in order to become who you're meant to be. As you travel this world, you'll meet more people who have more answers for you—that's why you're drawn to the road, and that's why you feel you must travel down that road. If the answers that you need were to be found by staying put, then your feelings inside would be to stay wherever you are, to search for answers there. You have to be patient, Walker, and allow the process of life to work within you—otherwise, you'll be dissatisfied for all of your days here on the planet."

Several weeks later, Gustav and many other people celebrated Christmas. It was a quiet time, and the bakery was closed that day. It was a time of reflection and peacefulness, Gustav told Walker. Marie had explained the origins of the day, and while Walker wasn't yet sure what to believe of the concepts behind religion, he did like the day and the mood that it seemed to put people in. He noticed that many people wished each other a "Merry Christmas" during the days before the holiday, and many people tended to be very cheerful, very positive, with a smile for everyone that they met. People seemed to find the holiday very important and very uplifting, and Walker enjoyed seeing them in higher spirits, even as he wondered why they couldn't be that way every day.

On Christmas morning, Gustav handed him a small package wrapped in plain green paper. Both of them had slept in as long as they could, but since they always woke up long before the sun came up, they were still up before the first light hit the sky.

"This is for you, Walker," Gustav said. "On Christmas day, it's a tradition that we exchange gifts, something small. Merry Christmas, Walker."

"Thank you," Walker replied, taking the gift. "Should I open it now?"

"Of course—it's Christmas."

Walker tore open the paper and found a small book and a pen. He opened the book, only to find blank pages inside. He looked questioningly at Gustav.

"One day when you learn to write, you can put down your thoughts," Gustav said. "Or perhaps you can start to record you memories so that you may be able to find some more. Sometimes certain memories are triggered by others."

"This is very kind of you," Walker said. "And I have a gift for you, also. Marie told me about the gifts on this day, and I have one for you now."

He went upstairs and pulled out a small flat package which he presented to Gustav, who looked surprised and fascinated to be receiving a gift from Walker. He took the package form him and unwrapped it carefully, to find a picture of his wife looking back at him from within a frame.

"Jack drew it. Mr. Stark. I saw pictures in his house when I delivered the bread, and he said he remembered your wife very well, and that he would be able to draw a picture of her for you."

Gustav was overwhelmed. "My, my," he said several times, and Walker saw a tear slide down his cheek.

"I didn't mean to make you cry," he said, concerned. "If you don't want to have it—"

"Don't worry, Walker. This is a wonderful gift, and I thank you for it. All this time, I've wished that I had a picture to remember her by, but I thought the chance had gone by for good. And now, here one is. Thank you."

"You're welcome," Walker replied. "Merry Christmas."

"And Merry Christmas to you, my friend."

As winter bore on, Gustav took the opportunity to start to teach Walker to write, though this skill didn't come nearly as easily to Walker as speaking or reading had. While he had no problems with the words, he had a difficult time deciding which letter to use to represent which sound. After many weeks of lessons, his writing was still very difficult for him; when he wrote he usually spelled almost every word incorrectly. It was very frustrating for him, but both Gustav and Marie were very encouraging.

By the time the weather began to warm up, he still had not been able to master the task of writing, and his blank book still had no words written in it. As the days grew more and more agreeable and the snow disappeared from everywhere, Walker began to feel the pull of the road once more. It started as a slight yearning, but grew into a strong desire very soon. He asked Gustav if the snow was finished for the year, but Gustav asked him to hold off for a few weeks for his own safety—one never could tell when a late storm was going to hit.

"Easter comes quite late this year," Gustav told him. "You'll probably be better off waiting until it comes—then you'll have a much better idea of what the weather will be like. You don't want to get caught in any spring storms—they can be just as fierce as any winter storm."

Walker took him at his word and spent his free time walking around the countryside. He was taking one such walk on the first very warm day of spring, a day when he needed only a heavy shirt to keep him comfortable. The breeze that came in from the south was welcome and welcoming, and more than just the warmth, Walker felt the change in the air. The whole world was changing: some of the trees were already getting leaves, some flowers were already making their way slowly through the few patches of snow that were still on the ground, the ground in the snowless spots was now soft mud instead of frozen, and the birds seemed to be singing more loudly, somehow more vigorously, now that the world was more conducive to song and outbursts of energy. Harmony seemed to be returning to the world after many months of absence.

He had gotten used to the cold, to being limited to doing things indoors or bundling up tightly against the cold before he ever went outside. He was used to coming inside and unwrapping the layers, never having quite enough space to put coat, gloves, sweater, scarf, boots, and extra socks, especially when they were all wet.

But now the world was a different place. The warmth was beautiful—it made him feel very much alive, very much refreshed. He had gone for many walks in the winter months, but he had not been able to foresee an end to the cold, and on those walks his skin almost never had felt the touch of the air, or the touch of the warm sun.

Now, though, the memories of his walks from so long ago came back to him. He remembered walking entire nights, never once feeling cold enough to have to put on more clothes. He remembered the warm sun, and he remembered the soft breezes against his skin. The memories were beautiful, just as beautiful as the days were becoming.

"The season of rebirth," Gustav told him one day as the two of them took a walk through the hills. "This is the season that many people spend all winter waiting for. They suffer through the cold months, just waiting for this kind of weather to show itself once more. It's kind of sad, in a way, for those people never really get much out of the days they have—they're too busy complaining about the cold and waiting for spring. I look forward to the warmth, also, but I try to make sure that I fill my days when I can't go outside because of the weather.

"Don't let this weather fool you, though—we still have some very cold days ahead of us. It almost always happens—we start to think that spring's here for good, then we get a furious storm that should remind us not to get too cocky—this world is much stronger and much less predictable than we give it credit for.

"It's a beautiful season. All of this life here has been waiting for the warmer temperatures, waiting for things to change enough so that they can come out and not be killed by the extreme cold. That's why the leaves fell in the autumn—the trees couldn't keep them alive in the cold of winter. They come out now because something in the trees signals them that the time is right, that it's time for them to put out the leaves that will gather the sun's light and energy and turn the world into a green place once more. The flowers come out from the ground—just wait until you see them all. The colors are magnificent." He stopped, looked at Walker, and then laughed. "But of course, you've seen flowers, haven't you? Sometimes I start to think that you're seeing everything for the first time. It's so strange sometimes—there's so much that you haven't seen, and I just take for granted with most people that they know everything they need to know. But with you, I start to think that you really don't know anything."

They walked on in silence for many minutes, enjoying the songs of the birds and the warmth of the sun. Gustav eventually broke the silence.

"Easter is in two weeks. I suppose it will be a good time for you to leave." Walker noticed the sadness in his voice, and he didn't know what to say. He wanted to go—he felt he must go—but he felt he was being unfair to leave his friends who had taught him so much, to leave Gustav with all of the work in the bakery.

Gustav seemed to read Walker's thoughts.

"You have to go, you know," he told Walker. "I can feel it, too—the road is very strong in you. You have so much more to learn, so much more to see. I know that it was right for you to be here in our village, for you've learned a great deal here, but I think you've learned all that we have to teach. And you've been a great help to me, too, not just in the bakery, but with my perspective. I've always been a rather enthusiastic person, or so I'm told, and I've felt myself losing a lot of that enthusiasm after Elissa died. Even more than the enthusiasm, though, I was losing my love for life, my appreciation for the everyday things that are so important to us, the beautiful things that surround us all the time, that help us to love this world if we truly see them rather than just look at them. You've helped me to uncover a lot of that enthusiasm, and I can see it now in almost everything I do. Even the bread tastes better these days—have you noticed how many people have mentioned that fact to us?"

"Yes," Walker replied. "I thought it tasted better because of the warmer weather."

"Spring. I thought so, too, at first. But the more I thought about it, the more I realized that I'm doing everything—bread-making included—with a lot more love these days. It's the love that makes it taste better, the love that people actually taste in the bread. I can get by without Elissa. The world was so bright with her around, but it's still a beautiful place without her here. And the memories I have of her are a very real part of me. The most important thing I've realized, though, is that if I were able to talk to Elissa, she would want me to continue to give love, to continue to live life as fully as possible, even if she's not here to share it with me. And I wasn't doing that—I was getting caught up in my feelings of loss and sadness, and I was dishonoring every principle by which my wife lived her life.

"The same thing will happen when you leave, though not to the same degree. We will miss you. We'll feel a sense of loss, and we'll miss your questions and your observations. But we'll get by, and we'll move on. New things will happen for us to deal with, and life will go on.

"So don't feel bad that you're leaving us. You owe us nothing. True friends don't owe each other—they help each other. And you need to leave, so there's no way that we'll hold you back. We'll send you off with food in your pack and all our love in your heart, and you'll do fine and we'll do fine."

"*All* of your love?"

Gustav laughed. "Love's like that, my friend. You can give all the love you have to someone, and then find that you have even more left than when you started. And you can give all of that to someone else, and end up with even more in your heart. In fact, the more you give, the more you have—it's a rule of life."

Walker smiled. "This is a lot of information. I hope I can remember it all."

"Oh, don't worry—you're bound to forget some of it. Some of it you'll learn again from someone else, and some of it you'll possibly reject as you learn different ways of looking at things. You have a lot ahead of you— these are all but small pieces of your present."

"It's very strange," Walker said. "I don't want to leave, but I need to leave. I wish I could stay—it's so pleasant here, with you and Marie and Jacob and Mrs. Johnston and the Hauck family and the Grahams and—"

"And all those people you've gotten to know in the last six months or so. I know. They're great people. But you've learned all you can from us. It's time for you to move on, to find new teachers, to learn new lessons that you'd never be able to learn here. You have to walk down that road and find what you need in your life to make yourself whole."

"Will God be on that road for me to find?"

"God's always everywhere. It's not so much a question of finding him as acknowledging him. If you need him, he's right where you need him to be. The question is whether you'll recognize him or not.

"So you can go down that road looking for God, if you feel that's what you need to do, but don't let the idea of a destination or purpose blind you to the beauty of the journey. If you walk with your eyes on just the road and your thoughts on where you're going, you'll see nothing and you'll find nothing. But if you keep your eyes open and watch all the beauty that is there all the time, you'll find your God, and you'll have a beautiful journey."

"Is all of life just lessons to learn?" Walker asked. "It seems that there's so much to think about, so much to keep our minds busy so that we can't see things clearly."

"I think that in your case, you're trying to cram a lifetime of lessons into a very short amount of time. It must be very difficult. I don't know why or how that came to be—maybe you lost your memory and now you're filling in all the empty spaces on a completely blank slate, but you have a lot of catching up to do. You have to realize that you're going to have to process much more information in a relatively short time than most of us do in an entire lifetime. It's challenging, I'm sure, but don't let it overwhelm you."

"Sometimes I feel overwhelmed. Sometimes I feel like no more information will fit in my brain, but then I go to sleep, and I wake up and I want to know more. Knowledge is a lot like love, isn't it?"

"The more you know, the more you want to know," Gustav said. "But keep in mind that the more you know, the more you realize just how little you know."

Chapter 11

The final snowfall came just four days before Easter, and it was anything but fierce. The clouds dropped perhaps an inch of snow on the village, and there was no wind at all. The snowfall was over quickly, the air never got extremely cold, and Walker could feel the snow starting to melt almost as soon as it hit the ground. In the winter, such a snowfall would have stayed around for a while, but all of this snow was gone by the next afternoon.

He spent Easter with Marie and Jacob and Gustav. They ate a simple dinner and discussed Walker's future.

"You know, Walker," Marie told him, "when you leave tomorrow, you'll be starting anew, starting an entirely new part of your life. You won't be the same person leaving this village that you were coming here—so much has changed in the last few months."

"And you won't be leaving behind the same people that you met when you arrived," Jacob added. "We're all different, partly from knowing you, partly from what goes on every day in our lives. Now you're going out in the world to continue your search for yourself, and I think it will be a very fruitful search. You're going to meet a lot of new people and make a lot of new friends. It should be great."

Walker liked Jacob. He was a bit taller than Walker, and he had very light blond hair. He was thin, yet somehow powerful, and Walker could see a great deal of strength in him, both in his physique and in his character. He carried himself with confidence, and he had a smile for everyone he met. He and Marie fit together very well, and after having known them as long as he did, Walker couldn't imagine them apart from one another.

"You will have to be careful, though, Walker," Marie added. "So far, it sounds like you've met kind and caring people, but not everyone's like that. I'd hate to say you've been lucky so far, but that may be true. You may run into some people who want to hurt you, and they don't need a reason for wanting to do so. That doesn't mean you should be suspicious of everyone and not trust people. Just be careful."

"I shall," Walker promised. "I'll take your advice with me and try to follow it whenever I can."

"And trust yourself, too," Jacob added. "Trust your instincts especially."

"I will."

The next morning, Walker left the village. For the first time, he felt tears in his eyes; one or two even rolled down through the little valley between his nose and his cheeks. For the first time, he cried, cried at the thought of not seeing his friends any more, at the thought of having no more walks or conversations with Gustav or Marie. He saw tears in the eyes of his friends, too. They had come as far as the edge of the village with him, then had sent him on his way.

He walked a few minutes, then turned, wanting to wave one last good-bye, but his friends were gone.

He smiled. That was best.

The day was warm and the sun was shining brightly on everything around him. The sun was higher in the sky than it had been for a very long while, and as he walked away from the village he felt himself grow closer to the sun, to the trees, to the road. While he was living in the village, he had seen the sun and had seen the road, but he always saw them in passing, for an hour here, a half an hour there. Now, though, he was a part of the outdoors, and he knew that he wouldn't be going indoors to work or to read or to talk for a long time. He had no more indoors to go into.

The realization struck him suddenly, and he knew that was why he felt the exhilaration that was working its way out into him somehow. It was a feeling that seemed to have been trapped inside him, hiding in some little spot somewhere within, but that was growing stronger and taking over as he walked towards the mountain range that still had quite a lot of snow on its highest peaks. Gustav had assured him, though, that since these weren't extremely high mountains and none of the roads went over the peaks themselves, he wouldn't have any problems getting through them even though it was still early spring.

Walker carried much with him. He wore shoes and socks, and he carried several extra pairs of socks in the pack on his back. He wore underpants and pants, and had three extra pairs of underpants and one extra pair of pants in his pack. He had on two shirts, and had four extras in the pack. He also had a blanket tied to the outside of the pack.

The pack also was filled with food that he would need to start his journey with—enough for at least three days, the amount of time Jacob said it would take for him to reach the last village before the mountains, just at the foot of the range.

As he thought about what he was carrying, he considered what it might be like to leave the pack at the side of the road, take off all his clothes, and continue on as he remembered starting, his bare skin to the wind, with no encumbrances at all. He knew, though, that it wouldn't work. He was no longer the same person who had started out so long ago. He couldn't point to any differences, and he couldn't name them, but he knew that he was much different. Even the fact that he was thinking about such things, he told himself, was proof that he was different, for he had considered nothing of the sort at the beginning of his journey. In fact, at the beginning of his journey he had considered nothing at all—instead, he had experienced all that was there to be experienced. He hadn't thought about it at all. Without language, such thoughts hadn't been possible.

And what bothered him as he walked was the fact that he didn't know where or when his journey truly had begun, and he had no idea where he was from. Everyone he met could tell him about their parents or grandparents and their other relatives, but he had none to claim for his, none to provide him comfort with their memories on the long journey.

Don't miss the beauty of the journey, Gustav had told him, and he shook his head, trying to clear out the thoughts that were distracting him from the beauty of the day. He stopped and stood still, just listening and looking and feeling. The world that surrounded him was, indeed, magnificent in its beauty. Before him rose a range of mountains, watching over the world just as the trees did, but with much more majesty than the trees. The mountains were impressively silent—they needed to make no noise to make their presence known. They spoke merely with their being, with their strength, with their gentle dominance.

Where Walker stood he was surrounded by trees, but not dense growths of trees as he had seen in the forest. These trees stood apart from each other, unwilling to share the same soil with their roots. They stood almost five times his height, he guessed, and they spread their branches out in all directions, giving themselves as much surface as they could to gather the sunshine that fell to the earth in such abundance. The grass on all sides grew almost to his knees, except under the trees, where it wasn't able to get the sun it needed to grow so swiftly.

The road itself ambled as far as he could see towards the mountains, and as his eyes followed the road, he could see his future playing out somehow; he could see himself standing at the crest of the next small hill a half hour in the future, even then a different person than he was at the moment.

As he stood there, alone with the world, he lost himself so much in his surroundings that he never noticed the other man approach from behind until the man was almost upon him, and said "Hello!"

Walker jumped, pulled out of his reverie, and turned somewhat sheepishly to the man. He was somehow wary, for the man's word had seemed to be more a challenge than a greeting.

"Hello," he replied. "I was just looking at how beautiful everything is."

"Beautiful?" the man asked, then looked around quickly. "I guess it is kind of pretty if you go in for that sort of thing."

The man looked hard—that was the only word that Walker could find to describe him. His face didn't have an unpleasant expression, but he didn't look open to receive anything—no love, no cheerfulness, no appreciation.

His face was thin and drawn, and he had brown hair that came down to just over his ears and that, while not neatly combed, wasn't messy or dirty, either. His green eyes surveyed everything quickly, moving restlessly from sight to sight, never resting on any particular thing for more than the slightest of moments. His nose curved in towards his face from his brow, then curved out again to create a small point at its end. He was unshaven, with the stubble of several days on his chin and cheeks and neck.

He was a bit taller than Walker, but Walker didn't see a lot of power in his thin frame. Even though he didn't look powerful, though, he did look tough, except for his hands—they looked delicate and soft. He wore a heavy shirt of green, and black pants and brown shoes. As he stood there, Walker got the impression from just his stance that he was challenging, that he somehow looked at everything in the world as potential conflict.

Walker thought back to the three people he had seen before reaching Gustav's village, but he didn't feel the same about this man as he had felt about those three—he didn't feel that he needed to get away, that he didn't want to be around this man. The man didn't appear to be as pleasant as Kennison or Gustav or Marie, but he didn't seem to be a threat, either.

The man finished looking, then turned to Walker. "I've seen better, though. There are plenty of places nicer than this. Where are you going?"

Walker pointed to the mountains. "There," he said.

"Into the mountains, huh? Well, so am I. I'm Brian, by the way. Looks like we're heading in the same direction, so we may as well hook up. It'll be safer that way."

"My name is Walker." Brian hadn't offered to shake his hand, so Walker didn't do so, either, in case it might offend him. "What do you mean by 'safer'?"

"Safer. A robber's much less likely to attack two people than one. That is, unless there's two or three of 'em. Then they'll attack pretty much anyone they want."

"Why would people attack us?"

"Why? Because people are cruel and vicious and mean, and they want what you have, but they don't want to do anything for it 'cept maybe put a knife in your back."

Walker picked up his pack, and rather unwillingly started to walk towards the mountains with the man. He suddenly found himself yearning for Gustav's optimism, or Tricia's innocence. He had the feeling that he was in for a different type of lesson during whatever time he spent with this man.

"So where you heading in the mountains? Where you gonna lay down your pack for good?" the man asked. Walker watched his eyes whenever he could, and they continued to dart back and forth from object to object.

"I have no end destination," Walker said. "I think I'm just looking for my past. And maybe for God."

Brian stopped dead in his tracks.

"God?!" he asked, and Walker saw the first glimpse of humor that he had seen in him. It wasn't the kind of humor he was used to. "You're looking for god?"

"Yes," Walker said. "I've heard many things about him, and I've heard that life is a journey that's meant to get us closer to God. But I don't know who God is."

"I sure do have a way of pickin' 'em," Brian muttered to himself. "Well, good luck. You ain't gonna find no god around here. As far as I'm concerned, you're not gonna find god anywhere—I don't know who you've been talking to, but I can tell you one thing for sure. There ain't no god."

"What do you mean?" Walker asked as Brian started to walk again.

"Just what I said, that there ain't no god. God's an invention, something that people have created to explain stuff that can't really be explained. Like how that tree got there. Nobody can really tell you exactly how the trees got here, and most everyone's too lazy or too stupid to find out, so it's much easier to just say this god did it. Then we don't have to have any real explanations for anything. And the religious types, well, they just use god to try to make people follow their rules, what they think people should be doing—including giving them their money. It's all a sham."

"But why would people want to do something like that? If they can't explain something, why don't they just accept it as unexplainable?"

"That's easy—they're afraid. People are cowards, in general."

"Afraid of what?"

"Death. Not having power. The bottom line, my friend, is that people are afraid of dying, and they need to have some sort of explanation as to what's going to happen after they die. If they create a god and heaven, then they can feel this false sense of security about what's going to happen after they kick it. 'Oh, I'm going to heaven,' they say. 'I have nothing to worry about because god will take care of me.' They're lying to themselves to make themselves feel better."

Walker was stricken by the difference in the words "my friend"—coming from Brian, the words didn't mean anything near what they had meant coming from Gustav or Amar or Kennison.

"But how can people be happy if they're living a lie?"

"It's not happiness—it's ignorant bliss. Look, I'll give you an example. Say you're walking towards the edge of a cliff, and you know when you reach the edge, you won't be able to stop, and you're going to fall to your death. It's going to take you an hour to reach the cliff. Now, if you know you're going to fall and die, how are you going to feel during that hour?"

"I'm going to feel afraid. Anxious."

"Of course you are." Triumph shone in Brian's eyes. "All of us would. Now what would that hour be like if you were to convince yourself that once you reached the edge of that cliff, you would be able to keep walking on thin air, that you would not only be safe, but be in a much better situation, able to walk on thin air. How would that hour be?"

"It would probably be very nice, because I'd look forward to walking on air."

"Exactly. And that's what people have done with god. They've convinced themselves that once their lives are up, their one hour of walking towards the cliff, they'll be going to heaven to be with god for a blissful eternity. So now their walks feel much more pleasant.

"The problem is that even though they've convinced themselves otherwise, they're still gonna fall when they reach that cliff. All that crap about walking on air was nothing but a lie."

Walker didn't answer. He was thinking about how complicated everything had just become, because he had to admit that there might be some sense to Brian's argument. Gustav had taught him a bit about logic, but this was the first time Walker had heard logic used to contradict something he had come to believe. And what should he do? If he couldn't argue his point with Brian, did that mean his point was less valid? Was Brian right? Even though Walker didn't feel as comfortable with him as he had with Gustav, that couldn't mean that Brian had to be wrong about this. Were Gustav and Marie and Jacob and Trish wrong?

He had thought that life had become complicated while he was staying in the village, but now, not even four hours out of the village, back on the road, life had become even more complicated.

"That's interesting," he finally said. "I've never heard that perspective before."

"That's because the people who believe in god want you on their side— they don't want you to see that they're living a lie."

"Why?"

"Safety in numbers, my friend—safety in numbers."

They stopped for lunch a couple of hours later at the side of a small brook that crossed the road. Walker was surprised to see how little food Brian had—he had nothing more than a piece of bread and some cheese. Walker offered him some food, commenting on how little he had.

"Well," answered Brian, "some of us are the haves, and some are the have-nots. I do my best, but nothing ever seems to come my way, no matter how hard I work. And believe me, I've worked pretty hard in my day. And I will again. But nothing will come of that but a few meals and maybe an evening or three with a woman."

"What do you mean?" Walker asked.

"You know, you ask that question an awful lot. What's up with that? It's like you don't know anything, like you want me to explain everything to you. Are you stupid or something?"

"No, I'm not stupid. It's just that you say things that I've never heard anyone say before. It's interesting. Because you say that nothing good ever comes your way, yet today you're eating a good lunch because I'm sharing my food with you. And you haven't even had to work for the extra food. I'm glad to share it, but it is something good that you haven't had to work for."

"Work for, no, but now you're throwing guilt at me, making me feel guilty for taking your food."

"That's not my intent."

"Intent be damned—that's the result."

"But don't you think that the extra food may be God's way of taking care of you, of making sure that you have enough to eat for your journey?"

"Here you go with god again. Look—there is no god, and when we die, that's it. Poof, we're gone. There's not going to be any grand entrance into heaven, no parting of the clouds, no angel wings, no being in the presence of the 'creator.' It's over. If you want to spend your time deluding yourself, then please, feel free to do so. Just don't drag me into it."

"If you would prefer," Walker said, wondering even as he said the words if it were an appropriate thing to say, "I could travel on ahead of you or behind you. I don't mean to upset you, yet it seems that everything I say is upsetting to you."

Brian looked at Walker with challenge in his eyes—he seemed to be prepared for conflict. Yet when he looked at his companion and saw no indication of conflict at all, his expression and his eyes softened.

"No," he said, "that won't be necessary. Almost any company's better than none, you know. And you may be annoying, but you may prove to be amusing, too. All this talk of god—next thing you know, you'll be trying to convert me or something. But you won't do it. Because you see, I've seen the world—I've been around. And no god in his right mind would create such a pit as this, such a place where people treat each other like they're treated here."

Walker suddenly thought of Gustav's words: treat others as you wish to be treated. But he didn't think it would be a very good thing to mention to Brian—was it possible that he saw the world as such a horrible place because he treated other people poorly, and was treated the same way as he treated them? Walker couldn't know, but since he knew next to nothing about Brian, it didn't seem possible to reach such a conclusion.

Hours later, when they stopped to sleep, he was again surprised at Brian's lack of preparedness. All of his food was gone, so Walker shared more of his food with him, then built a small fire in a small ditch where he would be protected from any wind. Gustav had shown him how to build a very small shelter that would keep him dry in case of any rain. He began to understand Brian's attitude when he saw Brian pull from his pack a small blanket that wouldn't even cover his whole body, then tried to wrap himself up in it.

Walker knew he would be warm and fairly comfortable, and that Brian wouldn't be so, yet he didn't feel at all compelled to share his bedding. He lay down and closed his eyes, quickly falling asleep. He was very tired from the entire day of walking.

Chapter 12

Two days later, they reached the next village early in the afternoon. The two days had been very trying for Walker, for he felt a strong tension inside, he felt a lack of balance and a negativity that he never had felt before. He was sure that the feeling came from Brian, who complained constantly about everything, who showed no sense of hope or optimism at all. To Brian, the world was an awful place, where the strong hurt the weak and the weak were completely helpless.

"It's been like that forever," he told Walker early in the morning on the day they reached the village. "All of the people who want to do good in the world get stepped on by the people who want to maintain their power. Even Jesus, who was supposed to be god—he's a great example of it. Here's a man who wants to do his thing and teach people what he wants to teach them, instead of what the powerful people have been teaching for years, and they kill him. Nail him to a cross and let him die in front of everyone. It was pretty ridiculous."

"Is it that simple?" Walker asked. "Weren't there other reasons?"

"That's what his followers want you to believe—it adds mystique to who he was. He was pretty much out of it, though—he said he was the only son of god, you know, and they claimed his mom was a virgin when she had him. Ain't no virgin in this world ever had a baby, though. It's not possible."

"A friend of mine told me that the essence of faith is the letting go of everything we see as normal, and accepting that there are many things for which we have no explanations."

"Sounds like your friend was trying to make excuses for his 'faith.' Faith is just a word people use to say they're dumb enough to believe in something that they can't see, can't touch, can't prove. Call it faith, and it's religion; call it belief in something that makes no logical sense at all, and it's stupidity. You make your choice."

"Are you happy?" Walker asked.

"What the hell is that supposed to mean?" Brian asked, with a sharp glance Walker's way.

Walker didn't reply. He was thinking of the words that Jacob had told him one day when Walker and Gustav had eaten dinner at Marie and Jacob's home. Jacob had told him that if anyone wanted to teach him something, Walker should first look at the teacher's own life to see if the teacher was living what he or she taught, and to see if the teacher was happy. He didn't see that in Brian.

When they reached the village that afternoon, Walker was surprised to see how large it was—it was at least four times the size of Gustav's village. As they walked into the town, as Brian called it, Walker saw a beautiful central square, much like the one where he had first met Gustav, except this one was much larger and much more beautiful. He wanted to see it and started towards it, but he felt Brian touch his arm.

"Come on," Brian told him. "I have some friends here—they'll help us out, get us something to eat."

Walker followed him with a glance back at the square and a wish that he were heading there. Brian led him down a small side street, and Walker couldn't believe how the street kept getting smaller and smaller as they went, and dirtier and dirtier. The homes went from being neat and attractive and well kept to being run-down and dirty and ugly. He stared at the houses. The windows were all dirty, some of them even cracked or broken. Inside the windows, Walker saw piles of junk, seemingly just thrown there without any effort to keep things neat. Some of the walls of the houses were cracked, and dirty rags and papers were stuffed into the cracks. Many of the doors were coming off their hinges, and everything needed to be painted—the areas that were painted were peeling and dirty. There was garbage in the street all around, and Walker couldn't imagine how people would want to live in such conditions, or how they could let themselves live there.

It seemed that no one cared, that no one tried to keep things up, to maintain things at any level of cleanliness or order. He imagined how Gustav would react if he were to live in such an area, or Kennison, or Tricia.

Through one window he heard two children arguing, calling each other names that Walker had never heard before.

Would Kennison ever let Tricia live in such an area?

Brian, on the other hand, seemed to be in the perfect place for him. For the first time since he had met him, Walker saw Brian gain energy, saw him show enthusiasm.

"Finally," he told Walker, "a place where I can feel at home. You see, Walker, this is how most people in this world live—this is where people actually live. Here, we don't have to put up with all those stupid social expectations; we don't have to make a show to be accepted. Here, people accept you for who you are, not what job you do or what kind of clothes you're wearing. Everyone stands out equally here, and people help each other out.

"I grew up in a neighborhood just like this, and I wouldn't trade it for the world. You grow up with money, you grow up with everything you need, and you grow up soft, you grow up not knowing how to take care of yourself. I feel sorry for those people—they're lost. And the worst part is that they don't even realize that they're lost. Pretty pathetic, isn't it?"

Walker didn't answer. He felt a wariness growing inside him. He wasn't comfortable, and his instincts were drawing him back to the square where they had entered the town. But Brian was taking him away from there. He remembered Jacob's advice to trust his instincts, but he didn't know if leaving Brian would be okay. He felt that at any moment, something could happen that could be dangerous and he'd have to react somehow. But he had no idea how to react.

"Here we are!" Brian exclaimed, stopping before a filthy wooden door that hung at a slight angle on hinges that were rusting. "This is 'The Eagle's Nest.' It's not well known, but we can get something to eat and a bed to sleep on in here."

Walker followed him inside. A voice inside told him not to go in, but he didn't want to offend Brian, who was showing him what seemed to be the first bit of graciousness that Walker had seen. He also didn't want to make Brian angry again, so he decided that he would go in and have something to eat, but then he would leave and find somewhere else to sleep. He was sure he didn't want to sleep there.

The place was one of the darkest rooms that Walker had ever seen in daylight. There was only one small window, and that was covered in dark cloth. There were three tables, all small with white coverings that wore the stains of many meals. A counter ran next to one wall, about three feet from it, and a small, stout woman stood behind it. Three stools stood before it, on the side where Brian and Walker were. On the other side of the room, a stairway went up to the second floor, and Walker saw that some of the steps were cracking. He wondered how long it would be before one of them broke completely.

"G'day, Maggie," Brian said with more enthusiasm than Walker would have thought him capable of. "How are you today, my dear?"

"My dear my ass," the woman grumbled, and Walker was shocked at her voice—it was the lowest, most gravelly voice he had ever heard, and his first thought that she was a woman was thrown into doubt. He looked at her again, though, more closely, and he saw that it was true—she was a woman.

She came up only to Walker's chest, and even though she carried some extra weight on her, she was drawn and frail-looking. Her skin was wrinkled more than Walker thought possible, especially on her face, and he couldn't imagine a smile seeing the light of day on her mouth. He could barely see her eyes, for the room was too dark and the shadows around her eyes were deeper than the shadows in the rest of the room. Her hair was grey and thin—Walker could clearly see her scalp through the little hair that graced her head.

"What do you want?" she asked Brian. "Didn't expect to see you back here again."

When she talked, Walker could see that she had very few teeth left, and those she had were dark and crooked. He thought of Mrs. Goodson, who had died, who had certainly been on the planet as long as this woman, but who wasn't nearly as decrepit, not nearly as old as this woman.

"Relax, Maggie," Brian said. "My friend and I just stopped in to grab a bite to eat, maybe get something to drink. You still have rooms upstairs?"

The woman looked at Walker as if she hadn't seen him enter at all, as if he had materialized before her without warning.

"You have a friend?" she croaked, looking back at Brian. "Lord have mercy—and I'll bet they're havin' a snowball fight down in hell even as we speak."

"Now, Maggie, don't be harsh. This is Walker. We've been traveling together a couple of days, and we're famished. Our food ran out yesterday afternoon, and we've been walking all day without a bite to eat."

"Walker, is it?" Maggie asked, then turned back to Brian. "Your credit's not good here—you know that."

"Walker, I'd like you to meet Maggie," Brian said, seeming to ignore her comment. "She's just like a mother to me whenever I'm in town. Maggie, this is Walker, but I call him Mark—you know, after that book in the Bible. What is it, Matthew, Mark, John and—" His voice trailed off as he was unable to come up with the last name.

"Matthew, Mark, Luke and John, you heathen," Maggie told him spitefully. "Then fine—eat your fill, but there'll be no problems here in this house, you understand?"

"Completely, my dear lady. Could you bring us some bread and cheese? And not any of that week-old stuff you give to those unsuspecting souls who don't know the depth of your kindness—something from today. And some wine. The strongest you've got."

Maggie glanced again at Walker when Brian said the last words.

"I'll get you what you want," she said, "but there'll be no problems in this house. You hear me, heathen?"

"I hear you loud and clear, m'dear," Brian replied with a smile. It was the first time Walker had seen him smile, other than the smiles of contempt that he tended to wear when he thought of other people's stupidity. This smile, though, had no sincerity or humor behind it at all.

Walker was confused. Brian had never called him "Mark" before, so why had he told this woman that he did? Something had happened during the conversation that Walker hadn't noticed at all—he had understood the words, but even though Brian seemed satisfied to have arranged things, Walker had no idea what had been arranged.

Maggie brought out the wine and cheese and bread, and Walker asked for water—he was very thirsty, and Gustav had warned him never to drink more than two small glasses of wine, for the effects of alcohol were very strong, especially for someone who didn't drink much. Walker didn't want to drink too much of the wine at all.

"Don't have no water," Maggie said brusquely, not even looking at him. "Water's no good for you, anyway."

"You tell him, Maggie," Brian agreed with a laugh. "Don't worry about it, Walker. There's not much alcohol in this wine. They water it down here, to make it last longer."

"But you asked for the strongest wine they have."

Brian laughed again. "That I did—you're right there. But I was talkin' about flavor, not alcohol. You can get some wines that have no flavor at all, just a tiny hint of the grapes of the vine. But you can get wines like this one, where you taste every grape that god put onto this planet."

"Don't you dare use God's name, you heathen," Maggie snapped at Brian with contempt. Brian looked down at the bar, but he didn't respond to her. "Doesn't even know the gospels," Maggie muttered, leaving the room, "but wants to use God's name for his own purposes."

Walker watched her leave.

"She doesn't like you," he told Brian.

"Sure, she does," Brian assured him. "She's just got a funny way of showing it. Here, have some wine and bread and cheese. If you go light on the wine, it won't be a problem."

Walker started to eat and Brian poured him a glass of wine from the bottle Maggie had put in front of him. He wondered why they had separate bottles, but he just assumed that it was customary in that place. He told himself that he would drink only one glass and then leave, but almost as soon as he took a drink, Brian refilled his glass. He tried to drink slowly, eating a lot of bread and cheese, but after a very few drinks the alcohol started to affect his judgment. He no longer knew what a little bit of wine was. The feeling he had as he started to get drunk was somewhat pleasing, somewhat disconcerting, and he didn't know what to think about the experience he was having.

He completely lost track of time, and he soon found it easy to laugh at almost anything that Brian said to him, even though inside he knew that Brian was saying nothing funny.

He noticed a change in Maggie, too—the looks that she gave him had somehow changed from disinterested to pitying. Walker didn't want to see that, though, or acknowledge it, for the wine in his bloodstream made him feel that everything was fine.

By the time he started thinking about sleep, he noticed that the lamps inside the place had been lit, and that there was no longer even the slightest hint of light coming in from behind the dark cloth over the window.

He told Brian, "I need to sleep."

Brian stopped smiling, then looked at something behind Walker. Walker tried to turn quickly to look, but he lost his balance because he couldn't turn nearly as quickly while drunk. He regained his balance, then turned slowly to see a very large man sitting behind him, watching him with eyes like those of the two men and women on the road so long ago.

"I have to go," he told Brian, noting that his words were slurred and unclear. Brian looked back at him with contempt.

"Not until you pay your bill," Brian said, and something clicked in Walker's mind, a sort of warning that he didn't recognize.

"How much is it?" Walker asked, somewhat surprised that Brian didn't seem to be feeling any effects of the wine. He pulled all of his money from the pocket where he was carrying it.

Brian quickly grabbed the money from his hand. "Get the hell out of here!" he yelled at Walker, then Walker watched in disbelief as Brian pulled back his arm, made a fist with his hand, and brought the fist forward with all its force to hit Walker squarely in the face. Pain burst through Walker's entire being with an incredible force, and he fell to the floor, not sure what was going on. Could this really be happening? He staggered to his feet, then reached for his pack, which was on the floor. As he bent over, Brian gave him as strong a kick as he could in the stomach. Walker lost his breath completely and fell once more to the floor.

"You won't be needing that," Brian said spitefully. "Now get the hell out!"

Walker was about to turn to the door, still unable to believe what was happening, when Maggie yelled out "Stop!"

Walker hadn't seen her in the room when this had started, but now she came back in and grabbed the money from Brian's hand. She took two of the larger bills and stuffed them into Walker's pants pocket.

"From now on," she told Walker gruffly, "stay away from garbage like this one. They're no good for you."

Walker heard Brian roar with laughter at the words, and the laughter sounded horrible—mean and angry and bitter.

He stumbled past the other man, who made no move to do anything, when he heard Brian yell "Wait a second!" He turned and watched Brian approach him, a look of gleeful malice on his face. Before he realized what he was doing, Brian punched him again, this time in the stomach just above where he had kicked him. The blow forced Walker to collapse once more— he had never felt such pain.

"That's for making me put up with all your asinine questions," Brian said viciously, "and all your stupid talk about god. Go on now—maybe god'll help you now. Maybe you'll find him in the gutter you pass out in."

Walker staggered out the door, bent over in agony. Once on the street, he vaguely remembered the direction they had come from, though the darkness was overwhelming. He couldn't concentrate at all because of the pain, and suddenly he felt a new sensation start in his stomach and work its way quickly up through his throat and mouth, and he felt the food and drink of the last couple of hours force its way out of his system. The vomit was bitter and foul-tasting, and he looked unbelieving at it. That had come from inside of him? He turned and staggered away, slowly making his way back towards where they had come from.

Somehow, he made it back to the point where he and Brian had left the main road—by that time, his head was clearing a bit and the pain had diminished somewhat. He walked slowly into the main square that he had seen earlier that day.

"This is where I should have come," he whispered to himself. But that chance was gone forever, so he turned and got back on the road that led into the mountains, the road that started uphill at the edge of the village, and he started to stumble through the night. He didn't want to stop, didn't want to think, didn't want to sleep. There was enough starlight to light his way, but he didn't notice any stars. Two hours later, the moon arose, giving him even more light, but he didn't notice the beauty of the moon.

A river flowed right next to the road, sending its music up into the valley formed by the hills that rose on either side of the road, but Walker didn't even hear it. He staggered on, and as time passed and the pain and the effects of the alcohol subsided even more, he was able to walk almost normally, though slowly.

He had never felt alone before, but that night, for the first time, he felt a sense of loneliness, felt the desire to be with someone else with whom he could talk, whom he could ask the important questions that were on his mind, like why someone would do this to someone else. Even more perplexing to him, though, was how someone could do such a thing to another human being.

But there was no one there with him, and he continued to walk as the night grew almost unbearably cold, continued to walk on without his pack or his blanket.

Sometime in the very early morning, though, a couple of hours before the sun came up, he found he could go no further. His strength had been waning for a while, and the pain from the punches and the kick kept coming and going—sometimes it was very strong, sometimes almost unnoticeable. Suddenly, the dizziness welled up inside him and almost took away his sense of balance. He turned to the side of the road and vomited once more, causing more pain to his insides. The taste in his mouth was the worst taste he had ever experienced—bitter and foul. His head became very light, and he found that he was unable to regain his concentration. Suddenly, he felt that he was completely detached from his own body, as if his arms and hands and legs were no longer under his control. He staggered off the road and collapsed behind a stand of bushes, and he immediately passed out.

The sun was already up when he regained consciousness. He had never felt that way when he had woken up before—his head and body ached, and he lay there where he was for several very long minutes, unable to move, unable to figure out where he was. Bit by bit, he pieced together what had happened the night before, and how he had come to be lying in the dirt with no shelter at all. He moved, and immediately felt soreness all through his body. The air was cold and he was shivering, but it took him several minutes before he was able to stand and move out into the sunlight.

He was hungry, but he was also nauseous. He felt that he might vomit again. It wasn't a pleasant feeling. The sun warmed him, but instead of feeling the rejuvenation that the sunshine normally brought him, he found that the part of him that responded to the sunshine was much deeper inside him, and he felt that it would take much longer for him to enjoy the sunshine as he normally did. First, he would have to recover, to reach a state at which that part of him that celebrated the sunlight could come out quickly and easily. Many barriers had been put in his way in the last hours, but mostly those of confusion and pain.

He was glad that no one was around, even if he was hungry. He felt bad, and he was pretty sure that he looked just as bad. He leaned against a large rock and rested, still tired from his lack of sound sleep and his ordeal of the night before. The simple act of getting up and moving out to the road seemed to tire him out.

He was thirsty. Never before had he felt such thirst—his mouth was parched, as if there wasn't a bit of moisture in it at all, and he knew that his first priority would have to be to find water. He vaguely remembered the sound of water from the night before, but he couldn't place it, couldn't remember how long it had been since he had last heard it until the time he stopped. He thought of retracing his steps until he came to the river, but he knew that it might take him an hour or more—it would be just as likely that he could find water by continuing on his way.

He started to walk, wincing at the pain of the first few steps. He held his left hand over his eye where Brian had hit him, for that was the most painful spot, and he watched the road with the other eye. The longer he walked, though, the more he woke up, and the better his body was able to cope with the pain. Soon the pain no longer overwhelmed him, though it did stay with him.

Soon he found water when the road crossed over the river, and he drank more than he believed he could. His thirst seemed to be insatiable. Soon he felt more discomfort in his stomach than he had from the thirst. He felt bloated, stretched inside, and he sat back, sighing, realizing that he had traded one source of discomfort for another.

He wished Gustav were there, or Marie, or anyone else. He wanted to talk, he wanted to ask questions, he wanted to know what could make people do such things. Gustav had told him about evil, but he didn't think that he had ever felt a sense of evil from Brian—he certainly wasn't a pleasant person, but evil?

Then Walker remembered the glance he had had of the man who had been sitting behind him, and he shuddered. Who had that been? Where had that look in his eyes come from? Why did it make Walker feel so cold inside just to remember him?

Could that man have been evil?

Walker sat for a very long time, not at all in a hurry to get back on the road. Soon his belly began to feel more normal, and he began to feel tired again. He knew he had not slept much the night before, and that he had slept fitfully at best, so he lay down in the grass far off the road and went to sleep. This time he slept well.

When he awoke again, the sun was well into the afternoon sky. He couldn't believe that so much of the day had gone by already. He had done absolutely nothing, it seemed. Normally he would have walked miles and miles by this time of the day, or he and Gustav had made an entire day's worth of bread and had gotten a start on the next day's work. There was so much he could have seen, so much he could have done, but he had done nothing but sleep.

He felt refreshed—the pain was still there, but it was quickly subsiding, and Walker realized just how healing the true sleep had been. His mind was clear now, not fuzzy and weak and distorted. Earlier that morning, thoughts had come to with difficulty, and they had come in fragments which he had found hard to string together in any sort of coherent fashion. Now, though, he was thinking as he normally thought, and he looked about himself and noticed that his surroundings were beautiful once more.

He sat next to a small river in a field of grass that came up to his ankles. A band of trees stretched along the opposite bank of the river, and beyond that was a broad, flat field that had been turned recently—all of the dirt had been disturbed, in a very regular pattern, and nothing was growing there. Behind him, too, stretched a field that had been disturbed but in which nothing grew. The sun was high in the sky and warm on his skin, and a slight breeze made its way through the trees, carrying with it the scent of the delicate flowers that stood at the ends of the branches, hiding most of the leaves, which were still very small. He hadn't ever experienced that particular smell before, and he inhaled deeply, trying to capture the fragrance in his memory.

He stood and stretched, feeling his muscles protest at first, but yield and even appreciate his efforts after a moment or two. The stretching did them good, and Walker smiled in spite of himself. He still had no answers for what had happened, but the need for answers was fading. He still felt much worse than he ever had before, but better than he had felt just hours earlier. He still was surrounded by beauty, and he would much rather focus on the wonderful things around him than the inexplicable actions of some people whom he probably never would see again.

He got back on the road and he started to walk again.

Walker soon noticed the valley in which he was walking. He must have walked for a very long time the night before, because all he could see behind him were mountains, and before him and to his sides stretched the valley. The ground there was very flat, and most of it looked to be barren of any growth at all. In the distance, he saw people walking over the ground, following animals, holding some sort of contraption in their hands. As he got closer, he saw that the large animals were actually pulling the tool, and the men who were following them were merely controlling its direction.

Very soon he came to a house that stood at the side of the road, and he decided to try to buy some food—his hunger was almost overwhelming, and it had begun to draw his attention from other things. He reached into his pocket and pulled out the two bills, and in doing so reminded himself of Maggie's action from the night before. He had just the slightest of memories of them. He didn't know why she had done what she had done, but he did know that he was able to approach this house and offer to pay for food, rather than beg for food, because of her action. He appreciated what she had done.

But hadn't she known what Brian was going to do, and allowed it to happen?

It was very complex, and he was very hungry, so he shrugged his shoulders and left those thoughts for another time.

He didn't get a chance to go up to the door and knock, for before he could do so, a man came around the corner of the house and stopped when he saw Walker. He looked surprised to find anyone there.

"Good day," the man said in a not-at-all-unfriendly voice. He started forward again, walking out to a box that stood on a pole next to the road and pulling small rectangular pieces of paper from it.

"I'm looking for food," Walker said.

"We got no handouts," the man said, not unkindly. "This time of the season is our hard time, too. Sorry." He had been walking back in the direction he had come from, but then he stopped and regarded Walker more closely. "Looks like you've been in a scrape or two."

Walker touched his eye. "Some people wanted to take my money," he said simply. "But I want no 'handout.' I would like to buy some food." He held out the two bills he had left.

The man looked at him several moments longer. He looked to have a great deal of strength, even though he wasn't very large. He was even a couple of inches shorter than Walker, but much thicker, much stockier. His arms were thick with muscles, and his chest very broad. The skin on his face looked tough, as if the man had spent many hours in the sun or in the wind, and his black hair was short, cut close to his head. Most importantly, though, in his clear blue eyes Walker saw a friend. The man walked up to him, looking Walker straight in the eye.

"You looking for work?" he asked. "We could use some help around here. We're right in the middle of planting season, and we're a couple of hands short. If you think you could handle work like that."

"I learn very quickly," Walker replied, interested in working again in spite of his desire to be on the road. He knew that he would need more money soon if he still wanted to eat, and right then he needed food badly.

"We have about two weeks of work, if that suits you," the man said.

"That will suit me," Walker replied.

The man held out his hand. "Name's Turner. Nate Turner."

"I am Walker." Turner's grip didn't disappoint Walker—it was the strongest grip he had felt, though he could feel that Turner wasn't putting all his strength into it.

"Well, Walker, let's get you something to eat, then get you out into the fields. We've got a lot of work to do." He turned and led Walker inside.

"Annie!" he called out as they entered, "Could you round up some food, please? We've got a new hand here who needs to eat."

Walker heard a door open upstairs, then the sound of feet hurrying down the stairs. He watched as a woman came into view—a lovely young woman with a bright smile on her face.

"Sure thing, daddy," she said, kissing him on the cheek. "My name's Annie," she said, holding her hand out to Walker. He shook it, surprised that her grip was almost as strong as her father's.

"My name is Walker," he replied.

"I'm pleased to meet you," she said, then turned to her father. "I was just working on my dress," she told him as she hurried into the kitchen. "It's going to be absolutely beautiful!" She looked very much like her father, though more feminine. Her hair curled down to the middle of her back, and she definitely had her father's eyes, but not his skin—hers was soft and smooth. She also didn't have his smile—hers was much different than his, much more open, less restrained, more welcoming and much brighter.

Turner smiled. "Annie's getting married next month. She and her mother are making her a dress for the occasion. I'll be out in the barn—Annie'll point it out to you when you've finished eating. We'll talk about pay later. I can't make you rich, but I can promise that I'll be fair. You just sit down at that table, and Annie'll bring you out a sandwich."

"Thank you," Walker said, sitting down.

"Don't be all day now," Turner said, then went into the kitchen and told Annie to show Walker the barn when he was through eating. Then he went out the back door, and Walker was left at the table, listening to Annie make a sandwich and wondering at how quickly things had changed.

Chapter 13

Though he was sore, Walker started work that day. Turner was a good teacher, and very soon Walker knew just how to plow a field, how to turn the soil behind the ox that pulled the plow. That's all he did that afternoon, until the sun was very low in the sky and Turner told him they were finished for the day. That was when he met Frank, the other hand, with whom he'd be sharing a room in the barn where Turner had told him he'd be sleeping.

He and Frank didn't eat in the house, as Walker had expected; Annie brought them out plenty of food, and they ate at a table next to the barn. Turner ate with them.

"I don't like to dirty up the house this time of year," he explained to Walker, "and I sure as heck don't feel like taking the time to clean up before I eat—by this time of day I'm too hungry to take any time cleaning up. Besides, everyone else eats earlier than we do, so there's no sense in making everyone change their schedule just for us."

Frank was quiet. He was very small, and his skin was darker than Walker's or Turner's, but not nearly as dark as Amar's had been. He seemed always to be in deep thought, and Walker found himself wondering more than once during their meal what Frank was thinking about. He seemed to be a very nice person, but it was hard for Walker to tell since he said hardly anything.

"Frank's the quiet type," Turner said to Walker. "His father runs the store in town, and Frank's worked for me during the sowing season for the past three years or so. Isn't that right, Frank?"

Frank looked up with his eyes, but barely lifted his head from where it had been bent over his plate. Walker got the feeling that he was somehow uncomfortable talking, so he didn't ask any questions himself even though he was interested in knowing more about Frank.

"So where you from, Walker?" Turner asked, taking another bite of his sandwich, "and how the heck did you get that black eye?"

Walker had noticed that often, when people asked two questions, the second question was answered and the first one forgotten in the course of answering the second one. So he gave Turner and Frank a detailed account of how he had come to be traveling with Brian, and how Brian had robbed him and hit him the night before. He saw that both Turner and Frank were listening closely, very interested in the details. He finished at the point where he had passed out on the road in the dark, not having any idea where he was.

Turner shook his head when Walker was done. "Bad stroke of luck, that," he said. "Any time you run into a piece of garbage like that, you're going to get hurt in the end, no matter how much you help him. That sort of thing makes me more angry than almost anything else—taking advantage of another person like that, then hurting the person on top of it."

"I just don't understand how anyone could do that to anyone else," Walker said quietly. "I couldn't even imagine wanting to hurt another person."

"You will. For most people, it takes something very extreme to make them want to hurt someone else. If anyone were to hurt a friend or my family, I'd certainly want to put some hurtin' on that person. Not that I would necessarily do so, mind you—that's a line we should almost never step over, the line between wanting to harm someone and actually doing so.

"But people like this Brian fellow, usually they just pull themselves back so far from other people, isolate themselves so much that they stop seeing the humanity in others, stop seein' that we're all in the same boat, trying to row as best we can. And the more they withdraw, the more they make themselves suffer, and the more they suffer, the more they blame others for their suffering. And of course, the more we blame others for things that have happened to us, the easier it is to hurt those people, the easier it is to see them as enemies rather than fellow human beings."

"So he blamed me for his unhappiness?"

"Only because you happened to be there. If I had been there, he would've blamed me. If it had been Frank, he would have knocked Frank silly. They stop caring, you know? They get so wrapped up in themselves, in pitying themselves because life's so unfair to them, that they lose touch with love. It's very sad, because they're the people who most need love, but they're the hardest to give it to."

"Why? I've heard that said before."

"Because if they feel love, it's hard for them to continue to feel sorry for themselves. And feeling sorry for themselves is pretty much all they know anymore."

"My brother's like that," Frank offered, the first words Walker had heard him say other than hello. "He thinks that everyone wants to hurt him and that everyone does things just to make him feel bad. So he feels bad, and blames it on other people. Sometimes, after we've talked with someone else, he'll say to me that the other person had insulted him. But I didn't see it that way at all. But then he gets mad at the other person, and the other person never knows it—only my brother becomes miserable, because he's so busy being mad at someone who didn't even do what my brother thinks he did. It's really weird."

"But so is life," Turner offered, getting up and starting to clear the table. "That's what keeps it interesting. Walker, Frank will show you your quarters—they're not much, but you will have a comfortable place to sleep. I'd suggest you get to sleep pretty early—we start as soon as there's light to work by. I'll be seeing you two in the morning," he said, heading indoors with a handful of plates and food.

"He's a really good man," Frank said when Turner was out of earshot. "Come on—I'll show you where we sleep."

Walker fell asleep as soon as he lay down, and his sleep was deep and untroubled. Morning came early, but Walker was ready for it, up as soon as Turner came into their quarters to wake them. The habits of the bakery hadn't left him at all.

After a quick, small breakfast, Walker found himself once again breaking ground with a plow behind a huge ox, who looked at him with deep dark eyes as Turner showed him how to hook up the plowshare. Walker touched the animal on the shoulder, holding his hand there for several long moments, feeling the power inside the animal. He knew that he couldn't even feel a small portion of the animal's true strength, but what he did feel almost overwhelmed him.

"We're fortunate that an animal this large wants to help us," Walker said to Turner. "If all this power were used to destroy, we would have a lot of problems, I think."

Turner grinned, and Walker saw the irony in his grin that he had sometimes seen before in Gustav's smiles when he had seen some humor in Walker's perspective or explanation of something.

"You're right," Turner told Walker, showing him how to cinch the strap that went around the animal's massive body. "This animal could do some great damage if it wanted to. But I'm not so sure that 'wants to' is the right way to explain why it works for us. A lot of that mildness is the result of a sharp pair of scissors when the animal's quite young."

Walker looked questioningly at Turner, who smiled more broadly. "Look," he explained, leaning down on one knee and pointing under the animal. "He's missing something the other oxen, the ones we use for breeding, still have. This particular ox will sire no calves, because we cut off his testicles."

Walker was aghast, and one hand involuntarily covered his crotch. He looked at Turner, then back at the spot where the animal had been cut.

"It sounds cruel, doesn't it?" Turner asked. "And in a way, it definitely is. But this animal is useless to us if we don't do that—not only useless, but often dangerous. This way, the animal helps us, and we feed the animal and keep it clean and healthy. The simple fact of the matter is that we couldn't do nearly as much work, and couldn't produce nearly as many crops, if these animals weren't helping us. It's one of those tradeoffs that have to happen, and I guess we'll never know if we're within our rights to do what we do to an animal like this. Inside, I don't feel that it's wrong. So I don't worry about it."

They were finished, and Walker took one last look in the animal's eyes before he took hold of the plow and started plowing.

The work was very pleasant, if a bit tedious. Walker loved the smell of the earth that was being turned after a long winter of being frozen. Something happened when he exposed the ground that had been underneath to the air, and the flat ground that stretched out before him quickly became broken ground behind him. The dirt was full of interesting things such as rocks and roots and worms and insects. Sometimes he would stop and reach down and pick up a handful of the ground, letting the dirt sift slowly through his fingers, watching for anything that might be interesting.

At times he saw small animals running away as he and the ox approached—a few rabbits left their winter homes, and several snakes slithered away as quickly as they could.

The morning air was cool and damp, and the ground was covered with a thick layer of dew. His shoes had been soaked after just a few steps in the grass outside the barn, and the dampness in the air made him feel colder than he did on most mornings. The air was still, though—not a breeze blew, and the only sounds were the songs of the birds that made their homes in the trees that bordered the fields.

Walker was glad the work was so simple. He had to follow the ox from one side of the field to the other, then he and the ox had to turn around and walk back to the other side, right next to the furrow that they had just plowed. This they did over and over, and Walker had to be sure only that they were the proper distance from the previous furrow and that the ground was being broken deeply enough by the plow in his hands.

He was glad of the simplicity because it gave him a chance to think, even while he was working to accomplish something. This job was much different than the work at the bakery—there, he always had something else to be doing, another batch of dough to make, another tray full of loaves to pull from the oven, another bag of flour to open. This job didn't demand as much thought, as much work, but it was pleasant in itself.

There also was something calming about working with the soil, working with the very earth that gave him sustenance. The work jarred his memory, and he felt a bit of the closeness to everything that surrounded him that he had felt when he had first stepped onto the road, when his mind hadn't been occupied by so many thoughts and ideas and feelings and contradictions.

He found that the work was soothing, and he went about it wholeheartedly. He found that his thoughts were calmer, slower, and he took advantage of the opportunity to think through many of the things he had been exposed to recently. There were so many contradictions in what he had heard from Brian that he had become very confused in a very short time. He remembered the stress he had felt just from being around him, and he was glad that they had parted company, even if the parting had been rather sudden and brutal. Most of all, though, as he worked he came to see the truth in Turner's words—Brian was a person who felt little or no love at all, and he was a person who needed love badly, but who didn't allow love into his life.

Brian had spent almost three days with Walker, and Walker had shared his food with him, talked to him, offered his friendship, yet Brian had gained nothing from those three days. Walker realized that Brian probably had spent most of that time planning how to rob him, and probably had never thought at all of how a friendship with another person was worth more than any money could be. For Walker's part, he would have been more than glad to share his money with a friend, and Brian wouldn't have had to rob him to get the money from him.

He thought of how Gustav and Marie were happy people, for they were satisfied with what they were doing, and they had good friends—people who cared for them and wanted to be with them.

Walker was realizing that he had choices to make—he could choose how he wanted to act, and he saw that if he acted one way, people would react to him in one manner, but if he acted another way, people would react differently, treat him differently. He knew that he never wanted to act like Brian, who pushed other human beings out of his life; he would much rather be like Kennison or Gustav, willing to love other people, and willing to be loved in return.

When he stopped to rest, he saw that his thoughts had kept him occupied for quite a long time—he already had plowed a great deal of the ground. As he looked back over the work he had done, he felt a sense of pride, of accomplishment, exactly like the feeling he had every time he finished baking bread. It was a very nice feeling, one that he appreciated and that he knew he would have to seek out more. And he was sure that the only way he could get the feeling was through working, and seeing the results of his work.

Annie soon brought him a lunch that he was to eat out in the field—she explained to him that if they were to plant all they needed to plant on time, they had to finish the plowing very quickly. She also told him that they were very lucky that Walker had come along, because the man they had hired had quit just the day before, and it had looked for a while that the plowing wouldn't get done on time for them to use all of their fields that year.

"Why did he quit?" Walker asked, taking a bite of the sandwich, relishing the heightened sense of taste he enjoyed from working hard outdoors and working up a hunger.

"Mostly because daddy tends to be rather strict—he's a very demanding man, and a lot of people don't like that. This man was plowing the furrows too far apart, so we wouldn't have been able to plant as much as we normally do, so daddy told him he needed to pay more attention to his work. He didn't, though, and he kept on plowing too wide, so daddy yelled at him. Mistakes like that are very costly, and they're such useless mistakes—all someone has to do is pay attention to their work, and do it right the first time. As soon as daddy yelled at him, he up and quit. Didn't like to be told he was doing something wrong, I guess."

"But if he wasn't doing something right, why didn't he want to be told? I don't understand."

"A lot of people take things like that very personally. Daddy says that if someone's criticizing our work, we shouldn't take that as a criticism of ourselves. But a lot of people can say that two plus two equal five, and if you tell them that's the wrong answer, that two plus two are four, they'll take it as criticism of them personally."

"Then how do they ever get corrected when they're making mistakes? Wrong is wrong, in many things."

Annie smiled. "Yes, it is. But whenever you try to let someone know they're wrong, you're taking a chance that you're going to insult them. I've been lucky—daddy and mommy are very demanding, but they're fair. And we've always known that when they corrected us, they were doing it for our benefit, not to cut us down or make us feel bad."

"It sounds like you're very lucky to have him as a father."

"Yes, I am. I'll miss him when I move out."

"When you get married?"

"Yes. We'll live close by, but I know it won't be the same. I'm sure it will be nice, though—just in a different way. I can't live with my parents all of my life, can I?"

Walker shrugged, for he didn't know the answer to that question. It seemed that Annie didn't even expect an answer. She took the bottle of water that Walker had been drinking from and pulled another from her bag, handing it to him.

"It's been very nice talking to you, Mr. Walker," she said, "but it's about time I got some food to Frank, or he'll be dying of starvation here pretty soon."

Walker gave her a surprised look, then looked over to the other field where Frank was doing the same work as he was. Frank was still working as he had been doing all morning. Annie's smile turned a bit perplexed.

"I don't mean that literally, Mr. Walker," she said, almost scolding him gently with her tone. "It's just a saying. Nobody who works for my daddy would ever so much as go hungry while working for us. My daddy takes very good care of people, even if he is very demanding."

Walker smiled. "I believe that," he said. "Thank you very much for the lunch."

"You're welcome. I hope you have fun with the rest of the field," Annie said over her shoulder as she walked away. "I'll see you later."

After many more hours of work and another, lighter meal in the afternoon, again delivered by Annie, Walker and Turner and Frank ended their day with another hearty meal outdoors. After the meal, Frank went for a walk, but he didn't invite Walker along. Walker almost asked if he could go with him, but then he realized that he was really too tired to go for a walk with Frank. It was all he could do to wash up and make his way to bed.

He fell on the bed more than lay down on it, and he had very few thoughts in his mind before sleep came over him in a great wave. He was smiling, though, as he fell asleep, for he knew that he had done a good job that day—Turner had told him so, and he was happy that he was able to help out someone like Turner by doing work that was so pleasant.

Walker spent many days doing such work, and soon he was used to it, so he didn't get nearly as tired at the end of the day. He was able to take some walks with Frank, who turned out to be much more talkative than Turner gave him credit for.

Within a few days the plowing was done, and the three men began the process of fertilizing the land. Walker didn't like the smell of the manure they used, especially after Turner told him what it was, and the job wasn't nearly as pleasant as the plowing had been. But it was soon over, and just in time—two days of heavy rain kept them inside, working in the barn, getting the seeds ready for sowing. Turner was satisfied with the timing of the rain, he told Walker, for it would work the manure deeper into the ground so the crops would have more nourishment.

On the rainy days the work didn't last nearly as long, and Walker and Frank had more of a chance to talk.

"Do you believe that there's a God, Frank?" Walker asked as they lay on their beds, listening to the rain outside. "Some people I've met believe in God, but Brian said that there is no God, that people made him up to explain things they couldn't explain themselves, and to make themselves fear death less."

Frank didn't answer immediately, but thought the question over a few moments. "And what do you think?" he finally asked.

Walker shook his head. "I don't know. I think that I would tend to believe Gustav and Marie more than I would believe Brian, because Brian is a very unhappy person."

"And very cynical, from what you've told us."

"Yes. But I've never seen God, so I don't know what to believe. I think that if I could meet him and see him, and look into his eyes, I would know whether or not I could believe in him. I think that I'm looking for God, in a way, but I don't know when or where I'll meet him."

"You'll never meet God," Frank said. "Not in the way you met me or Turner or your other friends. God isn't a someone—God simply is. You meet God in your heart, not with your physical self. That's why we were given a heart, and that's why we have a soul."

"But Gustav said that the heart is there to send blood through our bodies."

Frank laughed. "Not that heart. The heart I'm talking about is the heart that's part of your spirit. That's the part of you that allows you to feel bad for Brian, even after the horrible things he did to you."

"But he's a very unhappy person."

"Exactly. That's your heart talking. Your mind would give you all sorts of reasons for being angry with him, for hating him for what he's done. Your heart is the compassionate side, the side that tries to see the good in him. You have a very large heart. I've seen it."

"But if I hate Brian, then I'll end up being as unhappy as Brian."

"He's unhappy because he hates, and he's angry."

"Yes."

"My point exactly. If you keep looking for God, God will show himself to you in that part of you that allows you to think that way, that allows you to feel love for someone who has abused you, who's hurt you both physically and emotionally. The more people you meet, the more people will be able to open doors for you, more windows so that you can clearly see God inside of yourself. God isn't something that we find in the middle of the woods or on a pedestal somewhere. God is something we uncover as we learn more about how to love."

"But I met Brian, and he didn't help me at all."

"That's untrue. He's helped you just as much, if not more, than the other people you've met."

"What do you mean?" Walker was confused.

"Well, you've already told me that you don't want to be as unhappy as he is, right?"

"Yes."

"And you already understand why he's unhappy."

"I think so."

"So you know now what kind of attitude and what kinds of actions will make you as unhappy as he is. It's just as important for us to learn about what will make us unhappy, and then to avoid making those mistakes, as it is for us to learn what will make us happy. The other thing that Brian exposed you to, though, is one of the things that my mother told me over and over that we all have to practice if we're to live happy lives—forgiveness. It doesn't sound like you had much reason to forgive anyone before—the other people you've mentioned have been pretty kind to you, for the most part. And you've never mentioned anyone else who has harmed you."

Walker thought for a few moments, then said, "You're right—everyone has been very kind to me, and has helped me very much. Except Brian and the people in the place we went."

"Does Brian forgive people?" Frank asked.

"No. He stays angry with them, and he continues to focus on their faults and shortcomings, even when there doesn't really seem to be any there at all."

"So part of Brian's unhappiness comes from his inability or unwillingness to forgive?"

"I believe so."

"You see? He's proving my mom right. Are you mad at Brian for what he did to you? Are you holding on to anger? Do you continue to feel bad things about him, to wish bad things on him, because he's hurt you?"

"No. That would hurt me."

"Exactly. You've forgiven him. And that forgiveness will make you a stronger person. Most religions teach us that forgiveness is one of the keys to a happy life. My dad and mom say it's one of the most important things in life. Some people disagree with them, but I know it works for my parents—they have a lot of peace in their hearts and minds, and some people I know don't have any peace at all. I try to learn my lessons from people I don't want to be like as well as from people I do want to be like."

"Both you and Annie love your parents and want to be like them," Walker said, thinking hard. "I wonder what kind of father Brian has."

"My father says that if you look at the kind of father a man would be, you'll often see the kind of father that man has. What's your father like?"

Walker looked at Frank.

"I don't know," he said quietly. "I don't even know if I have a father. I remember nothing before last summer, when I started walking. Things were different then, but I don't know what was before then."

"That's really strange," Frank said. "I don't know what I would feel like if I knew nothing about my past. That's a part of me that I can't imagine being without."

"And it's a part of me that I can't imagine having."

Chapter 14

Time went by very quickly at the farm, and within a couple of weeks Walker was feeling the draw of the road once more. He knew that Turner needed him for at least another week, so he decided that he would stay on and finish up the work that he had started for him. The prospect of leaving didn't affect him so much now. He figured that it was partly because he had been there such a short time, and partly because of the nature of the work—he was out in the fields all day, and his contact with the other people on the farm was minimal because he was almost always working. Once, Turner's wife had eaten dinner with the three men, but other than that and Annie's deliveries of the meals, he never had any contact with anyone other than Turner and Frank.

He felt good about the work, though, and he was glad that he had had the chance to work on the land. They had timed Annie's wedding to coincide with the end of the first sowing season—Turner explained to him how they had several during the course of the spring and summer—so Walker would have to wait four or five days after the job ended if he wanted to see it. While he thought it might be interesting, he knew that no emotional bonds tied him with either person and that there was no social expectation for him to stay for the ceremony. He decided to heed the call of the road and leave when he finished working.

Before he left, he spent several evenings making a small tent, which Frank taught him to do. He also bought new clothes to replace what Brian had stolen, including a rather heavy coat as Turner had warned him of the coldness of the mountain nights. Walker didn't remember much of the night he had come into the mountains and he had been sleeping in a bed ever since, so he really had no idea of the temperatures of the very early morning.

The night before he was to leave, Turner thanked him and handed him his pay for the weeks he had worked.

At first Walker was hesitant to accept the pay, for he felt that money had been the cause of the robbery. But as he thought about it he quickly realized that that was not true—greed had been the cause of the robbery. Money had been the catalyst, the cause of the greed getting out of control and causing Brian to attack Walker. He took the money and put most of it in a hidden pocket that Frank had suggested he sew into his shirt, and he put the rest in his pants pocket.

"You know, Walker," Turner told him as Walker put the money away, "it's been a pleasure having you work here. If you ever need work again, feel free to come here. You'll have work whenever you need it. Though something tells me that I won't be seeing you again, to be honest."

"I believe you are right," Walker said, looking at the road. "Gustav said the same thing you just said, but then I wasn't sure whether I would be back or not. But I believe my road goes only in one direction, and I don't feel any urge at all to walk back in the opposite direction."

"I know that feeling—I've had it before, myself. It passes, though. The new is new for only so long, then it becomes the old. There will come a time when you're ready to stop and start searching out who you are."

"I don't know," Walker replied. "I don't feel it now, so I can't know how it will feel when it comes."

"It comes when you're willing to give up who you've been and become someone else. You'll see. The question is how far you will have gone by then, and how far you'll be willing to go when you stop. I don't think that you'll be making it back this far, though."

Walker smiled. "You're probably right," he said. "You usually are. Thank you for everything."

Turner held out his hand, and they shook. "Take care of yourself, Walker. Don't let any more Brians try to ruin your faith in humankind. There's too much that's beautiful in this world for us to focus on that which is ugly and horrible. Stay who you are, and stay true to who you are. If you do that, you're bound to be satisfied wherever you find yourself."

With that, Turner turned and walked into the house. Walker went back to the barn, where he was staying alone since Frank had gone home the day before. The night was quiet, and he slept well and rose early. By the time the sun rose to warm the morning, several miles lay between him and the farm.

He passed many farms that day and the next. He also climbed as the road climbed, and found himself ever higher. Sometimes he would climb for two hours straight, then reach a point at which he was in an even higher valley than the one before, and the people there would be working the land.

On the third day, though, after a particularly long climb, he came to a valley that wasn't being worked. Turner had told him that at a certain elevation, it was no long possible to grow crops. Walker knew that he had reached that height.

The mountains at this height also looked different. No longer did they reach high above him in the sky—now the peaks sat on the horizon, and he saw only the tops of the mountains. He was far above their bases, now, and he knew that he wouldn't be climbing much more because he was near the highest part of the road. He knew that the road didn't climb nearly as high as the peaks, as the road tended to follow the valleys where the going was much easier.

An hour later, the road began to descend, and he knew that most of his journey from that point would be downhill.

As he started down, he came across someone lying on the side of the road, wrapped in an old, torn blanket. It was the middle of the afternoon, as warm as it was going to get that day, and Walker thought it strange that this person wasn't taking advantage of the warmth and the light to do his traveling. He almost walked right past the person, except that he noticed something familiar in the form lying on the road. Walker approached him slowly and looked down at Brian's face.

He wasn't sure what to do. His first instinct was to continue walking, and he knew there was a time when he would have followed that instinct unquestioningly. But something was different this time, and he wasn't quite sure what it was.

Then he looked more closely at the sleeping figure, and he saw that Brian's face, which was mostly covered by his hair and a young beard, was bruised and cut. His breathing looked and sounded to be ragged and irregular, and Walker thought that Brian must be sick.

He sat down and thought it over for several minutes, trying to figure out what he should do. He knew that Brian would have walked right by him, not stopping to help, but he also knew that he didn't want to be a person like Brian. He didn't think that Brian presented a threat in his current state. He also knew that he was strong enough to prevent any sort of attack, especially now that he was aware of the type of person Brian was. Besides,

Brian had waited until Walker was drunk and confused before he had hit him, and that wasn't going to happen again.

Walker sighed, remembering how unpleasant the days with Brian had turned out to be. He stood and woke up Brian with his foot. He pushed him gently on the leg, but Brian didn't respond. He pushed harder, speaking Brian's name, softly at first, then louder. Finally, Brian awoke, but his response wasn't at all what Walker had expected. Brian immediately curled into a ball and covered his eyes with his hands, drawing his knees up to his chest, yelling out "No! No! leave me alone!"

Walker didn't know what to do. The arrogant, cocky, cynical man who had walked with him for almost three days was now lying on the ground, frightened of a push on the leg. Walker remembered his own journey through the night after Brian had robbed him, remembered how it felt, how little he had been able to think, and he wondered what would have happened if he had run across another person that night. What would his own reaction have been? There was no telling, of course.

He squatted next to Brian, though he wasn't sure if it really was Brian any more—it was the same body and the same figure, but it seemed that the person inside was different.

"Brian," he said quietly, "don't be afraid. It is Walker."

Brian seemed to stop breathing. After a few moments, Walker saw the fingers of his left hand—the hand over his eyes—start to spread apart just the slightest bit, and he knew that Brian was looking at him. The fingers closed quickly.

"Walker!" Brian cried out. "Don't hit me! Please don't hit me!"

Walker stood up. "I don't want to hit you, Brian," he said. "I want to know if I can help you."

Brian didn't respond, and Walker realized that he was probably confused. He knew that Brian wouldn't have considered the possibility that someone he had harmed wouldn't want to harm him in retaliation, so it probably surprised him that that anyone he had hurt could have wanted to help him.

"Go away," Brian finally said, his voice quiet.

."Okay," Walker said, then started to walk away. He was somewhat relieved that Brian had sent him on his way, for he hadn't wanted to deal with the man again. He knew that it wasn't entirely because of the robbery—that had been wrong, that had hurt, and that had been entirely unjustified, but it was over—but about the fact that Brian was a very annoying person who brought Walker down, who constantly bombarded Walker with negative ideas and criticism of everything that Walker said.

He had only gone about twenty yards, though, when he heard Brian yell out, "Wait!"

He stopped and turned. Brian was getting up slowly, obviously in pain.

"Do you have anything to eat?" he asked. "I haven't eaten anything in three days."

Walker nodded. "We should find water first, though. It's not good to eat without something to drink."

Brian limped towards Walker. He had cuts all over his arms, too, as if he had been pushing his way through thorny bushes. Now that he was standing, Walker saw that his face was even more bruised than he had seen before—the areas around both of his eyes was a deep blue, almost purple in some places, just as his own eye had looked. There were several places where scabs were growing over large cuts.

"What happened to you?" Walker asked.

"I was attacked," Brian said bitterly. His words were hard to distinguish, for he was talking through two swollen lips. "Three guys. It was a couple of days ago, and I've been walking up the mountain ever since. I couldn't go any further, though—with no food, it's pretty hard to keep climbing."

"Why did they attack you?"

"They robbed me. Took everything I had, too—" He cut his words off quickly, and Walker glanced at him. Had everything he had been Walker's possessions and money?

"Where are you going?"

"I don't know. Those guys said they'd kill me if I went back, so I figure I'll go to the other side of the mountain. I've never been there before—I'm sure there are plenty of places where I can find an honest day's work."

Walker was surprised at the words, but he didn't say anything. Brian didn't seem like the kind of person who would search out an honest day's work.

"I don't have the money I borrowed from you, by the way, if that's why you stopped," Brian said. "Those three took everything I had. The pack, too. Damn near killed me, too. So don't expect to get it back."

Walker was more astonished at those words than he ever had been at any other words. Just minutes ago, this man had been lying on the ground, begging not to be hurt, about as low as a person could get. Now that he was up and walking and seemed to be safe, he was just as arrogant and deceitful as he had been before. Walker didn't understand it. What would have happened if Walker had hit Brian, or kicked him? He thought that Brian probably would have cried out more, would have curled up even tighter. But now Brian had the promise of food and the knowledge that Walker wasn't going to hurt him, so he was back to being as arrogant as before.

Walker didn't know if he had expected an apology, but he knew that he never would have expected to hear Brian say that he had "borrowed" money from Walker. Walker almost would have expected Brian to ignore what had happened, not mentioning it at all. But to call a robbery "borrowing" was beyond Walker's comprehension.

Worst of all, now that he saw that Brian was back to the way he had been before, he knew that arguing the point with him would have been completely useless—there was no way he could get Brian to see that he had done wrong.

He wondered what went on in Brian's head, how his brain worked, what kinds of thought processes allowed somebody to deny reality as completely as Brian seemed to do. It didn't make any sense at all.

They found a small brook and sat down to eat, Walker sharing his food with Brian as freely as he had before the robbery. Frank's words came back to him clearly—Brian had given him the opportunity to learn about forgiveness, and he liked the way it felt, even if he wasn't too excited about being with Brian again. Brian probably had no idea at all of the meaning of the word, and Brian was a miserable person, somehow living his own truths that justified his cynical perspective on life. Gustav had told him of the concept of hell, and Walker wondered if Brian were already there, for he certainly was living in agony, without a bit of love for his own life or the people who surrounded him or the world he lived in.

Walker sighed. Brian was going in the same direction he was.

"I'll go with you," Brian told him, "but keep all that crap about god and how beautiful the world is to yourself. I've got no use for your delusions."

Walker thought about how Turner might have responded to such a comment.

"I'll talk about what I wish to talk about," he told Brian, asserting himself for the first time. "If you do not like it, then you can go on by yourself. But do not even think of telling me what to do or what not to do. You have no right to do so."

Brian looked at him with shock in his eyes, as if he couldn't believe what Walker had just said. His eyes went to Walker's pack, where the food had been put away.

"And if you even think of robbing me again," Walker continued, "you will regret it."

Brian lowered his eyes. "Of course you can talk about whatever you want," he muttered. "I was just making a suggestion, you know, so we could be more comfortable traveling together. So we wouldn't get on each other's nerves."

Walker found it rather pathetic to see how quickly Brian backed down when spoken back to. This man who claimed to be strong, who claimed to be completely independent in thought and deed and action, was in truth a weak person who merely carried a strong façade. Walker wished he had spoken back to him the first time they were together, but it had never occurred to him to do so.

"I'll tell you when you get on my nerves so that you can stop," Walker replied, knowing that Turner would be proud to hear him make a comment that asserted himself, but did nothing to insult or harm Brian. He merely spoke the truth in a more assertive manner than he was used to.

Brian's eyes grew wide, and he looked at Walker as if he had never met him before. But he made no reply.

Three days later they reached the bottom of the mountains. They had seen the plain before them for two days, watched it come nearer and nearer. It looked much different than the plain that Walker had left behind when he had reached the mountains, for that plain had been lush and green, full of life. This plain before them looked brown and empty as far as Walker could see.

Brian called it desert, and started complaining about it long before they ever reached it.

"The desert is a horrible place," he told Walker. "People die from hunger and thirst there more than anywhere else in the world. Everything there can kill you—even the snakes and insects. When they bite you or sting you, they put a poison into your body. And most of the plants have sharp spines that hurt you when you try to touch them."

Walker looked at Brian. "You may be safer if you go back, then."

Brian laughed nervously, looking back in the direction they had just come from. "No," he said, "I don't want to have to worry about you alone in the desert. I'll stay with you until you get to the other side of it."

Walker had come to see Brian as an open book—everything about his deception was obvious if one only looked. All of his comments were designed to make himself look better, or stronger, or braver than he actually was. Walker had found, though, that Brian had no bravery to speak of, but wanted everyone to think that he did. Brian was pure selfishness, though Walker could see at times that he longed to break out of it. It had to be difficult, Walker thought, to break out of behavior like that if Brian had been living that way for so many years.

"Please tell me," Walker said to Brian as they descended towards the desert, "why you don't believe that there's a God?"

"I've told you already—I don't want to talk about that." Brian's voice was harsh.

They walked on in silence for a few minutes while Walker thought that statement over. Then he continued.

"But you are sharing my food," he told Brian, "and my blanket at night to keep you warm. And I do want to talk about it. Talking about this is not something that will harm you. But if I am willing to share my food with you, is it so much to ask you to share your ideas in return?"

"You're blackmailing me," Brian grumbled. Walker waited, and Brian went on. "I don't believe in God, like I've already told you, because people are only fooling themselves. They're lying to themselves just because they're so afraid of what's going to happen to them after they die that they have to make up this deity just to make themselves feel better. And most of your people who believe in God are nothing but hypocrites—they talk about how kind and benevolent their god is, then they turn around and hurt people, use people to reach their own aims. They kill people who don't believe what they believe, and they grant special favors to those who believe what they do. It's wrong to do things like that in the name of a god—if they're going to hurt people, they should do it in their own names, and take responsibility for their own actions."

"So you don't believe in God because of other people, and how other people act. But you don't say anything about God."

"What are you talking about? Of course I'm talking about god. And god doesn't exist, so how can I talk about him as if he did exist?"

"When you explain to me why you don't believe in God, you always talk about other people, and what they do, and what they think, and how they act. But you never talk about having looked for God yourself and not having found him. If someone says there's no bread in the kitchen because they went and looked and found nothing, I would believe that person. But if someone said there's no bread in the kitchen because they think the person who owns the kitchen is a hypocrite, then I wouldn't be able to believe that person. Lack of belief in its existence doesn't make something not exist."

"And belief in something doesn't make it exist."

"You're right. But I have never heard anyone say 'God exists because my belief makes him exist.' I have heard people say 'I believe in God because he exists.' There's a big difference. Besides, if I don't know whether to believe or not believe, should I follow the example of people who believe and try to love other people and who are living happy lives, or do I follow the example of people who are constantly finding fault in others, hating others, and living very unhappy lives?"

Walker almost added the words "like you" to the question, but he didn't feel it was necessary to make his point. He had seen something important in Brian's argument, and he wanted to think about it.

"Your point doesn't hold up at all," Brian told him, almost gloating. "And I'm the perfect example to tear your argument apart. I don't believe in god, but I'm happy. I'm a lot happier than those fools who try to convince themselves that there's this god out there that loves them. They're just fooling themselves, lying to themselves to make themselves feel happy. They're not really happy, though. They're really miserable, pathetic creatures who are afraid to face reality. At least I'm willing to face reality and meet it head-on, not hiding behind the skirts of some god."

Walker felt sad. It didn't surprise him, though, with as much as he had learned about Brian, that Brian was willing to lie to himself about something as important as his own happiness. Brian was the most miserable human being Walker had met, yet Brian was telling himself that he was happy. Walker hadn't seen the slightest bit of happiness or satisfaction or contentedness in anything that Brian had done or said, and had heard only anger and hatred and contempt in his words.

If that was Brian's idea of happiness, then Walker wanted no part of it.

When they reached the desert, Walker found it fascinating. The temperature had been climbing steadily during their last few hours coming down the mountain, and by the time they reached the foot of the mountain the air was extremely hot and dry. The ground that they walked on had changed, too—it was no longer dirt and rocks mixed together, but hard-packed sand with a few small stones here and there. All around them the sandy ground stretched past the limits of their vision, broken up only by a few small trees, bushes, and cacti.

Walker carefully examined the first cactus they encountered, and he wondered at its complexity and beauty. The spines that protected it were long and fierce-looking, and a single red, waxy flower grew at the top of the two-foot-high plant. As they went on, Walker saw many more such cacti, as well as several other types of cactus and many small trees and bushes and plants.

So even there, in an arid, unwelcoming place, the potential for beauty was strong. The fact that such a beautiful plant could exist in such demanding circumstances made Walker realize that life could flourish almost anywhere, that no matter how barren the surroundings, life and beauty could make very strong marks upon the land.

He started thinking of just how much the desert was like Brian—parched and barren, seemingly devoid of hope and beauty and love. But he realized that within Brian lay the potential for beauty. Right now, all of his ideas were cacti, full of potential but protected by sharp, threatening spines that were intended to keep people away from them, to keep people from examining them closely and responding to them. But what if those ideas were defined, expanded, and further developed? What if he were to take the thorns off them and allow others to share them and add to them?

Walker sighed, for he didn't think that Brian would ever let such a thing happen. In that way, the parched, arid, seemingly barren desert was much richer than Brian. The desert, at least, allowed its potential to be fulfilled.

With the hot air and now-fierce sun, Brian began to complain more. He was thirsty, but Walker wouldn't let him drink all of the water that they had, which was very little. He was hot, but he didn't take off his shirt because he knew that the sun would burn his skin. He was hungry, but Walker didn't want to eat until they were ready to stop for the night.

After a couple of hours in the desert, when Walker saw that the mountains were already growing smaller behind them and now appeared much as they had before he had reached them from the other side, they saw a person walking towards them, towards the mountains. At first, the figure was no more than a small spot in the distance and neither Walker nor Brian was sure if it was even a person at all. As they came nearer, they saw that it definitely was a man.

Soon, they met up with him, an older man who wore a large hat and carried a long walking stick.

"Good day," the man said, lifting his right hand in greeting.

"Hello," Walker said with a smile. Brian grunted something that sounded like "Hi." Now that Walker actually was challenging some of his ideas, Brian wasn't nearly as talkative as he had been the first time he and Walker had traveled together, a fact that suited Walker fine.

"It's not too often that one runs across fellow travelers on a road like this," the man said. "May we sit down and share some bread?"

Walker smiled. "That's a wonderful idea," he said, taking off his pack.

The man took off his hat, and Walker got a better look at his face. It was very long—long forehead, long nose, long chin, and the man's skin was darker, but not like Amar's or Frank's—somehow, this darkness looked almost burned into the skin. By the sun? Walker wondered, for as he looked at the man's throat, he saw the skin there wasn't nearly as dark as the skin on his face. The man had deep brown eyes, the deepest that Walker had ever seen, except for those of the oxen. But that depth was different—that was a depth almost devoid of intelligence. This man's eyes were full of intelligence and of love. Walker saw a friend.

"I am Geraldo," the man said, moving his right hand with his hat across his torso and bowing deeply, "and I am very pleased to meet you."

"I am Walker, and I am pleased to meet you." Walker waited for Brian to introduce himself, but when he said nothing, Walker said, "This is Brian." He noticed that Brian was staring back at the mountains, a look of disdain on his face. He knew that soon, Brian would be telling him the many things that were wrong with Geraldo. He sat and pulled out some food. Geraldo did likewise.

Geraldo watched Brian. "You have no food to share?" he asked.

"No, I don't," Brian answered quite rudely.

"And why not? One could easily die in such an environment as this without food and water."

"That's none of your business, old man," Brian said harshly, and even Walker was surprised at his tone.

"You have a very unpleasant friend here," Geraldo said to Walker, and Walker saw a hint of laughter in the old man's eyes. "Or should I say, 'traveling companion'?"

Walker smiled, and Geraldo smiled back—he understood. Walker went on to tell him how he had met up with Brian this time, leaving out everything about the first time they had traveled together. It was a very short story.

Geraldo spoke to Brian, who was eating some of Walker's bread. "You are very blessed to have been found by someone who is willing to help you as this one has. Our God is quite good—we are always provided with enough to fill our needs. This is one thing that we can always count on."

"Your god had nothing to do with it. No god provided for me. It was a coincidence. If Walker hadn't come by, I would have gone to get help myself."

Geraldo smiled, but Walker saw a bit of sadness in it. "You had been beaten by three men in town. How did you come to be by the side of the road so high in the mountains?"

Walker was surprised—he hadn't thought of that before. He had assumed that Brian had come up into the mountains the same way he had—on foot, after having been beaten up. But Brian had been beaten much more severely than Walker had—how had he made it so far along the road?

"That's nobody's business but mine," Brian replied sharply. "You'll be wise to let it drop, old man."

Geraldo smiled again and turned to Walker. "You are very patient to travel with this one," he said.

"I learn much from him," Walker said quietly.

"Yes, I suppose you must. Just as one learns from being bitten by a rattlesnake—if one survives the sickness that comes from the strike. Snakes are beautiful creatures when left alone, but one must never forget that they're full of venom and they will strike when they feel threatened."

Walker smiled. "But the venom of some snakes, I have heard, is less potent than that of others, and a bite will cause just a bit of discomfort."

Geraldo looked back at Brian, then laughed quietly. "Your point is well stated," he said. "But I must warn you both—you are very poorly prepared for a journey through the desert. But you are fortunate—just three hours' walk from here, you will find an oasis where you can prepare yourselves much better. This oasis is ruled by a very powerful man—powerful because he controls the water, the single most important element to any traveler of the desert—and this man will ask you to work for your water. My advice to you is this: work for the water. He is not at all unfair, and the work is not too much when compared with the importance of the water."

"That sounds very interesting," Walker said. "What is an oasis?"

Geraldo thought for a moment. "An oasis is a miracle—a minute area of growth and flourishing trees and plants in the middle of a vast area devoid of anything that flourishes. In the desert, the plants and animals struggle to survive; at the oasis, life is full and rich. It is one of the greatest miracles that God has given to the traveler of the desert."

"An oasis is an area where underground water supplies reach the surface, and the plants have a plentiful supply of water. That's why they survive," Brian said sarcastically. "It's hardly a miracle."

"Cynicism," Geraldo said, without a trace of malice in his voice, "is a disease of the small mind. Do you see the beauty in this?" he asked Brian, picking up a small rock and holding it at eye level.

"It's a rock," Brian said disdainfully.

Geraldo sighed. "Yes, but in this rock lies the story of the ages. This rock has been here for countless years, and it will continue to be here long after we die. Just a rock? If you choose to see things as just a rock or just a tree or just a person, you will live just a life. You make that choice. Some people choose smallness as a way of being."

Walker reached out and took the rock from Geraldo. He studied it closely, noting every crack and mark on it. It was flat and circular, black with shades of grey running through it. It was only two inches across, but Walker saw the beauty there—it was perfect, just what it was supposed to be. He didn't see any story there, but he was somehow sure that Geraldo was right, and he was sure that one day he would understand what he meant.

"May I?" he asked Geraldo, holding the rock near his pack. Geraldo nodded, and Walker put the rock in the pocket of the pack.

Geraldo looked at Brian. "What was 'just a rock' now is part of all our lives, as real a part of our memories as anything else that ever has been a part of us. And only God knows what else that rock will become. Be a cynic if you wish, but you will live a very empty life.

"And you," he said to Walker, "continue loving life. You will find that those who love life lead lives that are lovable. To where do you travel now?"

"I have no destination," Walker replied. "I follow the road, but I'm not sure what I'm searching for."

Geraldo nodded. "If you're searching, though, you will find. Keep your faith, and you always will meet the people you need to meet, the people who will open the doors that you need to have open. Just be ready always to see those doors where you least expect to see them."

"I will," Walker assured him. "Thank you."

Geraldo leaned closer to Walker. "And just between you and me," he whispered, "lose this one. You've already learned all you can from him."

Chapter 15

Several hours later, as Geraldo had promised, they reached the oasis. They arrived there after nightfall and had been walking by starlight for some time, so the oasis first appeared to them as a dark mass in a dark world, rather than a lush haven on a barren land. There was a large fire burning, which seemed to Walker to be a welcoming sign.

The journey after their parting with Geraldo had been a quiet one—Brian seemed to have nothing to say, and Walker could feel a great deal of anger in his companion. It didn't bother him too much, for the silence was welcome, but he did feel bad that Brian's anger was making his companion feel so bad.

Walker was relieved when they reached the oasis, for he was thirsty and he wanted to sleep. They were met at the edge of the oasis by a group of three men carrying torches—one man stood before the other two, obviously the man who was in charge.

"Greetings, and welcome," he said in a very deep, powerful voice. "If you come in peace, you are greeted in peace."

"Yes, we come in peace," Walker said, a bit confused, for he couldn't think of any other way he would come. He was grateful to have reached the oasis.

"Good—then enter. I am Adam, the keeper of the oasis. I am very pleased to have you as guests." He turned, as did the two men behind him. They started back towards the large fire, the two men in the lead, then Adam, then Walker and Brian following them.

"I don't like this at all," Brian muttered. "This guy is trying to show off his power. People like that can't be trusted."

Walker didn't see the situation in the same way. He thought that it might be necessary for Adam to protect his home and his livelihood, but he said nothing to Brian.

When they reached the fire, Adam turned. He was a tall man, though very thin. The men who accompanied him were shorter, yet built more strongly. Adam had a thick black beard and moustache, and his black hair was very thick, though quite short. He wore a white robe that covered everything but his hands, neck and head, and that was tied at the waist with a red rope. He faced Walker and Brian.

"You are welcome here. We have already eaten, but if you wish to partake of our food, we can find some for you. You are welcome to all the water you can drink and carry, but on one condition—that you pay for it with one day of work. One day of work will earn you three days of rest at my oasis."

"We will be honored to work one day," Walker responded. He found the entire situation to be as interesting as anything he had encountered. He wondered if Kennison or Gustav knew that such places existed, where travelers would have to work one day for water and rest, in the middle of a vast desert that was so dreadfully hot.

Brian said nothing.

Adam gave Brian a penetrating look, but he seemed to be satisfied with Walker's use of the word "we."

"You may sleep anywhere you can find," he said. "There are no poisonous snakes here, or poisonous insects—we've rid our home of these, so you can sleep in peace. We begin work two hours after the sun rises. Do you wish to eat?"

"No, thank you," Walker replied. "I still have food. I think I need to sleep now—it has been a very long journey."

Adam laughed kindly. "As is any journey that's worth its while. Sleep well. We will wake you with the sun."

Walker and Brian turned away after Adam handed them a small torch, and they walked away from the fire until they found a spot near the water. The sound of insects and frogs was loud, but somehow soothing. Walker lay down his blanket and handed his other one to Brian, who was still in a foul mood.

"If that idiot thinks that I'm going to work for water, he's wrong," Brian said as he ate. "The water's here for everyone, not for some power-hungry fool like him to control. He's got no right to expect us to work for it."

"But if the land belongs to him, doesn't he have the right?" Walker asked.

"It's different when the land is out in the middle of nowhere, and people need the water to survive. It's obscene."

"I don't agree," Walker said, lying down on his blanket. "I'll see you in the morning." He wished for Brian's sake that Brian would wake up in a better mood the next day. He didn't think about it too long, though, for he was very tired and he fell asleep very quickly.

He was already awake when the people from the oasis came to wake them. He had awakened with the first light, and had sat in the stillness of the morning, watching the water in front of him as it slowly pulled more and more light from the sky to lighten itself. As he watched, the dark hole in the ground that reflected the stars became a bright pool of water, reflecting the blue of the sky that grew brighter and brighter each moment. There were very few sounds that early in the morning—even the frogs and insects seemed to be asleep, save for the few dragonflies that skimmed the surface of the water.

The trees gained color, too, as the light grew stronger, and their green seemed even more brilliant to Walker after he had walked for most of a day through the desert. The air was cool on his skin, but he knew that wouldn't last long—soon it would heat up to the intensity he had felt the day before. For the early part of the morning, though, he was content to feel the coolness and the freshness of the dawning day.

Adam himself came to wake them, and he smiled at Walker as he approached. He came close to Walker and bowed deeply, then straightened and extended his hand, which Walker shook.

"Ah, my friend—I see you are up already!" he said. "We had no time to meet yesterday, except through formalities. My name is Adam, and this oasis is mine. My parents owned it before me, and their parents before them. We have worked hard for many years to keep this haven for weary and thirsty travelers like yourself, and it is a great honor to serve you in any way we can."

"Thank you," Walker replied. "The honor is mine, to be your guest here. We thank you for your hospitality."

Adam frowned. "You say 'we,' yet your friend last night seemed less than happy to be staying here. Are you good friends?"

Walker shook his head. "No, we're not. We have been traveling together for a few days, but other than that, we don't know each other."

"I see," Adam said, and Walker thought he saw the man relax a bit. "That may be good to know. You see, much of my livelihood depends upon knowing which people will bring trouble to us, and which are the peaceful people. To where do you travel?"

"I have no destination. I'm searching. For myself, I guess. For God, for some answers."

"Ha! Then you've come to the right place!" Adam exclaimed enthusiastically. "God is all around us in this place, this haven of life in the middle of a world where life is so scarce. A man can not spend time in a place such as this and leave without believing in the existence of a God who gives us wonderful gifts in our lives. But you will see—keep your eyes and your heart open. We will eat in an hour, and we will begin to work in two. Please join us for our breakfast—the food is part of the wages for the time you spend working. And please, wake your companion so that he will be ready for breakfast and for work."

"I will do that," Walker said, glad to have met Adam. The man's enthusiasm was very refreshing, and Walker felt more enthusiastic about the coming day just from having spoken to him. He watched Adam walk away, then turned and woke up Brian, who was still sleeping somewhat fitfully.

"I don't want to wake up yet," Brian mumbled when Walker shook his shoulder.

"But you must," Walker told him. "We will be eating breakfast soon, and then we will start to work. We must be ready to do so."

"The hell with that," Brian sneered. "If that man thinks I'm going to do his filthy work for him, then he had best think again. There's no way someone can make me work for water that's here for everyone." He rolled over, his back to Walker.

An hour later, Walker went to breakfast alone, for Brian was still sleeping. When Adam asked him where Brian was and Walker told him, Adam nodded to two of the men who sat around the fire, and Walker recognized them as the two men who had accompanied Adam the evening before. The expression on Adam's face was knowing, but pained, as if he had expected exactly this to happen.

"We will be back soon," Adam told him. "Please sit down and eat."

"I will go with you," Walker replied.

Adam looked him closely in the eyes, as if he were judging whether or not Walker would be going to help Brian, but then he nodded.

"As you wish," he told Walker, "but please do not interfere."

"I have no right to interfere," Walker replied, following the three men.

When they reached Brian he was in the water, bathing and drinking deeply of the fresh water. One of Adam's men walked several steps on the shore past Brian and stopped; the other stopped on the land just where Brian would have entered the water. Adam stopped several steps short of the second man.

"Please get out of the water," Adam said firmly. "This water is not for bathing, but for drinking. You are spoiling our water."

Brian looked warily at the three men, and Walker could tell that he wanted to say something but held his tongue because he was afraid of the three. He walked slowly out of the water to where his clothes lay on the bank and dressed quickly.

"You have drunk of our water and spoiled much of it," Adam told him. "You now owe us two days of work for what you have taken."

"You told us last night it was one day," Brian challenged, doing his best to appear bold.

"One day for food and drink. One day for bathing in water that is not meant to be bathed in. That is our law."

"Your law has no force," Brian taunted. "What are you going to do? Throw me in prison for taking a bath?"

"Prison is a worthy place for thieves. If you do not work, we will hold you here until we can arrange passage to the nearest city with a prison, where you can spend the time that thieves spend as penalty for their acts."

"You won't hold me here. You have no legal authority. Come on, Walker—let's get out of here. These people are deluded."

Walker shrugged. "I agreed to work. I must work." He was gratified by the approving look that Adam gave him—this man who had treated him well approved of his words.

"You can work if you want to, but you're a fool if you do. I'm leaving." He reached down and picked up Walker's blanket, the one he had slept on the night before, and started to walk away. Adam nodded to the farthest man, who moved to cut Brian off. Almost before Walker could distinguish what was happening, Brian took a swing at the man, and Walker saw that his hand wasn't empty—he caught the glint of metal in his hand, something that surprised him. The man dodged deftly and swung back, hitting Brian in the stomach, and Walker saw in his hand, too, the glint of metal.

Brian froze, as if every muscle in his body had suddenly contracted, bent over in pain. Then, slowly, he toppled forward in the sand, and Walker saw the bright red of Brian's blood on his hands. He rushed forward, but by the time he reached Brian, he was already dead.

Walker stood slowly, confused. He turned to Adam, whose expression was one of sadness and regret.

"I am sorry," Adam said, placing a strong hand on Walker's shoulder. "We have had too many of our own people killed to risk allowing it to happen again. I will understand if you are not able to work, and you are still welcome to the water and the food."

Walker shook his head. "No," he said slowly, "I will work."

He looked back at Brian's body where it lay in the sand, and he knew that Brian had been released from his hatred and his anger and his pain, but he felt that there was something incomplete in the release, something that he couldn't name.

Adam named it for him. "It is very sad," he told Walker, also looking at Brian's body, "when a man dies with no peace in his heart."

Breakfast tasted strangely unsatisfying that morning. The food tasted good, Walker knew, but somehow he wasn't able to savor the flavors of the cheeses and bread and meats that his hosts provided. He found out at breakfast that eight people lived at the oasis, including Adam and the two men who turned out to be his oldest sons. Adam's wife, Sylvia, was small and thin, but full of great energy, and she provided everyone with breakfast. They had two daughters, one almost a woman and the other still a girl of Tricia's age, and both of them helped out with serving breakfast and cleaning up afterwards. Sylvia's father was a very old man with very few teeth but a great deal of pride and a bright smile in spite of his toothless mouth, and Adam's mother spoke a great deal to her daughter-in-law, but not much at all to anyone else.

All wore robes—the men's were of white, while the women's and girl's were of bright colors—brilliant greens and blues and purples that were astonishing in the desert sun.

There was one other traveler who already had worked the day before, a young woman who was crossing the desert alone to get back to her mother, who was dying. Her name was Stephanie, and she was dressed as the women of the oasis were dressed, in a bright orange robe with blue trim. Her skin was as dark as Adam's, and her hair was as dark as anything that Walker had ever seen.

"This is really a wonderful place," she told Walker after they had met and had sat down to have breakfast. "I've been here before—Adam and his family are great people. They share their water with every traveler, and they share their food, also. They are very kind, very generous people."

"But they make people work for the water. Some people object to that."

"You mean your friend," Stephanie said, then laughed, but without humor. "Your friend was a fool. Adam is building a temple—a very good-sized temple that probably won't be finished for many more years. His grandfather started it years ago. You see, living out here in the middle of nowhere, with no one nearby to help you or your family, life can get very dangerous. You never know who's going to drop by next—it could be a group of priests or a group of thieves. His grandfather devised the work as a check, a way to judge the character of the people who came. From what I understand, he figured there are four kinds of people—those who know the value of the water and are willing to work for it are the friends; those who don't want to work but grudgingly agree to do so are the companions; those who think that it's completely out of line to ask anyone to work for something as trivial as water and won't work are the fellow citizens; and those who are belligerent and disrespectful and pose a threat to other people here are the enemies.

"Your friend, from what I've heard them saying, was an enemy. Out here, they can't take any chances, and once he pulled the knife, they had no choice but to kill him or be killed by him."

"Please," Walker said, unsure of what drove him to say so, "he was not my friend. We traveled together, but we were not friends. I would not have chosen to travel with him because of the way he treated other people." Even as he spoke, he wasn't sure why he felt it necessary to clarify such a matter, but he thought that he might have had to clarify it for himself.

"I see," Stephanie said. "You certainly could have been luckier in finding a traveling companion. From what I hear about this morning, I would have had a good mind to kill him myself."

Walker's eyes widened, and his jaw dropped.

Stephanie laughed, this time with humor. "I'm speaking figuratively, Walker. I don't think I would be capable of killing anyone. It's a figure of speech."

Walker nodded and took another bite of cheese. It was a very strange figure of speech, he thought, but he believed her when she said that she wasn't capable of killing. He didn't think he was, either, and he suddenly hoped he would never have to find out. "You're from the mountains, then?" he asked, wanting to change the subject.

"Yes. I grew up in the mountains, but I've been away for five years now. I got married right out of school, and my husband wanted to move to the city to seek out his fortune. We left the mountains, crossed the desert, went through the forest and came to the city, where nothing ever really went right. We always had enough to eat, and we always had a roof over our heads, but we never really could get ahead, never could save enough money or make a fortune. We always were too busy working to be able to try anything new or daring or adventurous. We were always so tired in the evenings that it was almost all we could do to crawl into bed. Even making love became something of a luxury."

"Why did you stay?"

"I don't know. You get caught up in something, and it so quickly becomes normal that you feel you can't leave it because your life may fall apart if you do—you'll stop earning enough money to live on, you'll become poor and destitute and no one will help you.

"When I was growing up, my mother and I used to go for many long walks—that was a part of the day that I always looked forward to, for I knew that it was our time together, and our time with the world outdoors. I loved those walks. Since I've lived in the city, though, I could count on my ten fingers the times that Jack and I have gone for long walks, just for the sake of being outdoors and enjoying life. Those walks were normal parts of my mother's day, and my father did his walking, too, but he did his very early in the morning, so I didn't go with him. But both of my parents made time to get out of doors and walk. I miss that. I don't know anyone in the city who makes it a point to search out silence and tranquility on a regular basis—not that they'd be able to find much of either in the city."

"Why do you live that way, then, if you're dissatisfied?"

Stephanie looked at her bread, then spoke quietly. "I'll tell you the truth—I'm not going to any more. I took care of everything I needed to take care of, and I won't be going back. I'm going to stay with my parents. My mother is sick, but I don't believe that she's dying.

"Jack and I have lost what we had before. The city has beaten him down—he feels like a failure because he hasn't become incredibly wealthy, because his dreams of riches haven't come true. He's never seen that we had a treasure in each other—his treasure is money.

"And because he feels like a failure, he's begun to hate himself. He's even begun to hit me when he gets too angry with himself, and I can't live with that—I won't allow him to hit me. I don't deserve it. He's also started to sleep with other women, to convince himself, somehow, that he's still acceptable, that he's still worthwhile. He won't listen to me when I tell him he is—he looks for his own self-worth in the sexual acceptance of other women."

"Does he find it there?"

Stephanie smiled sadly. "Of course not. It's like a drug—it's a momentary high, a momentary fulfillment, but the very next day he's down on himself again, and he starts to look for acceptance again, either with the same woman or with another."

"It must hurt you very much."

"It did at first, but then I got used to it, started to harden myself against it. I thought about having a child to perhaps help the situation, but I realized that having a child under those conditions would have been horribly unfair to the child—I would have been using the child from the moment of conception to try to change the behavior of my husband. Jack is very dissatisfied with himself, and while the idea of a child might have given him momentary satisfaction, until he learns how to love himself, he's not fit to be a father. And we could not be a family."

"Your journey must have been a very long one, traveling by yourself."

"Very long, but very satisfying. I've been lucky so far, and I have only a few days more. Jack and I stopped here five years ago, on our way to the city, so there are many memories here for me. Then he was full of hope and expectation, and it was very easy to love him. Now he's full of anger and dissatisfaction, and I have no more love left inside me for him. Now I see this oasis with different eyes, and when I leave today, I know that I'll be heading home. I'm looking forward to that."

"You're leaving today?" Walker asked, surprised.

"Yes. I got here two days ago, and I did my work yesterday. Adam didn't want me to work, but I insisted. It makes me feel nice inside to know that I'm earning my keep, and not just taking advantage of people because of my gender. The women in my family have always worked just as hard as the men. I guess I'm no different."

Walker smiled. "I worked on a farm for a while. The women there worked hard, also."

"So you know what I mean."

"Yes."

Stephanie nodded. "I'm looking forward to getting back. Not just back to the farm, but back to the way of life. That way of life is difficult, but it fills you with life and vigor, if you let it. It doesn't suck the life out of you, as the city does."

They both looked up as Adam approached.

"We will start work soon, my friend," he said to Walker, then turned to Stephanie. "I am sending my son with you, the man I trust most in the world, for three days of the four. We have business we need to do in the mountains that we would have done in two weeks' time, but which can be done now."

Stephanie bowed. "Thank you so much," she said, "but truly, you mustn't—"

Adam held up a hand. "Please. You have come very far alone, and I know that you probably can finish the journey alone. But if anything were to happen to you now that you are so close to home, and I knew it was within my power to help to see you home safely, I would never again be able to sleep soundly at night. We do this for your parents, from two parents to two others, just as much as we do it for you. May your lives together be blessed always."

Stephanie was silent for a moment. "Thank you," she said quietly. "Thank you very much."

Adam smiled. "You are very welcome."

After he left, Stephanie turned to Walker. "To tell you the truth, I was beginning to wonder what it would be like to get so close to home, but then get attacked on the road and never make it. Now I won't have to worry about that."

Half an hour later, Adam led him through some bushes to a large structure that Walker had only glimpsed through the bushes before, the temple that Stephanie had told him about. It was one hundred feet long and fifty feet wide, though the walls were only about five feet high in most places. In some spots, though, they were already ten or fifteen feet high.

"This should be very pleasant work for one who is searching," Adam exclaimed. "We are building a temple to God, in thanks for the water that he has given us. Here, I will show you what to do.

He pulled a bag from a small stone structure, then poured what looked to be dust into a large metal pan. Then he took a large cup and filled it to the top with water, and poured it into the dust. With a stick, he mixed it up until it became soupy, then he carried the pan to one of the taller walls, where bricks were piled high next to it.

"You are young and strong, so you will work on one of the tall walls," he said, pointing to a ladder that leaned against the wall. He picked up a trowel off the ground and on a shorter section showed Walker how to put the mortar onto the bricks and how to fit a brick into the mortar, making sure the edges stayed even.

"Do you think you can do that?" he asked Walker, who nodded. Adam smiled. "Four bags of mortar," he said, "and as many bricks as it takes to use up the four bags. That is your job for today. Is that acceptable?"

"Of course," Walker replied. "I will be honored to have a part in building such a temple."

Adam looked at the structure before him. "Of course you will. A man in search of God or a man who has found God—both can find honor in any task that God puts before him. Just remember, though, that no matter how many temples we may build, the search for God is a search inside ourselves. We can not find God outside of ourselves." He clapped Walker on the back, then walked away, singing a song to himself.

In just five hours, Walker had finished his work. He was tempted to mix up a fifth bag of mortar and continue to work, but he had been told to do four, so he stopped. Then he lay down in the shade of the trees and took a nap. The oasis truly was a miracle—he had felt the heat while he had been working out in the open, yet there under the trees, the temperature was much lower, and the air was actually comfortable.

At lunch, he told Adam that he would leave that evening. He knew that he could have stayed another day if he wished, but the road was calling him and the memory of what happened to Brian was pushing him. As beautiful and as comfortable as the place was, he didn't wish to stay another night.

Adam understood, and that evening, at dinner, he handed Walker a robe and some hollow gourds that had strings tied through holes in them.

"Since you came from the mountains," Adam told him, "you have done the easy part first. You still have two days to go, though, until the forest. You are poorly prepared for that. Please take these things—the robe will protect your skin from the sun, and the gourds will carry enough water for one man for the two days. Travel all night, but when the day gets to be its hottest, find shade and rest. My wife will also give you food from our meal this evening to take with you. And may God bless you in your search."

Two hours later, both Walker and Stephanie left the oasis, Stephanie going home in the direction Walker had come from, and Walker heading off in the direction from which Stephanie had come. He knew little of what lay ahead, other than the fact that there was desert, a forest, and a city ahead of him. He didn't want or need to know much more.

The night was beautiful—he was sure he could see every star that was in the sky. Something about the desert air seemed to magnify everything in the sky, and when the waning moon came up an hour after it got dark, it started out huge on the horizon, then grew smaller as it rose into the sky.

The air was completely clear, and very dry—there was a slight breeze, but without moisture in the air, it did little to cool him. He was thankful for the moonlight, for it helped him to stay on the road, though he was sure that the starlight would have sufficed if necessary.

For a world that looked to be so devoid of life, Walker was amazed at the number of sounds that he heard—he seemed to be surrounded by animals and insects and birds, though he saw few of them. From time to time he heard the "who" of the owl or the howl of the coyotes, or he caught a glimpse of movement off the side of the road. Occasionally, a rabbit or lizard would cross the road just ahead of him.

Even in the noise of all the animals, though, he heard a profound silence, a wonderful peace that seemed to envelop him, that seemed to walk with him. He loved the feel of it, but he couldn't give it a name.

Chapter 16

As Walker crossed the desert over the next couple of nights, he couldn't help but think of Brian and his death. He didn't understand how a human being could cause so much harm inside of himself, and how that inner harm could lead to outer destructiveness. He had never found out why or how Brian had been injured, but he was sure it was because he had angered people. Brian had seemed determined to destroy himself through his own fatalism and destructive thinking.

Adam's son had been capable of violence, as had Brian, but Walker had seen no malice in that violence, only a desire to defend himself. He remembered Adam telling Brian that they would hold him until they could send him to a prison, which they seemed to have every right to do, and Adam had never threatened Brian with violence. But Brian had reacted violently to that possibility, and had acted with complete contempt of the rights of Adam and his family as owners of the oasis.

He knew that Gustav and Turner would have respected Adam's right to ask for work in exchange for water, and he saw how Stephanie had respected that right. And the work wasn't difficult—it hadn't even been an entire day's work. He was sure that Brian hadn't been protesting the work so much as he was reacting against Adam's right to ask them to work.

Adam's words about Brian's death stuck with Walker, and he wondered what it was like to die without ever having found peace within oneself. He had seen how miserable Brian had been, never being at peace with anyone or anything, always looking to blame and accuse. He saw negative in everyone's motives, never thinking that people's motives might have been honorable. Walker was sure that Brian's perspective of other people's motives mirrored his own self—because Brian always had selfish motives for whatever he did, he saw the actions of others as having originated from selfish motives, also.

He was also struck by the differences in the physical appearance of the people who saw the world brightly and those who saw the world darkly. Brian had been thin, almost emaciated, by the time he died, and his face was drawn, the corners of his mouth perpetually down in an unpleasant frown, his eyes never bright. Even his smiles were dimmed by the cynicism or criticism behind them. And though he had never spoken to the three people he had seen on the road so long ago, he was fairly sure that they would have been very much like Brian, judging from what he had seen on their faces and in their eyes. Likewise, the people in the bar where Brian had robbed him were somehow unpleasant, and he wouldn't have wanted to spend much time with them.

But how did such people feel inside? He couldn't imagine it. He loved seeing the world as a beautiful place, he loved being amazed at every new thing that came into his life. He couldn't imagine how it would feel not to see the beauty, not to feel the amazement.

And if he lost that, could he get it back? And if he couldn't get it back, what would fill up that part inside of him that allowed him to see the beauty? Would he be opening up a space inside of himself for negativity and hatred and anger? Were there even such spaces inside of him? How were such things as anger and cynicism and love and appreciation kept inside oneself, and was it possible for one to decide which ones one wanted to have more of?

It was very complex, but Walker enjoyed thinking about what would happen if he allowed anger to grow inside of himself, like one of the plants there around him in the desert. What would he have to do to get rid of it if he did allow it to grow? How would he go about changing the anger to something more loving, more productive, something that would make him happier as a person?

Somehow, he knew there were no simple answers. Gustav had taught him to bake, but he was sure Gustav had no recipes for happiness that would work every time as his recipes for bread worked every time. Even at that, though, when they ended up with bad yeast, the bread didn't rise as it should have, so even those recipes depended on the quality of the ingredients. Turner had taught him to turn the soil and sow the seeds, but he had also explained to Walker that the success of the crops depended on the amount of nutrients in the soil and the quality of the seeds and the amount of sunshine and rainfall during the growing season.

Was that how it was with people? If so, what were the ingredients? The skin and the body and the organs inside the body and the blood and the heart that pumped it? Just as the crops needed fertilizer and rain, people needed food and water. But the crops needed to be tended and nurtured, and the weeds had to be pulled so that the plants would get enough of the water and the positive nutrients that allowed them to grow.

Walker had first talked to a kind old woman who had shared her home and food with him for no other reason than she was kind. He had been given clothing by a man who didn't know him, but who had seen his need. He had learned to speak and had been completely accepted by Kennison and Tricia and Gloria. He had learned of work and love and death from Gustav and Marie.

But what if he had met Brian first? How would he be looking at the world if Brian's perspective had been the first one to which he had been exposed?

He liked to think that he might have rejected the pessimism and cynicism, but could he truly say that he would have done so? He was able to see Brian for what he was because of everything he had been taught by the other people in his life, but what if his teachers had shared Brian's feelings and emotions?

The thought was frightening.

He slept long in the afternoon in the shade of some large rocks that were piled on one another in such a way that they created shelter from the sun. Then he ate, and as the sun set behind him, he started walking again. He went another entire night, then another day and another night without seeing another person. By the end of the third night, he was feeling lonely once more, feeling the desire to talk with someone else, to share his ideas and feelings. The desert had turned out to be much more of an ordeal than he had expected, though he was glad that he had had the chance to see a world so different from anything else he had experienced. He also realized that the timing for such an environment was perfect—he had needed a chance to think about all that had happened to him, about all the people he had met and who they were and how they acted and what they did and what those things meant to Walker.

By the time the forest came in sight late in the morning after his third night, he felt sure that he was at least a step nearer to his goal, and that the thousands of steps he had taken since he had left the oasis had nothing to do with the fact that he was nearer to his goal—the advancement had taken place through his thoughts, through his consideration of all that had happened and of how he looked at the world and all he had learned.

Geraldo had told him that God would put the right people in his path on his journey, but Walker could see that sometimes it was best for there to be no people in his path. He knew that some people would complain about how lonely such a time was, but he also knew that others still would call such a time blessed.

By the time he reached the forest, he was ready for a change. He had gotten used to the heat, but it had become monotonous, as had the cloudless sky and the flat horizons. The forest came upon him gradually, first spreading out a few trees all about him, but always growing thicker and thicker as he walked. Soon the trees came together to form a canopy above his head, effectively blocking out most of the sun's light except for the stray beams that poked their way through the leaves in several different places here and there. No longer did he feel the vastness of everything that surrounded him in wide-open spaces—now he felt the closeness of limited space, of limited vision and movement. Out on the desert or on the plain or up in the mountains, he had been able to see almost forever, and he had been able to see the sources of most of the sounds that he had heard. Here under the canopy, though, the sounds were all muted, and he couldn't be sure of the direction from which they came. Even if he could make out where the sounds came from, so many trees and their branches and leaves stood before him and beside him at every step that it was usually impossible to find what had made the sound. The forest about him brought back memories of Tricia showing him her secret spot, and he smiled as he thought of her and the important lessons she had taught him.

He found himself walking more slowly, looking around more, paying more attention to his surroundings than he had for the two days previous. He didn't feel as comfortable moving quickly, for he had little idea of what lay before him and he felt it safer not to rush forward into anything he wasn't sure of.

The air was thicker in the forest, moister. His skin felt the weight of the humidity, but he also noticed that it was a bit more difficult to breathe the wetter air than it had been to breathe the drier air. The smells were rich in the forest, though a bit more pungent, and now and then he caught the smell of decay—a log or pile of dead matter that was breaking down into nutrients for other plants and animals and insects.

When he came upon a stream, he heard it long before he saw it. He was somewhat surprised when he finally reached it, for he had thought that it was far off to his right. But there it was, running right over the road he was on, and he stopped and left the road, looking for a place where he might fill that gourds that Adam had given him with fresh water instead of the hot tepid water that remained in them.

When he found a pool, he filled the gourds with the clear, cold, fresh water and sat down to rest a while, hoping maybe even to take a short nap. He was tired from having traveled all of the night, while sleeping only a few hours the day before. And he hadn't even slept well in the afternoon heat.

Before he knew it, he fell asleep. He didn't wake up until it was already dark in the forest. His decision made for him, he made a small fire and prepared his bed and shelter for the night. He knew there was no way that he could proceed in the darkness that was the forest at night.

He sat by the fire and ate his dinner, enjoying the noises of the world around him. At times, though, he heard rustling noises in the bushes around him, and he started to get a bit nervous. He had no idea what might be making those sounds. He remembered someone—had it been

Brian? Turner? Marie?—telling him that a good fire would keep most animals away, so he put a few more branches on the flames and lay down again.

The crackling of the fire grew stronger, and it blended well with all of the other sounds of the forest. Walker lay still, listening. And as he listened, he distinguished another sound, one that seemed to be human, one that he could barely make out. He strained his ears and had to listen for a while before he realized that he was hearing the sound of a child crying.

He stood, listening closely, trying to determine the direction from which the sound came. It came very softly, and when he turned his head a bit, the sound was stronger in one ear, so he moved in that direction. He went slowly, cautiously, for the light from the fire was not so strong, and he had no ideas what the shadows might have been hiding. As he went, the crying grew louder, and he finally stopped in front of a bush whose form he could barely make out in the light from the now-far-away fire. He listened to the very soft sobbing, and decided to return to the fire to bring a piece of wood as a torch, which he did quickly. Then he reached out and pulled back the branches of the bush close to the place where the crying sounded strongest, and he saw a child lying on the ground, crying in his sleep.

He wanted to wake the child, but his instinct told him not to; instead, he propped the torch against a stone, carefully picked up the child, took the torch in his hand, and went back to the fire. There he lay the child on the ground in his shelter, and he pulled his blanket from his pack and wrapped that and the robe around himself. He decided to stay awake and keep watch over the child, but he was more tired than he thought and soon he was asleep.

Very early the next morning he looked into the shelter to see that the child was a boy, and he was still sleeping in practically the same position that he had been in the night before when Walker had laid him down. Walker watched him for a while, wondering what the child was doing alone in the middle of a forest. He wasn't nearly as young as Walker had first thought—just very small—but since so many people considered such a place dangerous even for adults, the danger must have been even greater for a child.

Suddenly, the boy awoke with a violent start and a short, loud scream. Walker jumped at the sound, and the boy was on his knees before he even woke up. When his eyes did open, they were full of terror, darting back and forth, trying to see something that wasn't there. Finally his eyes focused on Walker, and he jumped again. Walker could see that the boy was disoriented and frightened, and that he had no idea where he was.

"Good morning," Walker said, quietly and kindly yet firmly. "My name is Walker. You were very cold last night, and you were crying, so I put you in this shelter."

The boy said nothing—he just stared at Walker as if he were trying to decide whether Walker was someone he could trust. Walker wanted to ask him his name, but he didn't want to make the boy feel threatened, make him turn and run before Walker could even find out who he was.

"Are you hungry?" Walker asked, reaching into his bag for bread and cheese. "I don't have much, but you're welcome to share whatever I have." He held out the bread to the boy, but he stayed on his knees, still staring at Walker. Then, suddenly, he started looking to the left and right, as if he were afraid that more people were around somewhere.

Walker held the bread out, not moving it any closer, but also not pulling it any further away.

Finally, the boy reached up and quickly took the bread from Walker's hand. Then he sat down on the ground and started to eat. Walker picked up a gourd of water and moved it closer to the boy, who picked it up and drank long and deeply.

"What's your name?" Walker asked when the boy had finished eating. He stared at Walker for several moments before he replied.

"Michael," he said quietly.

"Well, Michael," Walker said, "I am very pleased to meet you. My name is Walker."

"I know. You told me."

Walker hadn't thought the boy had caught his first words, but he was glad that he was at least responding.

"I found you last night when you were sleeping in the bushes. You were crying in your sleep, so I brought you here. You must have been very tired not to have awakened as I carried you."

"I didn't sleep for two days," Michael muttered. "I was afraid to sleep. So I was very tired."

"Why were you afraid to sleep?" Walker asked. "Because you are all alone in the forest?"

"No. I'm all alone in the forest and I'm afraid to go to sleep for the same reason."

"Why is that?"

Michael studied Walker's face closely, and Walker knew that the boy didn't yet trust him. This was natural, Walker thought, given the fact that the boy didn't even know who he was. But the boy seemed to see something in Walker's eyes that told him he could be trusted, for he dropped his head, looking at the ground, and quietly said, "They killed my parents."

Walker was stunned. "Who?" he asked. "Who killed your parents?"

"I don't know who they were," Michael said. "We were coming back from visiting my grandmother and grandfather when these men jumped out of the forest and stopped our coach. They were going to kill all of us, but my father told me to run and not look back, and I ran into the forest before they even saw me. I don't think they expected anyone to run so quickly. I ran, like my father said, but I looked back. I wish I hadn't."

He stopped. Walker said nothing.

"I saw them kill my father. He was just standing there, with his hands up, and they shot him. Then they pulled my mother from the coach and shot her, too. I couldn't see what they did to the driver. They would have killed me, too, if my father hadn't made me run. So I just kept running and running and running. I didn't sleep the first night, but I got really tired yesterday, so I fell asleep in the bush. That's where you found me, I guess."

"Why did they kill your parents?" Walker asked.

"I think they wanted to rob us," Michael replied. "My father had a lot of money. They know that people who ride in coaches usually do."

"They killed him just because they wanted to take the money?"

"Yes. I guess they wanted the money, but they wanted to kill them so that they couldn't tell the constable who it was who robbed them. They could be put in prison for a very long time for robbing people, even hanged. So they have to kill the witnesses."

Michael fell quiet, and Walker didn't know what to say. He felt sad that he wasn't surprised that people would kill other people over money—that should have surprised him more than anything else he had seen or heard, he knew, but though he found it a horrible thing to do, he wasn't at all shocked about it anymore.

"How old are you?" Walker asked after a few minutes of quiet. It looked to him that Michael was about to cry, but he didn't know what to do about that.

"I'm fourteen," Michael murmured, his eyes still looking at the ground. "I was going to go away to the university in just a couple of months, but I guess that won't be happening now. I miss them already." The tears started to flow down his cheeks, and Walker moved closer and hugged him. Michael hugged him back, and he began to sob harder than Walker had ever heard anyone cry before. He felt the sobs in the boy's body as he held him, felt the spasms of grief that overcame him. And as he held the boy, he thought of Brian and his anger, and he wondered if Brian had ever been able to cry like that. He was sure it would have helped him if he could have.

An hour later, after Michael's tears had ended and he had cleaned up and they had both eaten breakfast, Walker started out again, this time with a new traveling companion. They continued in the direction Walker had been heading, for that was the direction from which Michael and his family had come, and he now needed to get back to his grandparents, who would take care of him. They walked in silence for a while, then Michael asked Walker where he was from.

Walker started to tell him that he was from Gustav's village, but he realized that with Michael, he probably didn't need to do so—children didn't seem to need the concrete answers that adults demanded. They were satisfied with the truth.

"I don't know," Walker said. "I remember only a short time—a little less than a year, I believe, from what people have told me. I only remember that one day I started walking on a road, and I felt inside that I was meant to walk. So I followed that feeling."

"And you've been walking ever since?"

"Not exactly. I sometimes stop to work, to earn some money. And every time I stop, I learn many valuable things from the people I meet and the people I work with."

"I want to learn," Michael said. "I want to learn about everything— about what the stars are, about how fire works, about why the sun goes up and down. There's so much to learn, my father says, that if we spend an entire lifetime trying to learn it all, we'll still only learn about as much as one grain of sand in a desert full of sand."

"Your father was very wise," Walker said, gently changing tenses. "With every new thing that I learn, I find out that there are hundreds of other things related to that new thing that I could also learn about. I believe the process never ends."

"Even if we live to be a million years old. That's why I was going to school—father said that I was going to be the youngest student ever at the university, where I could learn a lot about everything. I don't know if I'll be able to do that now, though."

"One of the people I met recently told me that people can do whatever they want, as long as they set their minds to it and pursue it with all their heart."

"My mother and father said the same thing. So I guess it must be true. But what if I set my heart on it and it doesn't come true.?"

"I suppose that could mean several different things. It could mean that it was not meant to be, because there was something else that you were supposed to do in life. Maybe God is trying to show you a different path that would be better for you. It could mean that you have not committed yourself to it completely, that you have not put your whole heart into it. It could mean that there is something else you have to learn before you are ready to do it, and it will not happen until you meet the person who will teach you or go through the situation that will teach you what it is you need to learn. I am sure there are other explanations, too."

"Well, I want to go to the university, so I guess that one day I shall go. So you believe in God, then?"

"I think so."

"I think I do, but I'm not sure. My father doesn't believe in God—didn't believe in God—but my mother did. My father was a scientist, and he said that everything that people call miracles have scientific explanations. He thought that people use religion to justify their own weaknesses, and their own acceptance of their problems in life. He said people use God as an excuse not to take action, or not to take responsibility for their own condition. That people use belief in God like a crutch, like when you break your leg and you need something to help you walk. My mother was a scientist, too, though, and she believed in God. She said that since God created us, he was there to support us when we needed him. That he wouldn't have put us on a planet so full of heartache and pain and misery without some sort of support, and he offered himself as the support."

Walker was impressed by Michael's grasp of the concepts he was talking about, and he found himself thinking that he would have liked to have met this boy's parents—they certainly treated him with a great deal of respect to have discussed such things with him.

"One thing that both of my parents agreed on," Michael added, "was that it's a shame that so many people start wars and kill people because of what they believe God to be or not to be. It seems so contradictory that someone can believe in a peaceful, kind God, and then turn around and condemn their neighbors because they don't believe in the same ways. It makes no sense."

"No, it doesn't," Walker agreed.

They talked most of the rest of the day—Michael never seemed to tire of talking about his ideas and thoughts and feelings. Walker enjoyed talking with him, especially after having spent so much time with Brian. Where Brian had been cynical, Michael was full of wonder at everything there was to learn; where Brian had been full of distrust, Michael was full of good things to say about people, even after what had happened to his parents. The tragedy was only a couple of days old, yet Michael wasn't dwelling on anger or resentment or a sense of loss—Walker heard all of those feelings expressed in things that Michael said—but Michael never made them his primary focus, never let them control his thoughts or words, as Brian had done.

Was there a difference because Michael was still a child in most ways, or was there something else about the two of them that made one of them miserable and the other one fundamentally happy, even after having lost both of his parents to violence?

No matter what the answer, Walker was happy that he had met Michael, for the young boy was teaching him a great deal about a great many things. He only hoped that he could return the favor somehow.

Chapter 17

As they walked through the forest, Walker noticed more and more roads leading off the main one. They also began to see quite a few more people than Walker had seen on the road in the mountains, and certainly many more people than he had seen in the desert. Some of the people greeted them warmly, with smiles and kind words, while others looked at them and nodded and continued on their way. Still others didn't even look at Walker and Michael, choosing instead to look down at the road before them as they walked by without a word.

At times, Walker saw Michael's mood change quickly and drastically—he would go from speaking enthusiastically about something that interested him to walking with his head down, saying nothing. At those times Walker was sure that Michael was thinking about what had happened to his parents, and he didn't know whether he should try to cheer him up and pull him out of his mood, or let him be with his thoughts so that he could work his way through them. Walker saw the benefits of both actions, but he couldn't decide which the best would be.

By the time night fell, they had covered a great distance, and they were both very tired. They slept next to a stream after having eaten almost the last of Walker's food—there was just enough left for a satisfying breakfast. Walker slept soundly until some time in the middle of the night, when Michael woke him with a sharp cry.

Walker sat up, and in the glow of the dying embers of their fire he saw Michael sitting up, his face covered with sweat, a look of terror in his eyes.

"Are you okay?" Walker asked quietly.

It took Michael several moments to catch his breath. Finally, he nodded and managed to say, "I had a nightmare."

Walker didn't know what that was. "A nightmare?" he asked.

"A bad dream. A very bad dream. I saw my parents getting killed again. But this time, I wasn't able to run away. One of the robbers turned to me and started to come after me, and I tried to run, but my legs were so heavy that I could hardly lift them up. I was trying to run, but it took me so long just to get my feet off the ground and try to move them forward that he was just walking towards me, laughing at me. And I knew he was going to catch me and kill me. I guess that's why I screamed."

"I'm sorry," Walker said, wondering why Michael had to go through the same thing again in his mind. Wasn't one time enough? Why did his parents' deaths also have to be a part of his sleep? It seemed, it felt, unfair.

"Would you like some water?" he asked Michael, holding up a gourd. Michael took it and drank, then lay back down.

"I hope I don't have that dream any more," he said quietly.

Walker lay down, too, listening to the sounds of the forest in the middle of the night. He knew that somewhere above him, there had to be stars and a moon, but he certainly couldn't see them through the leaves of the trees. He was sure, though, that the fact that he couldn't see the stars didn't mean that they didn't exist.

That was an important thought, he knew, but he was far too tired to maintain such a train of thought. In moments, he was asleep again.

After their second day of traveling, when they saw even more fellow travelers than they had seen the first day, they came to the end of the forest. Walker hadn't seen anything like the land that stretched out before them—it was a mixture of farmland, of forest, and of buildings—houses and big rectangular buildings that were completely new to his eyes.

"They're factories," Michael told him when he asked. "That's where they make all sorts of stuff. Some of them are mills, where they make mostly cloth, and some are processing plants, where raw materials are turned into usable materials, and others are factories where the usable materials are turned into products, like pots and pans and chairs and tables and light bulbs and things like that. It's all a bit more complicated than that, but that's the basic idea."

"Why does the air smell so bad here?" Walker wanted to know.

"Do you see the smoke coming our of the smokestacks? That's what causes the smell. When they process certain materials, they give off horrible odors, and the smoke carries the odors outdoors. Most of the processing is done by heat, so there are a lot of fires burning here."

Walker was surprised at the sight. Not only did the air smell bad, but the view was extremely unpleasant, like nothing he had ever seen before. The factories were ugly, and the houses that were near them were built with no sense of order and no sense of beauty.

"They're just practical—a place to sleep," Michael told him. "The workers need a place to sleep—most of them don't really care how it looks. And they just rent them from the companies, they don't own them, so they don't tend to have as much pride in them."

"This would be such an unpleasant place to live. Even the farmlands look poor."

"I think that has something to do with the quality of the soil," Michael said. "My mother said the soil here is very bad, and they don't replenish it regularly like they do in other places."

"When I worked on the farm," Walker told Michael, "we used fertilizer that smelled very bad, but it smelled healthy—it smelled right. And the smell passed soon enough, mixing with the smell of the rest of the soil. This smells somehow wrong."

"Well, I think we should get through here as quickly as we can. We still have three hours until sunset, and I think we can put this far behind us if we try."

"I think that's a very good idea," Walker said. After they began walking again, Walker asked, "Why would anyone want to live in such a place when there are so many other beautiful places where one could live? I don't understand it."

"They need work, because they need money," Michael explained. "My uncle—my mother's brother—said he spent a long time working in factories like this. He said that he got used to it after a while, because he had to. He worked so hard and so many hours that he didn't really care what the living conditions were like, as long as he had a place to sleep. That's how he put it, anyway."

Walker smiled. "A man recently told me that if there were something I needed to learn, that there would be a teacher there for me when I needed it. You certainly have a wonderful education—is there anything you don't know about?"

Michael blushed, and smiled. "My father used to call me a pitcher, because he could pour knowledge into me, and it would stay like water. But when the knowledge wanted to come out, I would open my mouth and it would pour out."

"Your father was a very wise man."

They were walking by one of the larger factories, a huge brick structure that showed no imagination at all on the part of the architect—the sides were flat and rectangular, with no decoration. The windows were small and so filthy that they couldn't even see inside, even though there were many windows on the side that was facing them.

The atmosphere was glum, stifled, cold. There was no one on the road, not a soul to be seen. When Walker commented on that, Michael told him that he should wait for the whistle.

"When the shift is over, this road will be packed with people going home. Right now they're all inside, doing their jobs, probably the same thing over and over, all day long. My uncle said it took a lot of the creativity out of him, because it took most of his energy from him. He was a great guy, but he said that when he worked at a place like this, he used to get angry very quickly because he felt trapped, and he didn't feel that he had a way out."

"How did he change that?"

"He left. He quit his job and went to another place, a different job. He said it wasn't until he left that he realized that the job had had a hold on him, but he had created that hold himself through his own belief that if he left, he would starve, that he needed his pay every month in order to continue to survive. He said that when he left, he finally realized how free he was, and just how many other options there were in the world, just how many other things he could do to make a living and be much happier doing it.

"He told me that story over and over. He said he wanted to burn it into me because he didn't want his nephew to make the same mistake he did. He wanted me to learn from his mistake so I wouldn't have to waste years of my life learning the same lesson."

"That was very kind of him."

"Like I said, he was a great man. I mean, he is a great man." Michael paused. "I'm trying to get used to talking about my parents in the past. Now I'm talking about everyone in the past."

"It will take some time," Walker said softly. "It will come. For now, I'd just like to walk, to get past this place. It is very unpleasant."

"I agree."

They walked on in silence, and soon put that area behind them when they started climbing a tall hill that took them out of the valley. As they ascended, Walker noticed the air become fresher and cleaner. They heard a long, loud whistle behind them, and they turned to see people pouring out of the buildings, filling the roads, moving from the factories to the many rows of houses.

"They almost seem—" Walker started, but he didn't want to finish.

"Inhuman?" Michael asked.

Walker shook his head. "No," he said, "I was thinking that they seemed controlled, controlled by something else other than who they are as human beings."

"Well, their bosses control them. The time cards control them. The money controls them. Uncle David said that he felt a bit inhuman, because he never had to make any decisions. But he also said that a lot of the people who worked there liked it that way."

"It's very complex, isn't it?" Walker asked with a smile.

"It sure is. That's why I want to study so much."

They turned and continued up the hill, out of the valley.

After that point, they never really left people behind, as Walker had done for days at a time before. They passed houses and stores and more factories, though never as many in one place as they had seen when they had come out of the forest. At times they would go an hour or two without seeing a building, but over the next few days they did most of their traveling in sight of some human-made structure or another, even if it was just a small house off in the distance. Places to sleep in the open were getting harder to find, and on the second night, they ended up taking a room in a small inn.

Never having rented a room, Walker let Michael take care of the arrangements for the night. Michael suggested that they tell people they were uncle and nephew, for he still feared being discovered by the robbers who had killed his parents, and it would keep people from being too curious about who they were and why they were traveling together.

When they got to their room, Walker was concerned.

"I hear most people say that we should always be honest," he told Michael, "and that honesty is always the best of all possible ways. Yet you're the second person who has told me that my life will be much easier if I'm not completely honest. I believe you, and I believed Gustav when he told me the same thing, but I don't understand it. Why do we have to say something that isn't true in order to make our lives easier?"

Michael shrugged. "My father called it an unfortunate truth of life. You don't lie in order to deceive or cheat anyone, but because you want to avoid unfortunate reactions from people who think that they know how to react to your situation. If we tell people that we just met a few days ago, all it would take is for one person to become suspicious and go to the local authorities and get you in trouble or keep me here for some reason or another. And they would be doing what they thought was the best for everyone. But I want to go home to my grandparents, and you're helping me do that, and we don't want to be under suspicion for any reason. So we tell them something that will satisfy them. We'll never see these people again, and after we leave tomorrow, they'll never think of us again for the rest of time."

"So we say something that is not true simply because of the way other people may respond?"

"It's pretty sad, isn't it?"

"Yes, it is. But I do understand the need. Do the other people know that the way they often react is causing other people to tell lies?"

"I don't know. I hadn't thought of it that way before. It's a very good question."

Walker sighed and looked out the window at the lights of the houses that sat on the other side of the street. Michael laughed softly.

"One thing I learned from living with a mother and father who rarely agreed is that there's almost never a simple answer. If the answer is simple, it's either wrong or merely the first step of a much more complex answer."

"Somehow, though," Walker said slowly, "I miss the simplicity and the happiness that came with simple answers. If ignorance truly is happiness, can ignorance be all that bad? The more I learn, the more complex everything becomes, and the fewer answers I find for anything. I long for the simplicity—I long to be able to live life with simplicity, but the more I have to think about, the less simple my life becomes. It's all very strange— I used to be able to sleep by any stream I wished, but now I must rent a room at an inn, and I must have money to rent the room, and I must earn money to pay for a room, and I must find a job to earn money. And once I have money, I must be wary of thieves and greedy people who might want to take it away from me. Why must it be so complicated?"

"I can't tell you that, Walker," Michael told him. "I'm only fourteen."

"But you're a genius."

Michael looked down shyly. "That's what my parents said. That's why I was going to start studying so soon. But I still can't answer that question. That's simply the way things are."

Walker sighed. "It's time to go to sleep, isn't it?" he asked.

Michael smiled. "I think so—we're thinking too much for so late in the day. Let's sleep on it."

"On what?"

The next morning they left the inn after eating breakfast there. As Walker paid for the food, he was thankful that Turner had insisted that he take the money, for he had a feeling he would be needing more of it. Indeed, just after they left the inn, they stopped at a store and bought bread and cheese to carry with them for when they got hungry.

The day was cold and overcast, and Walker was glad that he had his coat and an extra blanket for Michael to wrap himself up in. He had thought about getting rid of them in the desert, and again in the heat and humidity of the forest, but he had thought he might need them again. The sun did manage to get a bit of its light through the clouds, but not much. The flowers that no longer seemed to grow wild, but that were confined to window boxes and gardens, shone dimly in the muted light, and the air was full of mist that never quite became rain.

After they were out of town, in another short stretch of undeveloped land, they came into the fog. Walker had seen winter fog before, a light fog that lifted early in the morning, but this fog was so thick that they could barely see a few feet ahead of them on the road. They walked quietly, and all the sounds were muted—it was as if suddenly the whole world around them had ceased to exist, and they were stuck in their own little space in their own time. Walker found the feeling strange, but interesting. When he heard a bird cry loudly, the sound was different than it normally was—he had no idea how close or how far away the bird was, as he normally did.

"It's great, isn't it?" Michael asked him. "We have a lot of fog where I live—I love to go outside and play hide-and-seek in it. It makes the game much more interesting."

Walker looked at him with a question in his eyes, and Michael went on to explain the game to him, as well as many other games that he used to play with his friends. They sounded like fun to Walker, and he wondered why none of the people he had met had told him about games—surely Marie or Gustav or Kennison would also enjoy playing games like that? He wasn't too sure about Turner or Adam, but maybe they, too, would like games. But they hadn't mentioned games to Walker, so he assumed that they didn't like to play them. But why?

The overcast lasted for two entire days of walking, and though Walker saw a lot of beauty in the greyness and wetness, he found that such weather made him miss the sun even more than being in the forest for several days had made him miss it. When they woke up at another inexpensive inn on their fourth day out of the forest, Walker knew that he would have to work once more if her were going to have any money. He told Michael.

"That's okay," Michael told him. "We'll just keep our eyes open—there are lots of people building around here—I'm sure someone could use some help."

So as they walked that morning, they watched for potential workplaces. They stopped at three sites where people were building homes, but none of them needed help. They weren't too worried about finding work, for Walker had enough money to last them for several days, so they still enjoyed the beautiful warmth of the sunny morning.

Early that afternoon, though, they reached a place where several men were working on a very large structure. They had only a frame up over a very large hole in the ground at that point, and Michael explained to Walker that that was going to be the basement. Walker was fascinated, for he had never seen the shell of a house without the house being finished—at all the other places they had stopped, the structures had been nearly complete.

They approached a man who looked to have authority and asked if he needed help. The man was young—much younger than Walker would have expected—and he looked pleasant enough, though not at all friendly.

"What kind of experience do you have?" the man asked, looking them both over with sharp grey eyes.

"None at all," Michael responded, "but we're both quick learners and we both work very hard."

"Do you do all the talking for your dad here?" the man asked, looking to Walker.

Walker smiled. "I'm not his father." He saw the look that crossed the man's face—a look that Walker couldn't describe, but that made him uncomfortable. "I'm his uncle," he added, and the look vanished from the man's face and he nodded. Walker understood Michael's point, but he couldn't help but think that this man's suspicious nature had just made him lie. Or had it made him? Hadn't he still had the option of telling just the truth?

"We've still got another week to travel," Michael added, "and about four days' worth of money. We were thinking maybe we could work to earn some money to make it home on."

"If you can give me four days," the man said, "I'll give you twenty a day," he nodded at Walker, then at Michael, "and you ten."

"That sounds fair," Michael said.

"My name is Lance," the man continued, "and while you're working for me, you'll do what I tell you to do. Nothing more, nothing less. I'm responsible for how this building turns out, so I have to have the final say on everything. Is that clear?"

"Perfectly clear," Walker said.

"Then come on. I'll show you where you can start."

Over the next three days, Michael was busy doing odd jobs around the site, separating nails, clearing areas of debris and extra materials, cleaning tools, and anything else that Lance found for him to do. Walker, on the other hand, helped Lance and his two other helpers, Enrique and John, to build the framework of the building, putting in the frames for the walls and the floor for the second floor, which was also the ceiling for the first floor. Then they put in the frames for the second floor's walls, and added the beams for the roof after that. The work was enjoyable—Walker liked to feel his body being used; he liked the feel of his muscles actually working hard, lifting and placing and cutting wood, pounding nails, climbing ladders. He was also using his mind every time he measured and cut and had to figure out the correct angles to cut, especially in spots where the corners didn't match up as evenly as he would have liked them to.

The sun stayed up, and Walker started working without a shirt, as the others did. Lance made him put the shirt back on after a time on the first day, telling Walker that he would be useless to him if he were sunburned. By the morning of the fourth day, their last day there, Walker had his shirt off the whole morning.

A few hours after they had started that morning, Walker came down from the roof to take a break and find out how Michael was doing.

"Great," Michael said. "I've never done this kind of work before—I like it a lot. Don't you?"

"Yes, I do," Walker replied. "It's great work. And look at the building—it's much different that it was when we started."

Indeed, the shell of the building was almost finished, and Walker could see that it was going to be a beautiful house. The outside walls and windows were all put up, and the roof was nearly complete. Looking up at the building, Walker felt a sense of pride, the same sense he had felt after finishing bread, but in a different way—this was on a much larger scale, an accomplishment that would stand for many years. How could it be, he asked himself, that there were so many different ways that one could gain a sense of pride and accomplishment, yet people like Brian rejected them all, denying themselves the pride that they could so easily gain?

Lance yelled to Michael from the roof, asking him to bring up another bucket of roofing nails, and Michael swiftly complied. Walker watched him with a smile—he admired Michael very much, for he did everything with a great deal of energy and enthusiasm, even though he had very good reasons to be angry and spiteful and distrusting. He watched him clamber up the ladder and give Lance the bucket, then stop and exchange a few words with him. Then he watched Michael turn and start down the ladder, and he watched as the top rung of the ladder cracked, and he watched as Michael fell with an awful scream thirty feet to the ground, landing on his back with a horrible thud.

He dropped his water and ran over to where Michael lay on the ground, moaning. Blood was trickling from the corners of his mouth, and his eyes were glazed over, unseeing. Walker kneeled over him and put his arms around him; almost as soon as he did so, Michael died with a terrible shudder that would never leave Walker's memory.

Walker cried as he had never cried before. He didn't even notice that Lance and Enrique and John were standing there by him, their heads down and tears in their eyes. They, too, had grown to like Michael very much.

Three hours later, Walker was on the road again, his pack on his back and the money that he and Michael had earned in his pocket. He hadn't wanted to take the money, but Lance had insisted, for he knew that Walker would need it—that was the main reason that Walker and Michael had stopped in the first place.

It had taken him a long time to stop crying, and in his heart, he knew as he walked that he was still crying. The four men had buried Michael deep in the ground in the woods behind the house they were building, and Walker's only consolation was the fact that he knew that Michael was at peace.

He didn't understand the death—Michael had gotten so much out of the world, and he would have given so much back to it. Brian's death had seemed to be a release—Brian had hated life and everything in it, and he was miserable while he was alive. His death didn't seem to be a tragedy, for it seemed somehow fitting, somehow the only thing that could have released Brian from the torment he put himself through every day.

But Michael had put himself through no such torment. On the contrary, he had loved life, even after his parents had been killed. He had felt the sadness of loss, yet he had put it behind him and continued to live each day as it came. He allowed the sadness and grief their places in his life, but he didn't allow them to control him or his thoughts. Michael's death was a great loss to everyone, even those people who would never meet him, such as the people at the university who would have been able to work with the fourteen-year-old genius who probably would have taught them many things about life, just as he had taught Walker many valuable lessons.

Michael's death seemed to be the useless destruction of potential, a meaningless, wasteful destruction of something very valuable, whereas Brian had shown no potential at all—no potential for accomplishment or change.

Walker was lonely now—he longed to have Michael there with him, talking to him, sharing his thoughts and ideas. He wanted to share his loss, he wanted to grieve with somebody. He wanted to let Michael's remaining family know what had happened to Michael and his parents, but he had always assumed that Michael would show him where his grandparents lived, so he had never found out their names or where they lived.

He stopped on the road and turned to look at a tree, a huge oak that stood twice the height of the house from which Michael had fallen. He tried to see the beauty there, but the loss in his heart was overpowering everything else, blinding him to the rest of the world, to the joy and the love that had to be there. He looked harder, knowing that Michael would want him to do so. He walked over to the tree and regarded a leaf, a leaf that Michael had explained to him turned sunlight into energy for the tree, that actually breathed, releasing oxygen into the atmosphere. The leaf went on—the leaf continued to do what it did, regardless of Michael's death. He looked down at his feet, where the huge roots of the tree made the ground bulge as they started their journey outwards, where they would both hold the tree steady and gather water and nutrients to supply the needs of the tree. The roots would keep on doing their job, also. The massive trunk stretched upwards, holding the branches that held the leaves and pulling the water and nutrients from the roots up to the very top of itself, so that each leaf got exactly what it needed to continue. In all ways, the tree was living up to its potential, just as Michael always had, just as Brian probably never had.

He returned to the road and smiled back at the oak, thanking it for its lesson. He would continue. He would go on leading his life as he felt he was supposed to, and he would carry the memory of Michael with him wherever he went, and he would carry Michael's lessons with him, also. There was no use in giving up his life, in giving up his potential for life, worrying about Michael's death, worrying about whether it was fair or not, grieving the loss of a great friend. The death made no sense, but he knew that Michael would want him to live as full a life as possible, and if he immersed himself in grief, he never would be able to do so.

He started walking again, his heart lighter, looking for the perfect place in his heart where he could keep his memories of Michael.

He stayed at another inn that night, for there were almost no places where he could sleep next to a stream anymore without being on someone's private property.

He found it interesting that when he had been with Michael, he had paid almost no attention to the inns where they had stayed, for he was busy talking with Michael and thinking about what they were discussing. He had hardly noticed the people whom he had paid, the people who had served him. He hadn't noticed decorations or architecture or furnishings, except in a very superficial way.

Now, though, he was noticing details again. He saw the ornate woodwork that showed many hours of work, and he saw the beautiful curtains that had been hung with a great deal of care. He also saw the eyes of the woman who took his name and money, saw that she was a kind person who cared about other people and who cared about her inn. She introduced herself as Alma, and she told him that dinner would be in an hour. He went upstairs and washed up, changing into his only other set of clothes, which were cleaner than those he had been wearing.

There were three other guests at the inn—young parents and their young daughter, who was no more than five years old. She was a bright girl with a bright smile which she seemed to get from her mother, for her mother's smile was identical. They greeted Walker as he sat down at an adjoining table, and he returned their greeting. He found that when Alma brought him his dinner, he wished to speak, to say something, but something inside stopped him. He recognized that something as his grief, and he let it keep its place and he didn't talk. Michael had been dead only a few hours, he realized, and he wasn't ready to talk yet. He thanked her for his food, then ate quietly and went up to his room.

He lay in bed a very long time before he was able to fall asleep. The feeling of Michael dying in his arms was with him, as was the horror he had felt as he had watched Michael plummet to the ground. There was nothing he could have done, but he found himself feeling somehow that he should have done something.

Finally, exhaustion took its course, and he fell into a fitful sleep.

At breakfast the next morning, Alma looked at him with a smile.

"You look a bit brighter today," she said with caring. "You were carrying a great burden yesterday, so I felt it best to leave you be. But your eyes show that your burden is lighter this morning."

Walker thought over what she said, surprised at all that she had seen—he had never thought that his own face could reveal so much, for he had tried not to show his grief to the rest of the world.

"Yes," he said to her. "A good friend died yesterday."

"I'm so sorry," she said quickly. "I had no idea. . . ."

Walker smiled, but he felt the sadness in his own smile, and he knew that she would be able to see it, too.

"That's okay," he said quietly. "It's very sad, because he was very young, but I know that he died at peace."

"That's the most important of all, isn't it?" Alma asked. "People who are at peace with themselves are very hard to find these days."

"Why is that?" Walker asked.

"You're asking me?" she asked with a little laugh. "I have a hard enough time figuring out my own life, much less the lives of other people."

"But you care, and you see things in other people. You saw what was in me."

Alma sighed. "I guess you're right. What I see in most people, though, is the need to get ahead, to get rich, to compare themselves to other people all the time and value other people's accomplishments more than their own. Few people are willing just to be themselves anymore. Few people realize that God made them just the way they are for a reason, and they spend so much time trying to become something else that they ignore the beautiful selves they are, or they would be, if they would just cultivate their own gifts rather than the gifts that they think everyone else values. But everyone wants to fit in, everyone wants to be recognized. They don't realize that they would fit in much better if they were true to themselves and true to what they were created to be."

"I see," Walker said. "My friend Michael wanted to follow his abilities— he wanted to learn. And he learned so much. But then his parents were killed, and he died soon after. But I think he died happy."

"Then God bless him. So many people die unhappy, miserable over mistakes they made during their lives or things that they never did but wanted to do. I've never made my mark on thousands of people, but I run a very nice inn, and people feel comfortable here. I've done what I always wanted to do, and my husband and I will both die happy because we knew what we wanted, and we worked for it. But we also knew what wasn't for us, and we didn't spend a lot of time worrying about the things we didn't have, like fame and fortune. We both think it's just as important to know what you shouldn't try to do as it is to know what you should try to do."

"You're very wise," Walker said.

Alma smiled. "Thank you," she said. "When one reaches my age, it's important that one have some sort of wisdom to pass on to the younger people who will be here long after we've passed on."

"Perhaps you could give me all of your wisdom and I won't have to learn it all on my own," Walker said with a smile. "It would save me many hours of thought."

"But getting there is most of the fun, Mr. Walker. I wouldn't want to rob you of the joy of the journey. Believe it or not, getting there is most of the fun. The destination isn't the most important thing—it's how we spend the journey on the way to the final goal."

After Alma had packed him a lunch, Walker started off on the road again, his heart a bit lighter, though still burdened with Michael's death. It would take time to pass, he knew.

Many hours later, when the sun was just about to go down, Walker crested a tall hill and looked down into a valley, the likes of which he had never seen before. Just below him lay a large town, stretching at least two miles into the distance, but soon the town stopped, right at the edge of a huge body of water that stretched as far as he could see, ending only at the horizon, which was even flatter than the desert's horizon had been.

He had never seen that much water before, and he wondered how it had come to be there. He saw many specks on the water, moving about very slowly, and he remembered a boat he had once seen on a small lake. The town looked to be crowded, for the houses were close together on the hills that reached down to the water. Floating on the water where the main part of town met it was a huge ship, which Walker could make out even from where he stood. Was it possible for him to get on that ship? he wondered. He thought that he would have to, or his journey might have to come to an end at the shore of the water. He wasn't ready for it to end, though, didn't feel inside that it was time for it to end. And he knew that he had to follow that feeling, for he didn't have anything else to go by.

He started down the road towards the ship, and he reached it in half an hour. The port was alive with activity, for people were rushing here and there, loading and unloading other, smaller ships that were docked near the large one. Walker saw people rushing by with trunks and boxes and carts full of very large fish, and he walked slowly to the stairs that were set up on the dock leading up to the large ship.

A man who was standing at the top of the stairs looked down at him.

"No boarding until tomorrow," he called down. "We leave at ten a.m., and we'll start boarding at eight."

Walker didn't move away. He looked around, unsure of what he should do. He understood what the man had told him, but he wasn't sure how he would be able to get on the ship, since they were obviously controlling who could get on.

"Tickets back there," the man said, pointing to a building just behind Walker. "But I think it's closed for the night. Get your ticket there, first thing in the morning. Now please get on with you—we can't have you blocking the way here. We've got work to do."

Walker went back to where the man had pointed, but a small sign that said "closed" hung over the window over which the word "Tickets" was written. Walker sighed. He would have to eat and find a place to sleep until morning.

He had seen a small inn about half a mile before he had reached the docks, so he walked back to it and paid for a room for the night. The innkeeper suggested a restaurant nearby, and Walker walked over there to find a bright, cheerful place with clean tables and a very friendly waitress. She greeted him as he came in and led him to a table near the middle of the room. To his right sat a family—a woman and a man and their two children, but the only other people in the place were sitting almost all the way across the room. Walker read the menu carefully, though he wasn't sure of what all the dishes were, especially the fish. He had rarely eaten in restaurants before, and he had never been exposed to seafood. He knew what potatoes were, though, and he knew what stew was, so he stayed with what he knew.

A few minutes after he had sat down, and just a minute after he had ordered, a woman came over to his table and stood next to the chair across from him.

"Is this seat taken?" she asked, rather innocently. Walker shook his head. "Would you mind some company for dinner?" she asked.

"Not at all," Walker replied, glad to have someone to talk to during the meal. She stood several moments longer, as if waiting for something, but finally she sat down and put her purse on the table before her.

"My name's Robin," she said, holding out her hand for Walker to shake. He did so, and was surprised when she squeezed more tightly than he had expected, and when she didn't let go nearly as quickly as he had expected.

"I'm Walker," he said. "It's very nice to meet you, Robin."

"Walker?" she asked. "What an interesting name—I don't think I've ever met anyone named Walker before. I'm very pleased to meet you, Walker. Where are you from?"

"From a village on the other side of the mountains, far from here," he said. "Where are you from?"

"I'm from here," she replied with a sigh. "I've lived here all my life. But I won't be here long—I'm going across the sea, and I'm going to start over.

I'm tired of this place. There's nowhere to go here, nowhere to get to. It's a dump. Are you traveling? Are you taking the ship tomorrow?"

"Yes, I believe so," Walker said. "I was going to buy a ticket today, but the office was closed, so I'll have to buy one in the morning."

"Did you just get into town?" Robin asked him.

"Yes, about an hour ago. Why?"

"Boy, are you lucky—this is the last ship for three weeks. If you hadn't made this one, you would've had to stay in this hellhole for three weeks. That would have been a fate worse than death, let me tell you."

When their food came, Robin continued to talk, hardly eating her food at all. Walker wasn't sure how he felt about her company. He was glad to have someone to talk to while he ate, but she talked about things that didn't interest him, much as Brian had. She mostly complained about how awful her town was, how badly people treated her, and how wonderful everything was going to be when she finally raised enough money to buy passage on a ship across the sea.

"It's really hard to get up enough money when you still live with your parents, though," she explained. "They keep wanting me to buy things for the house, like food, and every time I get a job, they don't like the hours or they don't like the job I'm doing or they need me around the house more. They even make me pay rent. Because of them, I've gone through ten jobs in the last four years—no one will hire me anymore, because they know that my parents will screw things up. It's horrible."

She was an attractive young woman, Walker thought as he listened to her talk, but she didn't allow her attractiveness to show through much—she hid all of her face's natural features beneath a great deal of make-up, more than Walker had ever seen any woman wear, and much of her long brown hair hung down over one side of her face, hiding much of what she looked like. Her brown eyes reflected her intelligence, but her words demonstrated none—Walker had never seen such a strong paradox in a person before. It struck him as rather sad, because in her he saw much of the same potential that he had seen in Michael, but on the surface he saw the same kind of person as Brian.

When they had finished eating, Robin ordered coffee for them both, and Walker drank his quietly. He wanted to know more about this woman, but he was very tired, and he didn't know how to ask her what he wanted to know without insulting her or hurting her feelings.

"You know," Robin said quietly, leaning on the table so that she was much closer to Walker, "I think it would be very nice if you and I could spend some time together tonight. We could get to know each other pretty well in the next few hours. Where are you staying?"

Walker told her the name of the inn, not quite sure what she was getting at.

"That's perfect. I know Jack, the owner. He and I get along very well. I know he wouldn't mind if you had a guest for the night, as long as you paid for a double room, of course."

"But why would I have a guest?" Walker asked. "I'm traveling alone."

"Exactly, So maybe you'd like to have some company. I think you and I could make a very nice time of it, if you know what I mean."

Walker didn't know exactly what she meant, but he was starting to get a good idea. And while the idea did hold a certain attraction for him, he wasn't ready to do anything like have sex with a woman he didn't even know, and whose company he wasn't all that fond of. But he had no idea how to respond gracefully, how to tell her he wasn't interested in what she was proposing.

"I can't do that," he said. "It's just not right. But thank you—I'm very flattered."

Robin immediately lost a great deal of her energy, became almost deflated with his refusal. She looked at him coldly, and the spark in her eyes had become ice. The energy she had lost was replaced almost immediately with the energy of anger.

"Don't be," she said, her voice tinged with venom. "Don't be flattered. Anyone who can get me a ticket across that damned sea is fair game as far as I'm concerned."

Walker watched the family at the next table leave—he hoped they hadn't heard any of their conversation—and then watched Robin storm out of the restaurant.

The waitress came over to him. "Will you be paying for her meal, also?"

Walker smiled sadly. "Yes, I suppose I will."

Five minutes later he was back at the inn, and he walked past the family he had just seen at the restaurant. The man was reading a letter at the desk, and Walker smiled and said hello to the wife and children. They looked like very nice people, and he found himself wishing that he had eaten dinner with them instead of with Robin. But he knew that dinner with Robin had been the best thing for him, unpleasant as it had turned out.

Twenty minutes later, there was a knock on his door. He opened it to find the man and woman of the family from the restaurant.

"Excuse me, sir," the man said, a bit uncomfortably. "We couldn't help but overhear at dinner that you will be taking the ship in the morning, and that you haven't yet secured passage. Is that correct?"

"Yes, it is," Walker said, a bit confused. "Please, come in."

The couple entered. "My name is Newman Smith," the man told him, "and this is my wife, Katherine. We have a great favor to ask of you. I have just received a letter that is delaying me on this side of the sea for several weeks—it's a business concern, and quite a complicated one at that. But Katherine and the children must continue on the journey, and I don't want them to travel alone, for various reasons." He paused.

"So I have a proposition for you. I overheard the woman's proposal to you at dinner, and I heard you turn her down. It is obvious that you are a man of no little honor, and I wish to ask you to watch over my wife and children during the course of the voyage. We will supply you with passage, though we'll have to put you in a separate berth in the morning.

"You don't have to answer right now, but I would appreciate it if you would think about it. The office opens at seven—you can give us your answer tomorrow at breakfast, if that would suit you."

"I don't really have to think about it," Walker replied. "I'll be on the boat anyway, and I can watch over them if you'd like. You don't have to pay for my passage."

Newman looked at him carefully, and Walker could tell that the man was judging whether or not he could judge Walker based on his response. Finally, Walker noticed that he relaxed a bit as he reached a decision.

"That would be splendid," Newman said. "I can't express how much I appreciate this. As far as the passage is concerned, though, we've already bought ours, and there is unfortunately no refund of the purchase price. It would be quite ridiculous for you to pay an extra fare when ours is already paid. We can deal with particulars in the morning, but for my part, I wish to thank you—I know that I'll sleep a great deal better tonight knowing that my family will be accompanied home. We shall see you in the morning, Mr. Walker. Good night."

"Good night," Walker said.

"Good night," Katherine added, "and thank you."

Walker closed the door behind them. They were thankful to him because he had agreed to do something that seemed to be an extremely pleasant task that he was already looking forward to doing.

"It's very complex," he muttered to himself as he lay down in his bed to sleep.

Chapter 19

Walker awoke early the next morning to another grey, cloudy day. This time, though, a soft rain was falling on the window of his room, and it didn't look like it was a rain that was going to stop any time soon.

He gathered what he owned and put it in his pack, leaving out his coat, and went downstairs to have breakfast.

Newman and Katherine were already there, and Newman waved Walker over to their table when he entered the room. Newman stood and extended his hand, and he and Walker shook.

Walker wished them both a good morning and sat down.

"Are you still willing to follow through on your decision of last night?" Newman asked him, looking him directly in the eye.

"Yes, of course," Walker replied. "I look forward to it, actually."

"It's not that my wife needs babysitting, mind you," Newman told him. "It's just that this particular ship has a reputation for having bad things happen on it, because of the type of people who tend to book passage on it here. The company is in business for profit, and they have a habit of selling passage to somewhat unsavory people. Quite a few people cross the sea to escape their pasts, much like the young lady you met last night. I'm not a paranoid man, but I am realistic, and I know that three days are a very long time, and anything could happen. Last year on the sister ship of this one, two people were killed during one of the trips. Fortunately, it was thieves killing thieves, so there was no loss of innocent lives, but one never knows."

"And I have to say that I'll feel much more comfortable knowing that everyone on board will know that I have a male companion," Katherine added. "I know that it's a lot to ask, but would you be willing to say that you're my brother? And that the children are your niece and nephew? We don't want to ask you to lie, but it would make things so much easier."

"I will say that," Walker agreed. "I just find it sad that people who don't honor the truth or other people can make others lie in order to ensure their own safety. It's very strange."

"Yes, it is," Newman agreed, "but it's one of those annoying facts of life. One day, when all human beings are kind and honest and good to one another, there will no longer be any need at all to tell any lies, for everyone will respect the truth. But I will never see that day, I fear, and until that day comes, we'll have to compromise our integrity from time to time."

Walker shrugged. "And life will go on," he said. "But we won't be getting any happier, or feeling any better about ourselves."

Newman put down the knife with which he had been buttering his bread and thought about those words for a few moments.

"There's a lot of truth in that statement," he finally said, "an awful lot of truth. My dear, it looks like your brother is a philosopher. You two should have a rather interesting voyage ahead of you. My wife," he explained to Walker, "loves to read the works of the great philosophers—Plato, Aristotle, Augustine—you name it, she's read their works. And she loves to discuss them, but unfortunately, I have little interest in their works."

"Are you familiar with Aristotle at all?" Katherine asked Walker, and he heard a touch of hope in her voice, but he had to shake his head.

"No," he replied. "I'm sorry, but I've done very little reading. I'm trying to find out what I need to know about life, so that I can know what I need to do with my life."

"Well, that's fine," she said. "Then we can talk about your philosophy of life."

"In order to allow you to talk about anything at all, we need to go over to the ship and change the ticket. Would you get the children ready, my dear, and bring them over to the ship?" Newman asked.

"Absolutely," she replied, standing. Newman stood and kissed his wife on the cheek. "I'll be there shortly."

Newman paid for Walker's breakfast over his protests, then they started down the road that led to the dock. As soon as they were outside the inn, Newman's tone changed. It was no longer friendly, but neither was it antagonistic.

"I'm usually a very good judge of character, Mr. Walker," he said, "but I know that mistakes are possible. I'm trusting my family to a complete stranger, something that yesterday I wouldn't have thought possible. But it must be done. I will tell you now that if any harm comes to my wife or children at your hand, I will hunt you down and I will kill you." They walked in silence for a few moments, then Newman spoke again, the friendliness back in his voice. "There—that's said. I hope that it doesn't offend you, but you need to know very clearly exactly where I stand."

"I understand," Walker replied. "And you've made no mistake. Your family will be fine—I'll do everything in my power to make sure they are."

Within ten minutes, the ticket was changed, and soon Walker was boarding the ship with Katherine and the children. Katherine and Newman introduced Walker to the children, Kathleen and William, who preferred to be called Billy, asking the children to make sure they called him "Uncle Walker."

"I'm sorry to rush things," Newman said, "but I've arranged to take a coach, and I have to hurry to catch it. I've already held it up half an hour." He kissed his wife and children good-bye, shook Walker's hand and wished him well, and left.

Katherine looked at Walker and smiled. "Well, Mr. Walker," she said, "we have a three-day journey ahead of us. Shall we get settled in our cabins?"

Walker followed her through a door that led inside the ship, down a hallway with a series of doors on either side, that looked very much like the largest inn he had stayed in. He found it incredible that such a large structure could be floating on the water, and he almost didn't believe that it could be doing so.

"Is this entire ship really floating?" he asked Katherine, and she turned to him.

"Of course it is. It's really quite a brilliant work, isn't it?"

"Yes, it is. It's very beautiful."

"Well, here we are," Katherine said. "Your cabin should be the second one down, on the right. I think we'll be staying in our cabin until we're well underway—I want to make sure that I don't lose either of the children before we embark. But I'm sure the children will want to be up on the deck as we leave, so we'll go up there once we start moving."

"That will be fine," Walker said. "Then should we meet for lunch?"

"We'll meet for lunch. How does one o'clock sound?"

"We'll eat at one o'clock," Walker said, and Katherine said good-bye and closed the door.

Walker was surprised at how tired she looked, and he was a bit worried about her. She had looked so different the evening before, so radiant, yet now her face wasn't nearly as cheerful as it had been. Then he thought of the fact that her husband had just gone one way, and she was going in another, and they had had no warning that they were going to be split up. It must have been very difficult for her.

He opened the door to his cabin and put the key into his pocket, then went inside and put his pack on the bed. The room was tiny, yet comfortable, considering how little space there was. Everything had been planned to be as functional as possible, he noted, and they certainly had done a good job. The bed was very thin, and it stood under two small round windows through which he could see the hills of the town around the port. He went to one of the windows and sat on the bed, looking out at the town he would be leaving soon.

For the first time that he recalled, he wondered what he was missing by walking through a town without exploring it at all, without getting to know anything about it. When he thought about what Robin had told him the night before, he realized that there were many human beings there, many people from whom he could learn many things, yet he hadn't even had the time to walk around the town, to see things other than the road, the inn, and the restaurant.

How many times had he walked right through towns without even thinking about what he might be missing by not staying? The times he had stayed seemed to be fortuitous accidents—Gustav had offered him a job, Turner had offered him work, he and Michael had worked on the house. But he had reached this town just some twelve hours before, and he was already leaving it, had already left it, without knowing it at all. The only indication that he had of what kind of town it was and what kind of people lived there came from the cynical words of an unhappy young woman who wanted only to leave it. They could hardly be accurate words, could hardly express just what the town was to the people who lived there and made their lives there and called the town home.

But what was it about the road that kept him going? What was this urge inside him that surfaced so often, this need to continue on, leaving behind people he had met and things he had seen? Why couldn't he stay here in this town and learn about people in depth, as he had gotten to know Gustav and Marie? He had learned much more about them after he had gotten to know them, after they had trusted him more and became more comfortable around him. What could he have learned about Kennison and Gloria and Tricia if he had stayed longer?

The question of course could not be answered, and he was a bit surprised that the question was coming to him for the first time. In all of the houses that he was looking at through the window—the expensive houses at the top of the hill, the cheaply built homes near the water—lived people, human beings with human stories and lives that they were living to the best of their abilities. They were learning, they were teaching, they were experiencing life all day, every day, in whatever form life was for them.

And he was seeing none of that.

He sighed. These new thoughts had come to him suddenly, and he was glad that he had a few days on the ship to think about them. He was almost tempted to get off the ship, to go into town and find a place to live and a job, but he had made a promise. Besides, the urge to continue moving was very strong inside him, and he knew he would watch the ship leave and know he had made the wrong choice.

He left the cabin and began to explore the ship. Everything that he saw amazed him, for everything was built on a vessel that was floating on water. When he reached the deck and looked down over the railing at the water, he wondered how the ship didn't tip over, for it certainly seemed that it should. There didn't seem to be any way that it could sit up straight with all the weight on it.

Suddenly there was a huge noise, and the ship began to tremble slightly as they turned on the engines below. Walker had never felt such a thing—in the trembling he could feel an immense power, a strength that he had never imagined before. Soon there was activity everywhere—yelling and running back and forth and throwing ropes off of the ship and onto the ship, and an incredibly loud whistle sounded from the top of the smokestack behind him. Then, ever so slightly, the ship began to move.

Walker stood in the rain, watching the dock. The movement was so slight that at first, not feeling any sense of movement at all, Walker thought the dock was moving away from him. It took several seconds for his mind to adapt, for him to realize that the ship that seemed motionless was actually moving. He watched as they pulled away from the town that he would never know. He walked to the front of the ship and watched as it turned towards the open sea, and within fifteen minutes, Walker could see nothing ahead of him except open sea.

"Fantastic, isn't it?" asked an old man who was standing near him.

"What do you mean?" Walker asked, looking at the old man who stood looking at the horizon. There was much that was fantastic about the experience, but he didn't know what the man was referring to.

"I mean that it's fantastic that we can see nothing ahead of us but open sea, seemingly endless open sea, yet we all have the faith that three days from now, we'll reach our destination safely and soundly. Yet it's a destination that we can't even see, can't even imagine from the perspective we have now. Are you completely sure that our destination is even out there?"

"Well, yes," Walker replied, though he wasn't completely sure that he was.

"I am, too—that is, I have no doubt in my mind that we will dock, three days from now, in the port at which we're supposed to dock. But why do you believe it's there?"

"Because," Walker said slowly, trying to grasp just why he thought it was there, "people have told me it's there. And this ship goes there regularly, right? And everyone else here knows that it's going to that place. Why wouldn't I believe them?"

"Why not, indeed?" the man asked with a smile. Then he turned and walked slowly away. "Have a nice voyage, young man," he yelled over his shoulder.

At lunch, when Walker was expecting to meet Katherine and the children, one of the stewards brought him a note instead. It told him that the three of them would be staying in the cabin due to Kathleen's seasickness. Walker read the note and thanked the steward. He was very hungry, so he ate lunch and then went to see Katherine in her cabin.

"Mr. Walker," she greeted him at her door. "Please, come in." Walker noticed that she looked a bit better, not as tired or as drawn as she had a few hours earlier. She still didn't seem as cheerful as she had the previous evening, though.

"I suppose I should stop calling you 'Mr. Walker' if you're my brother now," she told him, closing the door behind him. Walker saw Kathleen lying in bed, a wet washcloth folded over her forehead. Even though she looked quite normal, the expression on her face was one of great discomfort, and Walker could have sworn that he noticed a green tinge to her skin. He was sure that it must have been a trick of the light. Billy was sitting quietly on the other bed, reading a book. He looked up and said hello when Walker entered, then immersed himself immediately into the book once more.

"I'm really very sorry about lunch," Katherine told him. "Kathleen has a tendency to become seasick on the first several hours of any voyage—we've been on several—and I had to stay here with her. She should be fine by dinner—she usually pulls through it rather quickly."

"Then she'll be okay?" Walker asked.

"Yes, definitely. It lasts a few hours, then it goes away. She probably won't have much of an appetite by dinner, but by morning she should be just as fit as ever."

"Then we should meet at dinner?" Walker asked. He wanted to stay and talk, but he didn't get the feeling that it was the right thing to do— Katherine wasn't asking him to leave, but he didn't feel the time was right for him to stay, either.

"Dinner will be perfect. And I guarantee you that we won't stand you up this time. How does seven o'clock sound?"

"That sounds fine," Walker replied, turning back to the door. "I hope you feel better soon, Kathleen," he said, and was answered by a low groan that sounded a bit like "thank you." Then he turned to Billy and waved good-bye and took his leave.

As he walked down the hallway, intending to go back up on deck, he thought hard about the situation he was in. Yesterday he hadn't known these people at all, had no idea of who they were or what kind of people they were, yet today they were his responsibility to a certain extent. In any case, he felt responsible for their well-being because of a promise he had made. The feeling was much like the way he had felt about Michael when he was with him—that he was responsible for helping Michael find his way home, just because he happened to find him one night in the forest. Where did that feeling come from? Had Michael also felt that Walker was somehow responsible for helping him? Or had Michael simply seen him as a companion, someone to talk to while on the road?

Walker decided to go see the captain. He had seen him before, talking to a man and a woman who had called him captain, so he knew who he was. But Walker suddenly had an important question to ask him.

He found him on the deck, walking towards the back of the ship, alone in the rain.

"Excuse me, sir," Walker said, catching up to him. "May I ask you a question?"

"Absolutely," the captain replied, turning to face Walker, then extending his right hand to shake Walker's. "I'm Captain Stark. What can I do for you?"

"My name is Walker. I would like to know, how do you know where we're going?"

Captain Stark's eyes narrowed for a moment as he regarded Walker, then he realized that it was a sincere question, and he relaxed his eyes.

"I mean," Walker continued, noticing the look, "you can't see the place we're going, and it's very far away, so how do you know which way to go? And there are no landmarks to follow. How do you know which way to steer the ship?"

The captain turned to the wall behind him. "That's rather simple, Mr. Walker," he said. "Imagine this bolt is where we started, and this bolt way over here is where we're going. And in between the two is all sea, with no landmarks at all to show us the way. Are you with me?"

"Yes."

"Now, instead of looking at this as one very long voyage, try to look at it as a series of many trips that make up one. In other words, in the first three hours, we're going to go from our starting point at this bolt to this spot here just three inches from the bolt. So, three hours into the journey, we take readings and find out where we are, and make any corrections that we need to make in order to reach our second point three hours later. In other words, if we end up half an inch below where we're supposed to be, we turn the ship to point further north than we normally would, to compensate for being off-course. If we're on course, we're fine, but if we're off course, we need to compensate to get ourselves back on course."

"I see," Walker said. "And you're responsible for all the people on this ship, so that they reach that point safely when they're supposed to."

"You could look at it that way, I suppose."

"Isn't it difficult to have that much responsibility? To know that so many people depend on you?"

"Mr. Walker, my responsibility is to do my job. If I do my job as I should, all of these people will be fine, and they'll get where they need to go. If I looked at my job as being responsible for each individual on this vessel, well, then, I'm pretty sure that I would be completely overwhelmed very quickly. There are fifty crewmembers on this ship, all working together to get it to the other side of the sea. If each one of those people fulfills his or her duties, then the voyage will go smoothly, and we'll reach our destination. I have my duties, and I know what they are, and my job is to fulfill them. The men in the boiler room know exactly what they have to do, and if they fulfill their responsibilities, then we'll have the power to get across the sea. The only difference between them and me is that I'm trained to be a captain, and they're trained to work in a boiler room. One day, one of them may make a very fine captain."

"I see," Walker said, deep in thought. "Thank you. Thank you very much."

"It was my pleasure, Mr. Walker. Please, enjoy your journey." The captain turned and continued in the direction he had been heading when Walker had found him.

Walker walked slowly to the railing at the side of the ship and looked down at the water, which was now speeding by. He had a lot to think about, as always, and he wasn't sure what it all meant or how it fit together, or even if it fit together. He knew that he had to trust that if he thought about it long enough, he would find some answers.

That evening at dinner, both Katherine and Kathleen were cheerful once more. They had a nice dinner, then Kathleen and Billy left to explore the ship, which they hadn't been able to do before. Katherine and Walker sat at the table and had a cup of coffee to finish off the meal.

"Why did Newman tell me he would kill me if I hurt you?" Walker asked Katherine, and she regarded him with little surprise.

"He told you that?" she asked, and Walker nodded. "That's typical," she said. "Newman is a wonderful man, and a very caring man, but he has little faith in other people being able to accomplish what they need to accomplish on their own."

"What do you mean?"

"Newman needs to have as much control over any situation as he can. The problem is that he tries to control the results, not the actions that lead to the results. He gets very frustrated when he sees how something that someone else is doing should be, but sees that that person doesn't quite know how to reach the results he feels are necessary."

"I'm not sure I understand."

"Say one of the children is doing a puzzle—and this has actually happened. Billy is doing a puzzle that he can't see the results to. If Newman walks into the room and sees the solution to the puzzle, he'll solve it immediately to show Billy the answer, because he thinks the solution is the most important part of the puzzle. What he doesn't realize, though, is that puzzles are meant to be difficult, and it's learning the process of solving the puzzle that will help Billy learn how to solve other puzzles. If he's shown the solution without learning the process, he won't be any better prepared to solve the next puzzle that he runs into.

"And Newman doesn't do it because he doesn't want Billy to learn, it's just that he's so obsessed with finding answers quickly that he doesn't have the patience to watch other people reach their own conclusions. He spends so much time and energy trying to make sure that everything turns out fine that he pays almost no attention to the job itself, to the process of doing it."

"Then why did he threaten me?"

"I don't think he saw it as a threat. No—I'm sure he didn't see it as a threat. It was just his way of controlling the outcome—if he put fear in you of what might happen if you were to hurt us, you wouldn't hurt us. I don't even think he thought you might hurt us, but for him it was very difficult to leave us to make this journey on our own. He sees one of his responsibilities as protecting us, and when he got that telegram last night, he suddenly saw that he wasn't going to be able to fulfill that responsibility. So he took on the responsibility of finding someone else to take on that responsibility. And once you agreed to do it, he had to make sure that you would fulfill the responsibility exactly as he would—to see us safely home."

"But why would he say it if he didn't see it as a threat?"

"Because now he has more peace of mind than he would have had otherwise, if he hadn't told you what he told you. He told you that to make himself feel better, basically. Although I'm sure that if you were to do anything to harm us—and I don't believe at all that you would—he would do his best to fulfill that promise. Once he makes a vow, he sticks to it, no matter what the cost or consequences to himself."

"It sounds like he doesn't have much peace inside."

Katherine sighed. "People who need to have so much control rarely do. He can't ever relax, for example, because he's always thinking of too many things that 'need' to be done, too many things that he has to do himself. As soon as he finishes one thing he moves on to the next, because he can't delegate responsibility. He has to do everything himself because everything has to be done to his standards. It's not his fault, or anything like that. That's just the way he is. It's stressful for me because I prefer to leave results to turn out as they will—if I start to make a dress for Kathleen, I know basically what I want, but I'm open to changes along the way. I like to explore the process, experiment as I go. It drives Newman crazy," she ended with a laugh.

"The captain said that a long journey like this is like a lot of shorter journeys put together, and that at the end of each shorter journey, they must take readings to find out if they're on course."

"You'll never find Newman doing that. He'd make a terrible captain—he would focus on the destination only. I feel bad for him sometimes, for he means well, but he certainly doesn't enjoy the journey as much as he could. Actually, I take that back—he doesn't enjoy the journey at all."

"Do you think he'll ever change?"

"I don't know," Katherine replied. "To tell the truth, I don't know if I want him to. I love him just as he is. I'd like to see him enjoy life more, I suppose, for his own sake, but I don't know if I'd want him to change too much."

Chapter 20

The days on the ship passed quickly, for there was much for Walker to see and do and learn. He talked with the crewmembers of the ship and found out much about how the ship was able to stay afloat and how the engines worked to turn the propellers in the back of the ship, putting it into motion. He explored every area of the ship he possibly could, and by the third day he knew as much as he thought he could have learned in such a short time. He knew that Michael would have been proud of him, for Michael often talked about how things worked and how important it was to learn about such things.

He also talked a lot with Katherine and spent some time with Kathleen and Billy, though he didn't try to get to know them too well. He knew that his main purpose for being there was to watch out for them, not become friends with them. Besides, he felt more and more that he didn't want to get close to people that he soon would be parting ways with, and he was sure that something about what had happened to Michael made him not want to establish relationships with two more children right away.   They were very interesting children, though, and Walker was amazed at just how different two children from the same parents could be.   Kathleen was always smiling, always with a kind word for everyone she met.   She laughed often, and was interested in almost everyone and everything.

Billy, on the other hand, wasn't as outgoing as his sister. He was very reserved and spent most of his time reading, getting involved more in the worlds of his books than in the world that surrounded him. Katherine told Walker that she didn't mind him reading, that she had been the same way when she was young. She had learned a lot about life from the books she had read, and she knew that Billy also would learn a lot, and that he would come out of his shell when he was ready to do so.

During dinner on the last evening of the journey, Walker was looking forward to the next morning's arrival. He enjoyed being on the ship, but he missed traveling under his own power, missed the feel of the road beneath his feet. He had come many more miles in three short days than he would have been able to cover on foot, especially since the ship also traveled at night, but he much preferred traveling at his own pace, going where he wanted when he wanted.

"What will you do when we dock tomorrow?" Katherine asked him. "Do you know anyone where we're going? Or will you just continue to travel?"

"I'll travel," Walker said. "That seems to be what my heart is telling me to do. I'm still searching, and I know I must travel until I found what I'm looking for."

"Just remember, though, that if you're looking for God or for happiness, you have to start by looking inside. You won't find either on any road, or in any town you come across."

"I know that now," Walker said. "But when I travel, I meet the people I need to meet, and they teach me what I need to learn. There are so many different pieces that I have to see. Remember when you were talking about puzzles the other evening? About how the process of putting a puzzle together helps us to learn, as opposed to just seeing the puzzle already finished? You were telling me that to illustrate the kind of man your husband is, but I saw it in a very different way. I met a man in the desert who told me that if I were to search for God, then God would put the right people in my way so that I could find him. And I think it was very important for you to tell me that about puzzles, because later on I realized that I'm searching for a finished puzzle somewhere. I thought that somehow I would find the answer all put together for me, and I was looking for the wrong thing. I was blind to many pieces of the puzzle that are in me already, that have been given to me by you and by Kennison and Tricia and Michael and by all the other people I've met.

"But I'm not ready to put the pieces together yet—I know I don't have all of them, and I would rather wait until I have all the pieces until I try to put them together."

"And what will happen once you put all those pieces together? Once you have the puzzle finished?"

"I hope," Walker replied, "that I'll find another puzzle to solve."

Katherine smiled. "I would be willing to wager money that you already have—that some of the pieces you already have fit into a completely different puzzle, and that when you put your puzzle together you'll find that you have extra pieces that are the starts of two or three other puzzles."

Walker's eyes widened. "I never thought of it that way," he said. "You're probably right. There would be little purpose in life if we were to have nothing to strive for, would there?"

"There certainly would be very little purpose. That's why we must always keep looking and keep ourselves asking questions. I question my own faith very often, and I'm not always comfortable with the answers I get to my own questions. I'm never quite sure if I live up to my faith or not."

"I'm not sure that I even have a faith yet. Does that make me less of a person?"

Katherine laughed. "No—absolutely not. You're searching, and that's important, but you can't expect to find anything like faith without searching. You'll come to your own conclusions, and you'll find your beliefs when you need to find them."

"I hope so. Sometimes I feel like I'm being watched, like I have to live up to other people's expectations. Like someone's watching me and making judgments and deciding my future for me. And I don't know why I feel that."

Katherine didn't answer immediately. "Many people feel like that from time to time, Walker. You just have to accept that the feelings are there, and then they often leave. Try to learn from those feelings, and you may discover something important about them."

Walker looked into his coffee cup for several long moments. "That's a good idea. You're very wise, Katherine. Thank you for your help."

"Oh, I don't know how wise I am. But you're welcome. I've got a feeling that you're going to finish with your puzzle sooner than you think, Walker."

"I hope so."

After the ship docked the next morning, Walker accompanied Katherine and the children to their home. He felt fortunate, for it was located on the road that he would need to take anyway. Katherine hired a coach drawn by two large horses, and almost before Walker realized what was going on, they were off.

Walker was amazed and a bit dismayed at how quickly everything was going by outside the coach. He watched out the window at the houses and the trees and the people that were there, but he really saw none of it—he didn't get a chance to look closely at any one thing or person before it was gone, replaced by the next thing, which in turn went away just as quickly.

Katherine and Billy and Kathleen seemed quite used to such a way of traveling—Billy read his book, Katherine rested her head against the back of the seat, and Kathleen looked out the window, watching the world go by. Walker didn't know how to feel—he had wanted to feel the earth beneath his feet, to feel the sensation of standing on solid ground. But the deck of the ship had been replaced by the floor of the coach, and he couldn't have stood without stooping over even if he had wanted to. He was forced to sit and watch the world go by, even though he saw many flowers that he would have loved to smell and many trees that he would have loved to touch. There were also many people that he might have liked to talk to, but he was never to meet them.

The others seemed quite content to be where they were, and he could see the benefit of traveling much more quickly, especially since they were a woman and two children with a lot of luggage, but he ached to be outside, walking under his own power, enjoying the sunshine and the fresh air and the feel of his muscles being used.

Finally, over an hour later, the coach stopped. It had left the main road about a mile before, and Walker knew that he would have to backtrack. But he knew that even backtracking wouldn't take as long as it would have taken him to reach where they were by walking.

He helped them with their luggage, carrying it into a beautiful house that Katherine and the children called home. He was anxious to get going, but Katherine had offered him lunch, so he stayed a while as they all got settled and Katherine made the meal.

"Well, Mr. Walker," she said with a smile as they finished eating, "it looks like the time has come for us to part."

"Yes," he said with a smile. "It's time for me to be going. I have a ways to go still."

She looked at the road in front of the house. "In a way, I envy you," she said. "I would love to be on the same journey myself."

Walker smiled again. "But aren't you?" he asked. "Inside?"

She looked him in the eyes. "Sometimes I think so. But sometimes I think not. Sometimes I feel tied down, trapped, without any chance to go on any type of journey at all. Even inside."

She stood and started to clear the dishes and silverware from the table.

"I believe I shall miss you, Mr. Walker. You take care of yourself."

Walker stood and picked up his pack.

"Thank you, Katherine. You take care of yourself, too. Tell the children I said good-bye." Then he turned and left.

Within minutes the house was behind him, but he couldn't leave it behind him in his mind. For the first time, he was bothered in leaving when he did, feeling like there was so much more that could be said between him and Katherine. They thought so much alike about so many things, but there had always been a barrier between the two of them, some sort of wall that neither of them had tried to go over or break through. He felt that the wall was there for a reason, and they had both recognized it, and that it was right that they hadn't tried to get past it. But he had no idea just what the reason was.

He loved the feel of the ground beneath his feet once again—he was glad that he was finally able to walk again at his own pace, under his own power. The fresh air and sunshine on his skin were somehow more pleasant when he was walking, and he liked the feel of the air in his lungs when he was breathing more deeply.

Soon he was back on the main road, and he turned and walked away from the sea, in the direction he had always been going in. This time, though, his journey began to change, and he noticed it almost immediately. The road he was on was wide and busy, full of carts and coaches and people in coaches that had no horses pulling them, but that made loud noises and left a foul-smelling smoke behind them as they went. He felt out of place, felt that something fundamental had changed that couldn't be changed back, and he suddenly didn't feel so comfortable on the road. He even had to walk at the very edge of the road, lest he be hit by one of the vehicles that were going by so quickly. It was clear to him that he no longer belonged on the road—it was no longer welcoming to him.

Within two hours of walking, the road had changed from dirt to pavement, which wasn't as giving beneath his feet as the dirt had been. It was easier to walk on, for it was smooth and hard, but it wasn't as pleasant to walk on. Walker grew more and more nervous at the speed of the vehicles, and more and more nauseous at the smell of the smoke of the cars.

He reached a point at which he couldn't stand the noise and the smell any longer, and he took the first side road that he found, a peaceful road that led off to the right. He walked until he smelled the air clearing and the noise subsided, then looked back at the road he had left, at the many vehicles that sped in two different directions. He looked down in amazement—this road was paved just as well as the other one, yet no cars traveled on it. What was the difference? Were no cars allowed on this road, or was no one interested in traveling on a road that no one else took? Could it be that no one wanted to go where this road led?

Walker knew that he would much prefer to travel such a road, not even though few others took it, but just because few others took it.

He turned away from looking at the busy road and continued down the side road. It veered off to the left, and it ended up going in roughly the same direction as the other road, just a little more to the right.

Several hours later, he had left the busy road far behind him, and he was continuing down the same smaller road when it crossed a very different kind of path. This path was of dirt and rocks, and was almost as wide as the road he was walking on, but there was a very big difference—this path had two long, heavy pieces of steel lying on it, sitting on thick pieces of wood. The steel was made in a specific shape, and it seemed to stretch unendingly in both directions. The two pieces lay the same distance from each other for as far as Walker could see, and he saw that the path continued in exactly the same direction as the busy road had been going. But there was nobody at all on this path, no cars or people or noise or bad smells.

He decided to follow this path towards what Katherine had called the city, which is where she had told him the main road led. He would much rather journey to the city on a quiet road than on a busy one. He was soon satisfied with his decision, for the going was much easier and much less stressful.

After twenty minutes, though, as he was trying to keep his balance while walking on one of the steel rails, he suddenly felt it start to vibrate. He looked all around, but he could see nothing that might cause it to vibrate. Perplexed, he stepped off the rail and moved to the side of the trail.

In moments, he heard a low, steady rumble from the direction he had come from, and he knelt on one knee to wait for whatever was coming. The rumble quickly grew into a roar, and he actually could hear the vibration of the rails just before a huge train barreled around the corner he had just come around, seemingly straight at him.

He jumped back off the road, landing in the grass, looking back at the series of huge pieces of machinery that were flying by him at a speed that astonished him. In the shudder of the air around him and the vibration of the ground beneath him he could feel the unbelievable amount of energy of this machine. Twenty large coaches flew by him, and in the last four he saw people sitting inside, reading or sleeping or looking out the windows, and he wondered what it would be like to be inside the coaches, looking out.

Almost before he knew what was happening, the train was past him, and he watched it fade into the distance, becoming smaller and smaller with each passing moment.

"There's always something new," he muttered aloud, stepping back onto the road and following the train.

Never before, though, had his walking seemed so slow to him.

Chapter 21

Walker was getting tired, and he didn't know why. He had spent many days walking before, yet he had always had the energy to go on—even at the end of a day, he had usually slept because he knew that he needed to. But the kind of tiredness that he felt now wasn't just physical. His mind also felt tired, and it was getting difficult for him to think clearly. His impressions of the train were muddled in his head—he knew what he had seen, but he couldn't piece together all of the impressions into one complete picture, no matter how hard he tried. He attempted several times to decide just what he thought he had seen, but there was no answer forthcoming.

Finally, a good two hours before sunset, he sat down on the tracks, wondering where he would go and what he would do. He was much nearer to the city now and he was surrounded by buildings that resembled the factories that he and Michael had passed. But these buildings were old and hadn't been kept up. Many of them were run down, with broken windows and even holes in the walls. They weren't inviting places at all, and Walker wondered if people still worked in them.

But his main problem was finding a place to sleep—he hadn't seen any sort of inn all day, and for he first time he found himself doubting the path he had taken. Should he have stayed on the main road? The journey probably would have been more difficult and unpleasant, but he knew that he probably would have seen plenty of places where he could have slept for the night. And what if he was on the wrong road? Would he meet the people he was supposed to meet, or would he meet other people?

He breathed deeply, trying to relax, and immediately exhaled, for the air wasn't clean or fresh. He started to breathe more slowly, hoping to relax himself enough so that he would be able to think clearly.

Never before had he been in such a state—he had always been able to think clearly, except for a very short time after Michael's death. He knew he needed to sleep, but there weren't even any unpeopled spaces where he might lay out his shelter and blanket.

He was so caught up in trying to gain control of his thoughts that he didn't notice a man walking slowly up the tracks towards him until he heard his voice almost directly in his ear.

"Well, well, well," the man said loudly and heartily. "What have we here?"

Walker jumped, surprised at the man's voice. He looked up quickly, shocked and dismayed that someone had gotten so close to him without him even being aware of his presence. He got quickly to his feet.

"Hello," he said quickly, and the man roared with laughter.

"Gave you a scare, did I?" he laughed. "Too busy daydreaming to even hear me come up on you?"

"Yes, I guess so," Walker said. He held out his hand. "My name is Walker."

"Walker, huh?" the man asked, eyeing Walker's hand. "Well, Walker, you don't mind if I forego the social courtesies here, do ya? I mean, I have no idea where that hand has been, now do I?"

Walker looked down at his hand, confused. For a moment he thought that the man was joking, but a look in his eyes told Walker that he was serious. He was quite old—grey-haired and wrinkled, and fairly well fed. He was quite heavy, though his form was hard to see beneath the several layers of tattered, dirty clothes that he wore. The part of his face that

Walker could see above the heavy beard and moustache that hadn't been trimmed for a very long time was neither friendly nor unfriendly. The man looked at Walker with interest, his green eyes sparkling, as if Walker were something he never before had seen, and about which he hadn't yet made up his mind.

"My name is Verdad, young man. It's a name I adopted myself, not the one my parents gave to me. It means 'truth' in Spanish, you know."

"Spanish?" Walker didn't know what the man meant.

"You know—the language. Used to speak it myself, long time ago, when I was back at the school. But that was long, long ago, before I got out of that horrible world."

"What do you mean?" Walker asked, but before Verdad could answer, they both heard the soft roar of a train in the distance, and they moved to the side of the tracks.

This time, the train didn't sneak around a corner and surprise Walker. He saw it coming from a long distance, and he was able to watch it come towards them, wheels turning quickly and smoke pouring from the top. He watched the window of the first car and saw a man sitting there, watching them. Verdad waved to the man, but the man didn't wave back in the second or two that he was clearly visible.

This train was much longer, and Walker was able to pay more attention to it, to notice the connections between the coaches, to notice the sounds of the wheel hitting certain parts of the track, to hear the screeches and moans of the coaches as they swayed to and fro, testing their connections to one another. There was a certain beauty to it, to the power and the motion, but there was also a great deal of stress in the speed and noise. Walker wasn't too sure he liked it, and he wanted to ask Verdad what it was, but the noise was too loud for them even to be able to communicate. So he had to wait until the train had passed, and then he was able to ask.

"What is that?" he asked as the train and its sounds were fading into the distance.

"What do you mean, 'What is that?'?" Verdad asked, incredulous. "That, my dear man, was a train, and any fool who's walking along a train track who doesn't know what a train is is a fool, plain and simple. Now what are you doing here on the tracks that you don't even know from a tree?"

"I suppose I'm going to the city," Walker replied, looking in the direction of the buildings on the horizon. "That's where this road goes, isn't it?"

"This is not a road. I repeat: these are railroad tracks, and they serve as a pathway for the beast that you just saw pass, the train." He looked at Walker sternly, then his face softened, and he sighed. "Oh, my—what a shame it is. Another ignorant country bumpkin attracted by the allure of the terrible, terrible city. The promises of wealth and the fast life and extraordinary adventures have worked their magic on you, have they? You must go to the city to prove yourself, to make it on your own, to become rich and famous and glamorous, no?"

Walker was puzzled, but his thoughts had turned to Stephanie and the story of her husband.

"No," he said. "I'm going to the city because that's where the road leads."

"Then get on another road, fool!" Verdad roared. "What do you want to go to that place for, that hell on earth that robs people of their souls and spits them back into the earth as old, disheveled corpses without a bit of self-respect or love for life left in them? You don't want to become like them, do you? You don't want to waste your life in the soul-scarring search for wealth, do you?"

"Well, no," Walker said, becoming uncomfortable with the man's words and tone. "I'm just passing through."

Verdad's expression, which had become an awful grimace during his tirade, softened and turned back to normal.

"Oh," he said. "Good. Then come with me." He turned and started walking along the tracks, heading towards the city. He started singing aloud as he walked, but Walker had never heard the song before. He followed Verdad along the tracks, hurrying to walk beside him, confused because the man was ignoring him while he walked, completely immersed in the song he was singing.

Before long, Verdad left the tracks, following an extremely thin path through tall grass, a path that Walker knew he probably wouldn't even have noticed himself. He followed him closely, and soon they passed through a high fence into a clearing that at first glance Walker thought was full of garbage and useless old pieces of fences and houses and vehicles. But he soon saw that it was actually a group of structures built out of those things that other people had deemed useless.

"Welcome to our village!" Verdad roared with a laugh. "The most beautiful place in the world!"

Walker looked around in amazement. There were people all about that he hadn't noticed at first—they blended in so well with their environment that he hadn't been able to make them out until he looked more closely. Here and there, fires burned in large drums or in holes dug in the ground, and people gathered around the flames. It wasn't cold, though, so Walker guessed that they weren't gathered there for warmth. But for what, then?

All eyes seemed to be on Walker as he followed Verdad through the village. Some of the walls were made of steel, others of concrete blocks or bricks piled on top of one another, but none of the structures were made entirely of one material. They all were mixtures of brick and wood and metal. Some of them were quite ingenious, and Walker was sure they served as good shelters. Others were put together very poorly, and he knew they would offer no real shelter from the elements. The people were all dressed very poorly, some with no more than shredded remnants of what must have once been clothing somehow hanging on their bodies, somehow not falling to the ground. Everyone was dirty, everyone's clothes were dirty, and Walker knew from his own experience that he never could let himself get that filthy, for he didn't like the feel of being unclean.

He tried to look people in the eyes, but few of them would hold eye contact with him. In their eyes he felt he saw fear and suspicion, but he couldn't be sure. He even saw several children, and something in his heart reacted more strongly to seeing them in this environment than it had to seeing adults there.

"Society's outcasts," Verdad said with a wave of his hand, "one and all. We're all the people the world would have nothing more to do with, and the only thing we have any more is each other. Now here is my humble abode." He stopped before one of the more sturdy structures.

Walker noticed for the first time that all of the shelters seemed to have one thing in common—none of them were tall enough for anyone to stand up in. The ceilings in Verdad's shack were only four feet high, which meant that one must sit or kneel or lay down in the rooms, which Walker imagined could get to be rather irritating, especially when the weather didn't allow one to go outside much.

"It's not much," Verdad said, "but it's home, and I much prefer it to the beautiful home that I used to have when I was teaching at the university. This home has no chains."

"What do you mean?" Walker asked.

"What do I mean? What do I mean?" Verdad almost shouted the question the second time he said it, his face becoming angry, then the anger faded and the calmness returned.

Walker was suddenly on edge. That was the second time he had seen the rage enter the man, and he knew that if this man weren't anything else, he was definitely unstable. Walker knew that he would have to keep an eye on him, for he didn't want the same thing to happen here that had happened with Brian.

"You think those people in the beautiful homes and the beautiful yards with the beautiful children are happy, don't you? That's because they want you to think that they're happy, because they're supposed to be happy, and they wouldn't want you to think there was anything wrong with them because they weren't what they were supposed to be. They're successful, and they want the whole world to know that they're successful. What the whole world doesn't know, though, is that they're being eaten up inside by pressure and envy and resentment of others who are better off than they are, and they're spending their entire lives trying to be something that they're not—they're not trying to become who they were truly meant to be—they're trying to become what they think the people who are better off want them to be. So they can never truly be what they were meant to be. Does that make sense?"

Walker thought a moment. "Yes, it does."

Verdad went on. "I spent twenty years teaching the art of economics, teaching people how to make money and become 'successful' in terms the world defined as successful. I spent twenty years teaching people that success equaled monetary wealth, and that monetary wealth equaled success. And I was successful. I had a high income, I made wonderful investments, I acquired a massive fortune, I bought a wonderful home and gave money to our church and had a lovely wife and three lovely children."

"What happened?" Walker asked. "Why did you leave that—for this?"

Verdad glared at him from beneath bushy grey eyebrows. He said nothing for a long time, and Walker began to get nervous, fearing that he had asked the wrong question. Finally, Verdad spoke, his voice quiet and subdued.

"I don't know why I'm about to tell you, Mr. Walker, what I have never told another human soul. Why isn't important. That was my life as Roger Brown, Dr. Brown, as my students and colleagues called me. But all they ever saw was the bright side. They didn't see the dark side of my life, the dark side of my self. They never saw me hit my wife Sara after I had drunk too much and she said something that annoyed me. They didn't see the years of abuse that she endured because she loved me, and because she hoped I would change and did everything in her power to help me change. But I drank because I was dissatisfied—even though I had everything I could possibly want, I wanted more. I was on a social level higher than most people in the world, but I wanted to be on the next higher one. I wanted people to respect me for my achievements, for I had achieved so much. When they didn't respect me as much as I felt was my due, I took it out on my beautiful wife, on the woman who loved me more than anyone else and who stood by me for so long.

148

"But it wasn't until I took it out on my daughter, my youngest daughter, my lovely little Emily, that Sara took the children and left. The next day, after I had returned to a sober state, I saw the black eye on Emily's face, I saw the fear in her eyes when she looked at me, and I lost all desire to be what I was. My wife left that day, and my life left that day. I spent several days in that large, cold, empty house, then I sold it for a fraction of what it was worth. I converted all of my assets into liquid funds and signed them all over to Sara. I left that world, and I came here."

"But why?" Walker asked quietly. "Why come here?"

"Quite simply, Mr. Walker, for penance. These are the very people I most despised, the very people that I mocked and insulted in the classroom, the very people whom I accused of disrupting the economy, of undermining our economic stability. I accused them of turning their backs on us all and ignoring us. In the last four years, though, I've come to see things differently—these are the people on which the rest of the world has turned its collective back, not the other way around.

"I'm ashamed now of how I used to see it, of how I used to see the poor as living in their own filth, filth that they made themselves. While some of them are doing just that, many others aren't. Just a moment, Mr. Walker." Verdad turned his head towards the shack next to his and called out, "Maria!" A woman stuck her head out and then came out slowly, followed by a young boy.

She came over to where Walker and Verdad were sitting, greeting Walker, and sat down next to Verdad.

"Maria," he said softly, "would you tell Mr. Walker how you came to be here?"

Maria looked awkwardly at Walker, then back at Verdad, shaking her head. "I don't know him," she said. "It's difficult for me." Walker looked closely at her. Beneath the dirt and the tattered clothing, he saw an attractive woman somewhere in there, much as he saw youth in the faces of older people. All he had to do was look in a different way. But Maria's eyes made him sad, for he saw a great deal of pain there, a great deal that he didn't understand. But he saw no joy, no hope.

In her son's eyes, though, he saw curiosity, he saw a desire to know, to understand, and he saw a lot of love as he looked at his mother. The child was about four years old, Walker guessed, and cleaner than Maria was herself. His clothes were in fact almost new, and Walker wondered how she had been able to get them.

"Then may I tell him?" Verdad asked. "It's important to me."

Maria nodded after several moments.

"Maria was married to a man much like me," Verdad explained, "except that he wasn't successful, wasn't wealthy. But he wanted more, and when he was unable to achieve it, he took it out on his wife, beating her severely. Finally she had enough, and she left, for her sake and for the sake of her son. She left her husband and tried to make it on her own.

"But it wasn't easy for her to make it on her own, especially since she had married early and left school to do so. She was able to get only jobs that paid very poorly, and when her son became sick, it took all of her money to buy him medicine. Because she had no money, she was kicked out of the home she had. Her husband didn't help her to support her son at all, so she was left alone on the streets. I found her one afternoon, and I brought her here. Her parents died several years ago, so she has no one to go to for support. It's not a wonderful place to live, but at least she has food and shelter."

"And I'll be working soon," Maria interjected, "so then I'll be able to afford rent for an apartment."

"Of course, the problem with finding work is that she needs an address," Verdad said. "We're trying to work our way around that. Her husband seems to be doing very well on his own, and he shows no interest at all in either of them. Can you imagine how a person can do that to another human being?"

"No, I can't," Walker said quietly. His heart felt very heavy, and he suddenly felt very discouraged and very tired. He reached into his pack and pulled out most of the food he had, giving it to Verdad and Maria.

"Please, eat," he said. "I must sleep."

Verdad turned and pointed to his shelter. "There's a small room on the right," he said. "You can sleep there."

The last light of the day hung silently in the sky, but there was little light in the room in which Walker was to sleep. He spread out his blanket and lay down on it, noticing that he could see some of the night's earliest stars through holes in the ceiling. He was glad it wasn't raining.

He thought he would fall asleep immediately, but he kept thinking of Verdad and Maria and her son and the lives they were leading. He heard their voices as they spoke softly outside the shack, and he heard an occasional yell from someone else, somewhere else in the village. After a while, he heard Verdad enter and lay down in the other room. He thought of the changes that had come over Verdad's face so quickly, but he wasn't sure what they meant.

How could these people's lives be so different from the lives of the other people he had met? How could they have so little when others had so much?

He could see why Stephanie would want to leave a place where people could live like this.

Chapter 22

Walker awoke very early the next morning. He had woken up quite often during the night, not quite sure where he was. It had taken him several minutes each time to figure out just where he was and how he had come to be there. The world was very dark, but there were sounds all around— some from a distance, some from nearby. One time he heard a dog barking somewhere near, and another he heard an animal sniffing at something on the other side of the wall of the room he was in.

The sleep hadn't refreshed him at all, and he felt drained when he got up and crawled outside on his hands and knees. He already had his pack with him, for he meant to leave very early to get to the city. He probably would have left immediately if Verdad hadn't been up already, eating some of the food that Walker had given him the night before. He picked up the plate he was using and handed it to Walker.

"We very much appreciate the food, Mr. Walker," he said quietly. All around them, Walker knew that people were sleeping, so he sat down and took some bread and meat. "You look like hell," Verdad said. "I take it you didn't sleep very well?"

Walker shook his head. The very act made his head hurt, a fact that he attributed to his poor sleep.

"You know," Verdad said, looking at the bread in his hands, "I didn't tell you what I told you last night because I wanted to scare you or make you feel bad or anything like that. I told you because it was the truth. That's why I've adopted my name—I'm dedicated to the truth in life, and the truth of life. Sometimes, the truth is the hardest reality of all to accept. I know that—it took me years even to recognize any truths, much less live by them. But you seem to be a man in search of answers. Am I right?"

Walker nodded. "Yes, you are. But I'm not so sure any more that I know the questions. I believe that I'm close to answers, but the questions keep getting less clear."

Verdad smiled. "Welcome to real life. There are millions of answers everywhere, but we're not always clear on which questions we want to have answered."

"It seems to me that we should have the questions before we search for the answers. And if that's the case, then I'm going about this the wrong way."

"I don't believe there is such a thing as a wrong way to search for answers. You'll find the answers that you need to find when you need to find them."

"That's what I've been told. But I don't understand why you stay here, when you have the possibility of doing so much more. Couldn't you be much more helpful to Maria and her son if you had money?"

Verdad was quiet. "It's not that easy, Walker. I don't fully choose to be here. There are certain things that I have to go through that I don't understand completely, but which make me change very quickly. I don't have any control over it, and I change as a person when it hits me. Nobody wants me around when I'm like that, and it happens more than I'd like it to. I don't usually even remember when it happens."

Walker nodded. He had seen that.

"Perhaps one day I'll go back to being Roger Brown," Verdad continued. "Perhaps not. Either way, I'll finish my life the best way I know how."

"I wish you good luck," Walker said, standing. He looked at the shelter next door, where he knew Maria and her son were, and felt a touch of sadness. He reached into his pocket and pulled out his money. He gave half of it to Verdad.

"Please give this to Maria," he said. "Perhaps it will help her to start out when she does start."

Then he turned and left. As he slowly walked out of the village towards the path they had come in on, he realized that all of the people who were sleeping there had their own stories to tell of how they had come to be in such a place, living in a way that their fellow human beings so despised and misunderstood. He knew that if he could hear their stories, his heart would be very heavy, and he would have to listen with the knowledge that he wouldn't be able to do anything for those people. So many human beings, living outside of their potential, having fallen so far that they could no longer see that potential, though it surely still lay there in their hearts, unused, unacknowledged.

Walker wiped the tears out of his eyes as he started through the high grass towards the railroad tracks.

Three hours later, he could clearly see the city ahead of him. He crossed many more roads running across the tracks, and he felt the energy from the vehicles and the people and the trains and the factories and the stores all around him. There was an intensity about him that he felt growing stronger with each mile that he put behind him.

He wasn't sure, though, how positive that energy was. The air around him smelled bad, and the closer he got to the city, the more garbage he saw, the more broken-down buildings, the fewer trees and flowers. He saw much that was made by people, but little that was natural, and he didn't know what to make of that. Had humans replaced nature in the city, turning their surroundings into their idea of what reality should look like, or was it just necessary to change things in order to provide so many people with places to live and work and buy their food and clothing?

Not far to the sides, he saw roads running parallel to the tracks, and they were almost constantly filled with vehicles that moved along quickly with little noise, leaving the smoke behind them, just as those he had seen the day before had done.

The noise was what he most noticed, though. No longer did he hear the birds and insects; instead, he heard the vehicles and noises from people working and traveling almost everywhere he looked. He walked right by many people who seemed to be working, but none of them seemed interested in any contact with him—some looked and nodded or said a quick hello, but most dismissed him with a glance and got back to whatever it was that they had been doing before they noticed him.

Within an hour, he was close enough to see just how tall the buildings actually were, and he saw that the tracks went straight towards the middle of the city. The roads that surrounded him grew more and more numerous, and he saw some of them that were wider than houses, with four or five vehicles traveling side by side, and others that raised into the air, supported by huge columns that held up what must have been an incredible amount of weight.

He knew he had to make a choice—stay on the tracks or move to one of the roads that were filled with vehicles. On those roads, he saw life going on, he saw people and homes and parks, but the closer he got to the heart of the city, the more tracks joined the original set he had begun to follow, and the fewer people he saw near the tracks. There were now seven sets of tracks where he was, and he saw even more join them not far ahead.

He left the tracks and started up a street that ran parallel to them towards the center. The closer he got to there, the more of everything there was, and the less he felt he was able to figure things out easily. He had never really tried to be in control of anything, being content to let things work out as they would, but he felt that any control he might have had slipping from him as the intensity of everything around him grew greater. He was very close to being overwhelmed, and he knew he had to find a place to sleep. Perhaps some rest would help him to deal with the vast amount of sensations and feelings that were coursing past him and through him.

Walker longed for a peaceful stream to sit next to, with the songs of the birds to stimulate him, to help him think things through. He had never felt so overwhelmed before, and it wasn't a pleasant feeling.

He simply continued walking towards the tallest buildings, for he was sure that they were at the center, the most important part of the city. He knew that it was important to reach the center so that when he decided to leave, he would be leaving the city with his very first step.

Even with all that was going on in his mind, even through his confusion and exhaustion and powerlessness, he couldn't help but feel a sense of awe at the size of the buildings that stood before him almost as beacons, leading him to the center. The closer he got to them, the more amazed he was—no, these weren't the same as the mountains or the huge trees of the forest, but they were awe-inspiring in their own way, for they were truly miraculous.

He was very tired when he reached the center, and it had already been dark for some time when he finally knew that he had reached his destination. He was surprised to find, though, that there were still many, many people on the streets. He had never been anyplace where so many people were out so late, and he had never seen so many lights on at one time in one place, illuminating the streets so that people could get around almost as easily as they did during the day. When he looked up at the sky, though, he couldn't see any stars at all. He wondered if the clouds had covered the sky so quickly, even though he hadn't seen a single cloud all day.

He was very hungry, too, and he found a store that was open where he bought a sandwich and a drink. He took out what he thought was enough money to pay for the food, but he was surprised when the woman who took the money told him a price that was more than double what he was used to paying for such things. He hesitated, suddenly realizing that his money wasn't going to last him nearly as long as he had expected it to. He had to eat, though, so he paid and left the store, sitting down on a small stone wall that surrounded a fountain to eat his sandwich.

The people who were out paid him no mind at all—they were oblivious to his existence, just doing whatever it was they were doing, seemingly completely unaware of anyone who was around them. They were laughing, talking to one another, walking with each other with no words, walking alone. Walker knew none of them, and he thought it would be best for him to find a place to sleep very soon.

The streets around him were so full of lights and activity that it was difficult for him to distinguish what was what—just which lights were for inns, and which restaurants, and which for whatever else there was in the city.

Across the street he saw an old man dressed in rags, and he thought of Verdad. The man's destitution stood out in stark contrast to the affluence that most of the other people on the street showed, and Walker wondered how there could be such a great disparity in what people had. He was about to cross the street and ask the old man where he might find a place to sleep when the man started screaming at a young couple walking by. The couple gave him a wide berth and continued on, and the old man continued on his way, now yelling loudly at no one in particular.

The soothing sound of water behind him reminded him of days before, when he hadn't been surrounded by concrete and metal and glass and people who didn't even know he existed. And he knew he had a choice—did he truly want to learn the lessons of this place, or should he continue on, having learned very quickly that this place was not for him?

He realized immediately, though, that he was far too tired to leave right then. He needed to find a place to sleep, so he started walking slowly down the street until he came to a place called "hotel" that had a sign in the window that said "rooms."

He walked inside and saw a set-up similar to that of the inns he had been staying at, though the place itself was very different—it wasn't filthy, but it wasn't at all clean, either. It wasn't a place where he would normally stay, but he didn't have much choice, he knew. The man behind the desk simply looked at him without a word. He looked overfed and less than clean, as if he hadn't bathed in days, and his eyes were completely expressionless, dark and lifeless in a pasty face that didn't seem to have gotten any sun for years. Walker was too tired even to think of looking for another place if he didn't have to, so he asked the man if he could rent a room for the night.

"Thirty a night," the man said in a gravelly, somewhat unpleasant voice, his expression not changing a bit. That was again more than double what Walker had been paying, and he started to realize just how expensive the city must be. He pulled out his money and set out enough for that night. The man took it and counted it, then put it in a drawer and set a key on the counter.

"Room twelve," he croaked. "Up two flights, first door on the left."

"Thank you," Walker said quietly, starting up the stairs. The carpet on the stairs was filthy, as were the walls, and Walker wondered if he had made a mistake. When he reached the room he was even more appalled— the walls were covered with filthy wallpaper that was peeling off, and the room smelled musty, as if the air were many years old. The covers on the bed looked as if they had been washed, but even washing them couldn't take out the old stains that they bore. When he pulled down the covers to look at the sheets, he found that they were so thin that he could almost see through them, and he was sure that if he tried to rip them apart he could do so quite easily.

With a sigh, he pulled the covers back up over the sheets and pulled out his own blankets, rolling them out on the bed. When he lay down on them, though, the bed sagged beneath him as if there were nothing there—his hips were a good six inches below his head and feet. He sighed again, too tired to be upset, and he moved his blankets to the floor, where he lay down and fell asleep almost immediately.

He awoke in the morning with the sun in his eyes, not quite sure where he was. A look around the room reminded him, and his spirits fell once more. But he was somewhat refreshed, and the headache of the morning before hadn't returned, so he got up with the thought that maybe this day would turn out better—maybe this day would be much nicer than the previous day had been.

He checked his money and found that he had enough probably for a few days, but not much more. He sat down and tried to think of what he wanted to do first with his day, but then realized that the first thing he wanted to do was get out of the filthy hotel room. Then he could think better. He washed up at the sink, not even thinking about taking a shower there, then he put everything into his pack and went downstairs. The same man was at the desk—how could that be? Could someone work that long?—and Walker said thank you and left. The man made no response at all.

The city looked much nicer in the early-morning light. Though it was still rather dirty, it wasn't as crowded as it had been the night before, and the light on the stone of the buildings made them look strong and secure. He started walking down the street, looking for a place to eat.

In almost every doorway that he passed, someone was sleeping—dirty men and women who seemed to be content lying on the concrete. Walker was amazed—how could it be that so many people had no place to go? Even Verdad's little village would have been much preferable to this, to sleeping on the street with no security, no cover, no comfort.

Several people passed him as he walked, but no one made eye contact with him, no one greeted him. He felt a bit inhuman, as if he had somehow changed, become something different that people no longer wanted anything to do with. It was very strange to him, very humiliating.

He found a small restaurant and went inside, sitting at the counter. A waitress approached, and without a word of greeting asked, "Coffee?"

"Yes, please," Walker said, expecting her to tell him what was available as she poured. Instead, she tossed a piece of paper that was covered in clear plastic onto the counter and walked away.

Walker looked at the menu, searching for familiar meals, and was relieved to find that the food was about the same as he had seen for breakfast in most of the places where he had eaten.

The waitress returned shortly. "Whatcha want?" she asked. Walker was feeling less and less like a person. This woman looked nice enough, but she was treating him as if he weren't a person at all. She was short, not at all old, it seemed, though she looked old. Her face was full of wrinkles, though it had a youthful quality to it that made her look younger than the wrinkles might have indicated—a kind of flush to the cheeks that Walker wasn't sure was her own color or the color of the make-up she was wearing. Her eyes were beautiful—crystal-clear green eyes—but they had no shine to them, no love of life, no joy at all. Perhaps that was just because it was still early in the morning, though. Her uniform was clean and ironed, and she moved quickly and gracefully, accomplishing all of her duties efficiently.

Walker ordered, wanting to ask her some questions about where he might find work, but everything about her body language indicated that she wouldn't want to answer any questions that Walker might ask.

He ate his breakfast in silence. He had never been in such a place before, and he wasn't at all sure what the customs were there. He was especially unsure about tipping; Michael had taught him about the practice, but he was never quite sure of how much he should tip, or even if he should tip. He was pretty sure he should here, so when the man a couple of seats down at the counter got up to leave, Walker looked and saw two coins next to his plate. He decided to do the same thing, so when he finished, he paid and left two large coins next to his plate.

When he stepped outside, he realized that he was in the middle of a huge city and he knew absolutely no one there. He had no friends, no place to stay, nowhere to work, no one to ask for advice. Worse still, he couldn't remember which way he had come from, so he didn't know which direction he should walk in if he were to leave. At least, though, he had a full stomach and money in his pocket for whatever he might need for a few days.

As he walked down the streets, he was surprised to notice that most of the businesses had "closed" signs on their doors, and he wondered how he would be able to find work if nobody was working. The hour already had passed when most places should have opened for the day's business, but nobody was opening up except for a few restaurants. He realized what was happening when he saw one business's sign that read "Closed for the Holiday."

So he had arrived in the city on a holiday, and he knew that meant that almost no one would be working.

He passed a park and decided to sit down and relax, to try to think things through. He found a bench that nobody was sleeping on and sat down next to a rose bush that was in full bloom—the scent was wonderful, though very much out of place there in the city.

He knew that he could stay there or leave, but either way he would have to earn more money soon. And in order to have money, he would have to work. He could look for work in some of the restaurants, or he could try to find a farm or a bakery somewhere outside of the city, assuming that there were farms on the other side. He realized with a shudder that it was possible that on the other side of the city, there were just more cities. What would he do then?

He sighed. What he would do then wasn't important—all that was important was what he would do now.

He felt completely alone, and he wished he had someone there to talk to—Michael or Gustav or Amar or even Verdad—someone who could give him advice or just listen to him speak his concerns aloud. He thought of all the things that he had had in the past year—the mountains and the trees and the streams and the sunrises—and he wondered why he wasn't with them now. He had been with so many truly caring people, yet they were all somewhere behind him now. He was now surrounded by an untold number of compete strangers, people whom he didn't know and who didn't know him.

So much was going through Walker's mind that he longed for the simplicity of the days before, even for the simplicity of the days before he had learned to speak. But then, he had wanted to learn to speak, and now he had gained what he had wanted.

The contradictions piled up, one after another, confusing him, sending his thoughts into completely different directions, and he found himself losing control of them. He tried desperately to bring them back into a clear focus, but they went where they wanted, spiraling up and up, out and out, leaving him behind in the middle of the city where he knew no one and could turn nowhere for help. He needed to pull them back, needed to get control of them.

Instead, his thoughts leapt to Katherine and Kathleen and Billy, and he suddenly wondered how they were. Why had his thoughts gone there? he wondered. And then a voice came into his head: "You're not what you think you are, Walker," it said loudly, clearly, unmistakably.

"Then what am I?" he asked aloud, and suddenly realized that he was still in the park, still in the middle of the city. He looked around quickly, and sighed in relief. He was still alone.

He looked up at the blue sky that still stood watch over him, even though there was so much less of it there in the middle of the city. He missed seeing it all around him, and he wondered if he ever would see it all again. The thought suddenly froze him.

Why had he thought that? All he had to do was walk out of the city, and he'd have it back. So why was he worried about losing the sky?

Chapter 23

He went to the first restaurant he found and asked the woman who was at the door if there was any work for him to do. The woman laughed.

"You've got to be kidding," she said. "You're looking for work on a holiday? Sorry, but no one's here who can help you. The managers don't come in on holidays. Sorry." She turned away from him, getting back to the work she was doing.

Walker left, trying to figure out her response. Did that mean that no one would be hiring anyone? And why had she been so distant with him, not even looking him in the eyes? So far, he hadn't seen a single person who was interested in who he was, what his name was, what he was doing. Before he had arrived in the city, almost everyone had been interested in him as a person, yet here, people didn't seem to be at all interested in other people.

He tried several more restaurants, receiving the same negative response with each try. In two of them, he noticed a difference—the people he talked to were actually sympathetic, actually looked him in the eyes when they talked to him and wished him luck as he left. So there was some sympathy in the city, some compassion. One just had to look a bit harder to find it. He found a couple of stores open, but the people there gave him the same answer—they didn't need anyone at the moment.

By the end of the afternoon, he had asked at twenty places, at least, and hadn't found any work. At the last place he asked, the man at the cash register was one of the nice people who looked him in the eye and actually talked to him instead of at him, so Walker asked him what someone could do to find work in order to be able to eat in the city.

The man shrugged his shoulders.

"If you want to work just for food," he told Walker, "you're not gonna find much. People need workers for the long haul. Plus, you've got salaries to worry about, taxes, paychecks, identification numbers—there's a lot more involved in getting work than you'd think. But if you want a meal, then I'd suggest you head down to the food kitchen. It's about five blocks down this street. Opens up in about an hour, I think, and they can feed you there. May even be able to put you up for the night—depends on how many beds they have open."

"Thank you," Walker said. "Thank you very much."

"No problem," the man said. "Good luck to you—the city can eat you up if you're not careful. Lots of opportunities here, but lots of traps, too."

"Opportunities for what?" Walker asked.

"Why, pretty much anything you want to do or to see. Entertainment, sports, parks, movies—you name it. You can make it big if you work at it, make yourself a fortune here that you couldn't make anywhere else. You just have to pay attention and make sure that the price you pay isn't worth more than the reward is worth, if you know what I mean."

"I think I'm starting to understand that," Walker replied as he left. He was thinking again of Stephanie and her husband. As he walked down the street to find the food kitchen, he thought how easy it would be to get trapped into something that he didn't necessarily want—after all the rejections he had received while looking for work, he knew that he was ready to take the first job that came up, no matter what it was. And that thought frightened him—he didn't want to have to take just any job just for the sake of earning money.

All day long he had been regretting his decision to stay, and several times he almost started walking out of the city. Certainly, once he left things would be better again, and he would be able to find the peace around him and inside himself. But he realized that compared to how he had felt the day before, he was starting to feel much more at peace despite his surroundings. He was where he was, and it was his choice to feel bad about it or to accept his situation for exactly what it was. There had to be something to learn here, for so many people wouldn't live in such a place if it were all bad. He would hate to leave before he learned it. Right now, all he wanted was a chance to earn some money, yet he was being denied that opportunity by the people who wouldn't hire him.

He stopped in his tracks, dismayed at that thought, dismayed at how similar to Brian's thinking the thought had been. Would he start blaming the people who wouldn't help him, too? Could he somehow become as cynical as Brian had been, as hateful and as negative? He hadn't understood Brian's thinking at all, couldn't see how the man went through life blaming others for his own misfortunes, yet he had just had a thought similar to Brian's thoughts.

He had a choice, though—he could accept that others had denied him and let it be, or he could bear a grudge against those people and hold on to resentment and anger as Brian had. He knew that the fact that he had walked through the doors of those places looking for work in no way obligated the people to hire him, especially if they didn't have the means to do so. So why should he take it as a personal affront?

Life seemed to be growing more and more complicated.

He found the food kitchen, and found that the man was right—it would be opening soon. He decided to rest in a park he had seen nearby, and he went there and walked around, looking at the plants and the flowers.

So even in the city, people tried to remind themselves of what nature was like, giving themselves a small piece of what the world was like outside the city. They hadn't lost their love for nature, it seemed, just the access to it. It was rather sad, when he thought about it, but it was better than nothing, he was sure. This particular park even had a small pond with fish in it, and a small wooden bridge spanning a thin part of the pond. It was quite pretty, even if it was artificial. It was definitely better than nothing.

Even there in the park, though, the air smelled quite bad. he was glad it was a holiday after all, for he was sure that the place would have been very crowded if it had been a normal day when everyone had to go to work.

Soon he went back to the food kitchen, where there was now a short line outside the door. People were passing through the door rather quickly, and Walker joined the line, not quite sure what was going to happen. He was behind an older man who smelled very unpleasant, so he tried to keep his distance from him.

He noticed that none of the people in the line were looking around, none of them seemed to be in the least interested in their surroundings, in the people who were there with them. When several people joined the line behind Walker, he looked back at them and saw that they were looking down at the sidewalk, almost as if they were ashamed of where they were. Suddenly, Walker was no longer quite sure if he should be there—he had been told he could get a meal and a place to sleep here, but why were these people ashamed to be here? It didn't make any sense—didn't they have a right to ask for help when they were down? Walker knew that he wouldn't be there if someone had given him work, but no one had done so, so there he was. He didn't see that it was anything to be ashamed of—he had tried his best, but he had found nothing.

He was soon inside a large room that had many tables set out in three long lines, and the line of people that he was in moved past a series of small tables. He did what the man ahead of him did—he picked up a tray and a napkin and a plastic knife and fork and spoon, and he took a plate of hot food when it was handed to him by a young man with a long beard who didn't even look at him, but watched the food with a great deal of concentration, making sure that everyone got the same amount. Then a young girl put some salad on his plate, next to the hot food, and he smiled and thanked her. She smiled back and said, "You're welcome." A woman who looked very much like the girl—possibly her mother, Walker thought—put a piece of bread and an apple on the plate, and he thanked her also. She, too, smiled and said, "You're welcome."

Walker couldn't believe that most of the people in line weren't thanking the people who were serving them, but when he thought about Brian, he realized that he probably wouldn't have thanked anyone, either.

He sat down at one of the tables, across from a young man who was already half-done with his food. Walker ate a few bites, then said, "It's pretty good food, isn't it?"

The man glared at him, and Walker wondered what mistake he had made. The man grunted something, then went back to eating.

"Do you come here every day?" Walker asked, and the man glared once more.

"You've got your food," the man said rudely. "Shut up and eat."

Walker shut up, wishing that he had chosen a different seat. He was thankful for the food, but he already had decided that he would leave the next day, no matter what. He was tired of the city, and he knew that whatever lay before him on the road had to be better than the way things were there.

The man soon finished and left, without even a glance at Walker. A few moments after he left, another man came and sat down in the same seat. This man was different, though—he was clean and dressed well, and he looked Walker straight in the eye and smiled. He also didn't have any food.

"You're new here," the man said in a friendly voice. "I don't think I've seen you here before."

"No," Walker replied. "I haven't been here before. I just arrived in the city yesterday. I tried to find work today, but there was nothing."

"Well, you're welcome here. What kind of work were you looking for? Long-term? Short-term?"

"I don't want to stay in the city long," Walker said. "I don't like it here."

"I can understand that," the man said with a laugh. "The city isn't for everyone. We get a lot of disillusioned people here, people who came here to make their way in the world, but who leave with all their dreams shattered. It's a shame that so many people think that the city can solve all their problems for them, that the city can help them—the fact is that they've got to help themselves. The city couldn't care less what or who they are, or what they need. The city's completely impartial. What brought you here in the first place?"

"I was traveling," Walker said. "The city was in my way."

The man laughed. "That's a nice way to put it, Mr.—"

"Walker. And you are?"

"John. John Davis. It's nice to meet you, Mr. Walker."

"Just Walker," Walker said with a shrug.

"Okay, just Walker. In any case, I may be able to help you out. We try to keep an eye out for people who are willing to help themselves out—most of the people who come here, unfortunately, are either unwilling or unable. But I know a man who's looking for some help for a few days. He'll pay cash for ten days' work, and if you're willing, you can even sleep in his garage while you're working for him. It's nothing illegal, don't worry about that. It's just that he can often use some help, and he likes to help people to get back on their feet. He'll work you pretty hard, but I think you'd be able to handle it. Are you interested?"

Walker thought a few moments. "Is it here in the middle of the city?"

John shook his head. "No, it's not. He lives in a nice neighborhood on the outskirts of town. I think you'd like it there."

"When would I start?"

"I'll give him a call right now, if you'd like. You may be able to start tomorrow morning."

"That would be very nice," Walker said. "Thank you very much."

"It's my pleasure. I'll go call him now, and I'll be right back."

John left, and Walker watched him go. Things had fallen into place again, and Walker's plans had changed very quickly once more.

In five minutes, John came back and told him that everything was set—Walker would start work the next morning, and he could sleep there in the shelter for the night.

Walker was curious. "Why do you do this for me?" he asked John. "Most of the people I met today wouldn't even talk to me, but you've even found me work. I don't understand."

John thought a few seconds. "You can't be too hard on those other people," he said. "They've got a lot of worries of their own, trying to keep their businesses afloat and their heads above water. They're trying to make a living and feed their families. They don't see how helping someone else can help them. They don't realize that you're only truly prosperous in this world when you're sharing what you have, your abilities and your love. They don't realize that life isn't about getting and spending money, but about what you do when you've made it—what you do with it, how you use it. A great poet once wrote, 'Getting and spending, they lay waste their powers,' which means that because they focus so much on money, they don't see the things they can do that don't involve money.

"All of us who work here are volunteers. Except for the director, and she earns very little, from what I understand. But we volunteer our time mostly because we know what it's like to be without hope, without opportunities, not to know anyone who can point us in the right direction. Many of these people don't want our help—they want the free meal, and that's it. But many others could use a hand, a suggestion, a temporary job that will help them get back into life, to stand on their own power once more. It's very gratifying, to tell you the truth."

Walker looked around the room at the many people who were eating, almost all of whom were dressed poorly, and almost none of whom showed any enthusiasm or friendliness.

"Who are these people?" Walker asked. "How did they come to be like this?"

John looked around. "I couldn't tell you. We ask no questions here—if someone wants a meal, we feed them. If they need a place to sleep, we let them sleep here until it's full. I've found that most of them have gone through rough times—they've lost jobs or lost savings in bad investments, and have ended up losing pretty much everything. For the most part, these are the people who let those bad times or drugs or alcohol get the best of them. They haven't made any effort to fight back, to reclaim what they had before. Most of them have lost any faith they might have had, and they haven't been trusting enough to try to get it back."

"Faith in God?"

"Faith in God, faith in other people, faith in the government, faith in life. They see themselves as victims, and they don't see any way past the victimization. Often, people like you come through here, people who don't really seem to be down for good, but who have experienced temporary setbacks. How did you come to be here, if you don't mind my asking?"

"A man told me about the place, and I came to see it. I asked him for work, but he didn't have any."

"But what led you here? How did you reach a point that you came to a place like this?"

"My money's running out, I guess. The city's very expensive, and I didn't have much to begin with. I just wanted to get a night's sleep before I started traveling again."

"So you were going to be leaving tomorrow?"

"Yes, but not any more."

John smiled. "Well, I'm glad I found you to give you the job. Old man Richards just called about an hour before I talked to you, saying he needed someone, and there you were—the perfect person for him. I'm glad things worked out the way that they did."

Walker thought for a few moments. "Things always seem to work out perfectly for me. Either I'm a very lucky person, or something is different about me."

"What do you mean?"

Walker shrugged. "I don't know. It's very odd."

"Well, of course we're all different—we're all unique individuals. And you certainly did stand out in the crowd here."

"I guess that's true."

John stood to go. "I have to get to work now, though. When you're through eating, just head through that door over there and you'll be shown where to sleep. There's a small breakfast in the morning—just bread and jam and coffee—but find me after breakfast and I'll drive you over to where old man Richards lives."

He walked away, leaving Walker sitting alone at the table. Walker felt much better after his meal, and his mind turned towards his recent thoughts. There seemed to be pieces missing from the puzzles of his thoughts, and he had no idea how to put them together without the other pieces. Everything seemed somehow incomplete, and he wasn't sure why.

Chapter 24

Early the next morning, John drove him twenty minutes through the city to an area that was almost all houses and few stores, with no tall buildings at all. It was Walker's first time in a car, and he felt very constricted, very limited being locked inside a small vehicle, even though he was impressed with its power and speed. The holiday had passed and the city was full of people, traffic, and noise. But as they made their way out of the center and into the neighborhood where Mr. Richards lived, Walker saw the traffic diminish and the noise lessen—things weren't nearly as bad there as they were in the center.

John pulled up to a small house on a corner, and he and Walker got out of the car. They were met there by an older man who walked with a lively step and had the bright gleam of a love for life in his eyes.

"Good morning, John," old man Richards said enthusiastically, "and good morning to you, too, Walker. It's very nice to meet you. I'm Timothy." He looked Walker up and down as he shook his hand, nodding approvingly. Timothy himself was a robust man, though quite thin—he seemed to look weaker than he was. He was just as tall as Walker, and his face was serious and trustworthy. There was a twinkle in his green eyes, and his grey hair framed his face in a dignified manner. Nothing about him seemed out of place, nothing seemed not to fit. He wore a green plaid shirt and loose blue jeans, and seemed to be someone who dressed for comfort rather than what others might think about him. "Very good choice, John. Here's a man who can do a good day's work and who can be trusted. You're a fine judge of character, no doubt about that."

John smiled. "Thank you, Mr. Richards," he said.

"How many times have I asked you to knock off that 'Mr. Richards' crap?" Richards asked. "The name my mother gave me is Timothy, and I'd thank you to use it."

"As you wish, Timothy," John said, laughing.

"That goes for you, too, Walker. My father was a good-for-nothing gambler who gambled away everything we had, and I'm not at all proud to be addressed by the name he passed on to me. Call me Tim or Timothy, please."

Walker nodded. "I understand," he said.

"I'd like to stay, Tim," John said, "but I have to get to work myself. I'll leave you two to take care of whatever arrangements you need to make. Good luck, Tim. And Walker, good luck to you, too. I wish you all the best."

"Thank you, John," Walker said. "Thank you for everything."

"You're very welcome. God bless."

Walker and Tim watched John drive away, then Tim slapped Walker on the shoulder.

"We've got some work ahead of us, son," he said. "Let me show you where you'll be sleeping and show you what kind of work we'll be doing." He started walking up the driveway towards the garage, and Walker followed him.

First he showed Walker the garage, and the corner in the back that had been set up with a bed and a small chest of drawers.

"This is where you'll sleep," he told Walker. "I know it's not much, but it's quite a bit better than the shelter, I imagine. It's a good bed—used to sleep on it myself, before I got a new one. You can use the bathroom inside. I'll show it to you when we get there. Feel free to make yourself at home out here—fix things up as you'd like."

He entered the house then through a side door, and he and Walker were standing in a small dining room.

"This is the house," he told Walker. "This is the kitchen and dining room, and over there is the living room. Upstairs, we have two bedrooms and the main bathroom—the one you'll be using is right over here." He walked over to a door and opened it. "You've got your own shower in here, so you're all set. But the most important part of the house is where we'll be working, down in the basement.

He flipped a switch and opened another door, and Walker saw a stairway leading downstairs. Timothy started down the stairs, and Walker followed him. At the bottom, they entered a huge room that looked like a library, full of empty shelf after empty shelf, with some of the most ornate woodwork that Walker had ever seen.

"This here's Terry's room," Timothy said proudly. "Terry was my wife for many, many years until she passed on two years ago. I had been working on this room for years, getting it done little by little, and before she died, she made me promise that I would finish it before I died."

"Why?"

"Don't rightly know, to tell you the truth," he said. "I suppose to keep me busy, to keep me out of trouble. But it doesn't matter why. The thing that matters is that I promised her that I would finish it, and finish it I shall." He walked into the room, running his hand over a mahogany desk and an oak dresser, beautiful pieces of furniture that could have been called works of art, in Walker's opinion. "I made all of these pieces myself, as time went on, but time's taken its toll—I'm not as young as I used to be, and my eyes and hands aren't as sure as they used to be. They work fine, but I can't depend on them like I used to. And I have only one section of that main bookcase to finish, and the room will be done. Just in time, too, if this feeling that I have inside is at all right."

"What do you mean?" Walker asked.

Timothy sat down on the chair that was the match for the desk—a beautiful mahogany piece that was ornately carved and shined to an exquisite finish.

"You see, Walker, my doctor told me about a year ago that I had only six months left, tops. Well, I lived past that six months, but I've been feeling that I'm living on borrowed time ever since. My heart's not what it used to be, and I've already had one stroke. The next one could kill me, if there is a next one, or worse, leave me lying in a bed, not able to get up and finish this off. I have to finish it, and I'm pretty sure the time is now. I figure that with you and me working for two weeks, we'll have this baby done with no problem. I want to take my time and do it right, but I don't have a whole lot of time to take. Do you understand?"

"Do you mean that you're dying?"

"Absolutely. This time next year, I won't be around to enjoy this room. Heck, this time next week I may not even be here, for that matter. You never know. But I don't want to take my leave until I fulfill my promise. I know it sounds kind of silly, like some old man's ridiculous quest, especially when the woman he made the promise to is dead and buried. But I know in my heart that this needs to be done. I won't be free to leave until I finish this, and to tell you the truth, I'm getting pretty antsy to see Terry again. I miss her quite a bit, and I'm looking forward to seeing her real soon."

"So we only have to make the last part of the bookcase?" Walker asked. "That doesn't look like it will take two weeks."

"It will if you've never done any carpentry before, now won't it? And I'd be willing to bet that you haven't done any, have you?" Walker shook his head. "There now, you see? This whole room is perfect because I've always taken the time to do things perfectly. This whole room was meant as a gift to Terry, and she used it a lot before she up and left, but now I've got to finish it so that I can join her. But I've got to finish it right—this last section has to be perfect, too, and then we have quite a bit of finishing to do. You know, polishing and such. Then the room will be done."

He clapped his hands suddenly. "But come on—from what I know, they didn't give you much of a breakfast at the shelter, and I've never known anyone to do any real learning on an empty stomach. Let's go see if we can get Lisa to make us some breakfast."

"Lisa?"

"My daughter. We couldn't have any children of our own, so some thirty years ago, Terry and I adopted a little girl named Lisa. The best thing that ever happened to us, other than each other. She's been home the last few weeks. She's a schoolteacher, and she has the summer off and comes home to take care of me every year. This summer's different, though—I think she feels that it's my last summer, too."

Timothy went up the stairs, back into the kitchen, then called Lisa's name up the other stairs. In a few moments, Walker heard a door open, then shut, then he heard footsteps coming down the stairs. Timothy gave her a hug as she reached the bottom of the stairs, then took her hand and walked over to Walker and introduced the two.

"This is my daughter, Lisa," he told Walker, "and this is Walker. He'll be helping me out with the last little bit of the library downstairs. I believe we should be finished in a couple of weeks."

Lisa smiled at Walker and said hello, but the smile was a polite one, not a happy one. He had seen a shadow pass over her when Timothy had said that they would finish the library, and Walker was intrigued. Her eyes were beautiful and bright and expressive, and he saw in her a nice, caring, loving woman, much as Katherine had been, much as Marie had been. But he also saw something else, some sort of emptiness, something missing. It was something that struck him as incredibly sad, for he sensed that she wasn't who she could be because of what was missing, and he didn't know what it was.

"Your father says that you're a teacher," Walker said, and she nodded.

"Yes. I teach ten-year-olds. They make for a rather challenging group." Her voice was soft and firm, but somehow unsure, somehow lacking in confidence.

"I was wondering, dear," Timothy said to her, "if you're going to be making breakfast, could you make something for Walker also, please?"

"I'll be glad to," Lisa said, though with little enthusiasm.

Timothy turned to Walker. "Lisa's such a help to me these days—I don't know what I'd do without her here. I'd probably have to work myself to death."

"Which you're doing anyway," she said sweetly, though Walker sensed that the sweetness was false. "I came here so you can rest, yet you're working now more than ever. Just on other things."

"Lisa has picked up on chiding me where her mother left off two years ago," Timothy said with a smile. "She worries far too much about me."

Lisa walked past him into the kitchen. "I'll have breakfast ready in twenty minutes," she said brusquely.

Timothy smiled after her, a great deal of love and a great deal of sadness on his face and in his eyes. He motioned for Walker to follow him, and they went out into the garage.

"I'll warn you about Lisa, he said when they were outside. "Don't expect her to be too friendly to you. I've got a feeling that she'll see you as someone here to take me away."

"Me?" Walker asked, incredulous. "What do you mean?"

"It's rather simple, really. I know and she knows that once this library is finished, I'm going to die."

"How can you know that?" Walker asked. "You're not going to kill yourself, are you?"

"No, no—it's not that at all. I'm an old man, Walker, and I'm on my way out. Lisa knows that, and she knows that I know it. She wants me to prolong my life as long as I can, by sitting around and doing nothing and somehow getting healthier without getting any exercise. But it doesn't work that way. I have to live my life, right up to the end. I don't want to be a passive bystander, watching other people live while I vegetate and grow old. If my life ends tomorrow, then so be it. If it ends in a year, then so be that. No matter when it ends, I want to be doing what I love to do up to the end."

"That makes a lot of sense."

"Yes, when you can see it objectively. But Lisa has had a lot of problems with trust, ever since her parents died. As a child, she saw it as them abandoning her, and she was left with nothing and nobody. Even after we adopted her, she never had many friends because she was afraid they'd leave her alone, just as her parents did. We were all she had, and when Terry died last year, it was a terrible blow to her—she had been abandoned again. She's never been able to get it into her head that people leave for many reasons, and most of those reasons have nothing to do with leaving someone behind. But it's something that's been with her since she was a child, and it started with her parents dying when she was four. She's never been able to get over it, really.

"Now it's worse, because I'm the last person she has, and I'm the only person she truly trusts. And I'll be leaving soon. It's such a shame, because at heart, she's a happy, loving, intelligent woman, and this part of her holds her back from being what she's meant to be. She's using her gifts to teach children, but I have no idea how effective she is at it, how much of herself she's able to put into it."

"It's very sad when people don't reach their potential," Walker said.

"It sure is," Timothy replied. "A person can have all the God-given gifts and talents possible, but if they don't use them, they're worth nothing, now aren't they?"

"No, they're not," Walker agreed.

Lisa yelled from inside that breakfast was ready, so they entered and ate. After breakfast, Timothy took Walker outside to show him the tools that he would be using, the saws and the planer and the sanders and the hammers and nails and glue and everything else. By the time the afternoon came and Walker had learned the purposes of all the tools, he was ready to make his first project—a bookcase that was much smaller than the ones downstairs, out of a cheaper kind of wood.

Walker understood well what Timothy taught him, and he was sure that he would be able to do the job very easily, as long as he went through the steps properly. He soon saw, however, that it was very easy to make small mistakes that would ruin the project as a whole. By the time he was finished with the bookcase later that evening, he knew that the finished product was full of minute errors, mistakes that caused instability in the bookcase's structure and unattractive flaws in the looks of the piece.

Timothy smiled as he examined the work. "Not bad for a first shot," he said. "In fact, it's quite good. But quite good only as a first try. You've already shown me where all the mistakes are, but can you tell me how you'll avoid making those same errors when you make you next one?"

Walker was perplexed—the errors seemed to have happened almost on their own. A slip of the wood on the planer, too short a cut here, and they added up very quickly. He had been very careful throughout the whole process, wanting to do the best job he possibly could, yet he had still made so many mistakes. Finally, he saw the point Timothy was trying to make.

"Practice," he said softly.

"Practice," Timothy repeated. "There's nothing like it if you want to improve your skills at something. And you've already got some pretty good skills in carpentry—you're a quick learner, just like at the bakery and the farm. You could do some great work if you put your mind to it."

"Thank you," Walker said.

"No thanks necessary," Timothy replied. "I call them as I see them, and that's how I see this. But speaking of calling them, I think it's time we call it an evening, don't you? Let's go have some dinner."

Lisa had prepared dinner, and she ate with them. She wasn't at all talkative, and Walker was too tired to talk much himself. Besides, so much about carpentry was going through his mind that he wouldn't have been able to focus on a conversation. He did offer to help Lisa with the dishes after the meal, but she told him no with a small smile and a shake of her head.

The second day went much as the first had, though Walker's second attempt at a bookcase had far fewer mistakes than the first had. On the third day, Timothy had him make a piece on the lathe, a simple piece that took three tries and three hours to make, and which turned out far from perfect.

"Remember," Timothy told him, "perfectionism is usually a curse, and people drive each other crazy if they always expect everyone to do things perfectly. Perfection is not inherently a human trait. But as a tradesman— a carpenter, a mechanic, a plumber, a smith—you're bound by duty to make your work as close to perfect as possible. You've seen the work downstairs—it's not at all perfect, but it sure would take someone an awfully long time to find any of the flaws there."

At the end of the third day, Lisa let him help her with the dishes, after his third offer in three nights. When they finished, she thanked him and went upstairs, while he went outside to read.

Twenty minutes after he went out, there was a knock on the garage door, and he went to open it. He was surprised to find Lisa there, and she looked just as surprised to see him at the door.

"Hello," Walker said, and went back to his bed, sitting down on it.

"I don't mean to bother you," she said, walking over near the bed and sitting down on the armchair that was there. "I just wanted to thank you again for helping me with the dishes. It was very sweet of you."

"But you already thanked me," Walker said, confused. "Besides, you make all the meals that I eat. The least I can do is help clean up afterwards."

"Not everyone sees it that way, but it's nice that you do." She sat there for several long moments, saying nothing, and Walker didn't know what to say, or if he was expected to say anything.

"You know," Lisa finally said, "You're a very strange person."

"Thank you," Walker said with a laugh.

"No, I didn't mean it that way. I meant that you're very polite, very intelligent, you're a hard worker, yet you were at the shelter. You were at a homeless shelter. One usually doesn't picture someone like you at a place like that."

Walker shrugged. "I was hungry, and someone told me I could get a meal there. I saw no reason not to go."

"Well, some people see a handout like that as a negative thing. It's nice to see that you don't."

Walker wanted to reply, but he couldn't think of anything that sounded right as a reply to that statement.

"Where are you from, anyway?" Lisa asked.

Walker thought—Gustav's village, or the entire story? He liked Lisa, and he was in no hurry, so he told her the entire story.

When he finished, Lisa's eyes were wide with disbelief. "So you have no family?" she asked, aghast. "No one to be there for you when you need them? I thought I had it bad—my parents died when I was four, but at least I've always had Timothy and Terry since then. They've been wonderful to me. I don't know how I would feel if I were in your position."

Walker shrugged. "That's the way things are, so there's nothing I can do to change them. I just try to live today, without worrying about what might have happened in the past. I'm sure that I'll know what I need to know when the time is right. There has to be a purpose to my life."

"And what might that purpose be?" she asked, a bit of a challenging note creeping into her voice.

"I don't know. I believe it has something to do with learning all I can about all I can. But beyond that, I couldn't tell you. I'm still searching for the other pieces of the puzzles."

"It's nice to see someone who trusts life so sincerely and so. . . simply. I don't have a whole lot of trust left in me."

"What do you mean?"

"When my parents died, I lost just about all my trust in life. They were everything I had, and then they were just—gone."

"But then you had Timothy and Terry, didn't you? And this nice place to live? Besides, you can't lose something like the ability to trust. A friend of mine once told me that something like that we can hide behind walls inside ourselves so that we don't have to use it any more. It's easier to go through life without it, some people think. But it's still there, just waiting to be used."

"That's easy enough to say," Lisa countered, "but I've tried. For years. I just can't trust any more."

"But it's still inside you," Walker said. "Is it hard because you can't, or because you won't?"

Lisa shook her head. "I don't know for sure. I think about that question a lot, to be honest. I just don't have any answers."

She stood abruptly. "It was nice talking to you, Walker. Thanks so much for your time. And your story—it's just amazing. I hope you find what you're looking for."

"Thank you," Walker said as she walked away. "Have a good night."

Chapter 25

The next morning at breakfast, Lisa treated him the same way she had treated him all the other mornings—politely, but from a distance. Except for one thing that Walker wasn't quite sure of: he thought he saw her looking at him a little more often out of the corner of her eyes.

Walker found that time went very quickly at Timothy's house, and he enjoyed himself very much there. The days of work were interesting and intense, and Walker was learning more about woodworking than he ever imagined there was to learn. Timothy had him make piece after piece until he got them right, working with each of the tools he would use to work on the library bookshelf. His days with Timothy were fulfilling, and he spent hours talking with him about the wood and the art of carpentry.

By the end of the first week Timothy had him make another bookcase, just like the first one. Walker went about it as confidently as he had before, but with much more skill, with practice behind him. This time he worked more quickly and easily, and an almost-perfect bookcase was the end product.

Timothy looked at it with a great deal of satisfaction. "Can't see a single flaw," he said proudly. "I know they have to be there, and I'm sure I could find 'em if I looked hard, but I sure can't see any."

That evening after dinner, Lisa asked him if he'd like to take a walk around the neighborhood. Walker had been surprised to find it quite peaceful where they lived, even though they were still in the city. He was still uncomfortable with the lack of trees and grass and flowers, for the barrenness made everything seem stark and lifeless. He knew that outside of the city, there were many beautiful places to be seen, many wonderful places where he could sleep next to a stream under the stars, rather than in a garage or a shelter or a filthy hotel.

"You know, Walker," Lisa said as they walked, "I have a lot to thank you for."

"What do you mean?"

"Do you remember our conversation the other night? The first night we talked? Well, you gave me a lot during that conversation, and I appreciate it."

"What did I give you?"

"Perspective. A dose of reality, I guess. Here I've been focusing so much on all that I've lost during life that I haven't been able to appreciate all that I have. No, I didn't have parents or grandparents when I was young, but I have had a family and a home. Timothy and Terry have taken great care of me. They've pushed me when I needed to be pushed, and they've loved me when I've needed to be loved. And I haven't ever allowed myself to accept them fully into my heart; I haven't allowed myself to trust them. And I even blamed Terry for leaving me—she died, for goodness' sake—she had no control over that.

"And here you are, with much less than I've ever had, with no support from anyone else, living today, getting all you can out of life just because you love to live. I've never lived life with love, you know. I've always feared life. I've always feared people, and I've always feared God. But you've opened my eyes. I don't know how you did it—I guess just by being the completely honest person you are. You're a great example, Walker."

"So you don't fear people any more?" Walker asked. "You don't fear being left alone?"

She looked down at the ground. "Well, I'm sure that will take some time to completely work its way out of me. But at least I have a start now. You're so much different than all the others who have worked for Timothy."

"All the others?"

"Yes, all the others who have worked on the basement. Timothy's a brilliant man, you know—he did promise Terry that he would finish that library in the basement, but did he tell you why she made him promise?"

"No."

"Because of all the wonderful work he was doing with people. You've just had an intensive, week-long crash course in carpentry. In another week, you'll have even more skill. When you finish your section of the library, you'll have the beginning of a trade, and you'll easily be able to find work as an apprentice somewhere. You're about the tenth person from the shelter who's worked on that library. Timothy uses money from his own pocket to pay for the materials and to pay you, but he does so gladly. He feels like he's contributing something to the world, to society, by teaching people a trade instead of giving them a handout."

"Wow," Walker said. "That's amazing."

"No," Lisa said, "that's generosity. That's love."

Three days later, Walker had finished half of the pieces he would need for the bookcase. They were all works of art, even in their unfinished state. There wasn't a flaw to be seen in any of them—he put extra effort into each stage of making each piece for Timothy's sake, for he felt that a man who had been giving as much during his life as Timothy had deserved to be given something back. Walker was sure that the best thing he could give was his effort. When they finished that day, Timothy seemed more tired than he normally did, and instead of going up to the dining room for a snack, as they usually did, they stayed in the basement. Walker went up and got the snacks and brought them back down.

"Take a good look at it, Walker," Timothy said, gazing at the empty shelves that lined the walls of the basement. "A beautiful library with no books. My life's work. A beautiful desk that nobody uses to work or write on. But all of it was taking steps in a very different direction, you know."

"Yes, I do," Walker replied. "Lisa told me about all of the people you've helped."

"Helped? I don't know about that. Pushed along, maybe. They were all good men and women, and I felt it was my duty to give back to this world that's given so much to me. So instead of giving them a fish, I taught them to earn the money to go to the market and buy all the fish they need. It's been very gratifying, Walker, I'll tell you. Lisa looks at it and sees the ten people I've helped, but I can't tell you what it feels like inside to have helped. There's no substitute for the feeling I've gotten, knowing that I was helping others and contributing in my own small way to the world. I've helped to shape people into the drawers or shelves they were meant to be."

"What do you mean?"

"Look at it this way—before any of this wood became parts of the shelves or the desk or the chair, all of it was in pieces—just pieces of wood. But the wood was full of potential. It could be shaped into anything that a carpenter wanted it to be shaped into, turning it into a beautiful finished product. Now, not all carpenters are equal in skill—you know that. If a piece of wood is shaped by a poor carpenter, the finished product will be lacking somehow, in some way. But if that wood is shaped by a master carpenter, then that piece will fit into this world precisely as it's supposed to fit, whether it be a desktop or a cabinet shelf or a doorstop. And the way that I work wood is the way I try to work with people—with love and attention and caring—so that the wood and the people can reach their potential. And if someone lets you teach them, and is open to what you have to teach, then how can you go wrong?"

Walker and Timothy sat quietly for a very long time. "Why do so many people make it so hard for anyone to help them or to love them?" Walker asked finally.

Timothy chuckled. "Ah, Walker—if I could explain all of humanity's foibles, I'd be a rich man indeed, at least as far as money goes. I believe people are like that because of fear. They fear being loved because they fear that if they're loved, they'll have to love back. And if they love back, they may get hurt. And many people aren't ready to put their hearts on the line like that. Mostly because they don't have anything to fall back on. It's quite a shame, really, because they don't hurt themselves by trying to avoid getting hurt. But we have to be willing to die many times if we're ever going to get on with this business of living."

"What do you mean, 'willing to die'?" asked Walker, very confused by the words.

"That, my friend, is something that you have to learn all by yourself. We die many deaths all through our lives, if we allow ourselves to move on. If we're unwilling to move on, of course, we die no deaths, and we never remake who we are, never move on to the next level. Some people call it being born again, and others call it letting a part of you die. Either way, it's leaving something behind as we move on with life."

"Someone once told me that before I would be ready to stop my journey and turn around and search for something in my past, I would have to be willing to give up who I am and become something else."

"It sounds like that someone was very wise. But remember, just because you become something else doesn't mean that you leave everything behind. If you become a husband, you leave behind your focus on yourself and open up a focus on others, but you still bring with you all the traits that you've developed over the years. We all have many beautiful qualities, and many people feel that if they change their lives, they'll have to leave behind all that's beautiful, all that's fun, all that they love. But nothing could be further from the truth—they leave behind all that has been holding them back and take those things that help them move on. What's holding you back, Walker?"

Walker shook his head slowly. "I don't know," he said. "I don't feel a pull from behind—I feel a barrier up ahead, and I don't know what it is."

"You will," Timothy replied. "One day, you will."

Three days later the bookcase was done, and Walker gazed at it with pride. His mind, though, was a whirlwind of activity, as it had been for a very long time. He felt the pull of the road once more, a pull he had been feeling for several days. He had told Timothy and Lisa earlier that day that he would be leaving when he was done with the work, and they both seemed sad that he was leaving. At dinner that night, there was little talk, and Walker went to sleep with a heavy heart.

The next morning when he woke up, he got dressed and started out, only to find Lisa sitting outside the garage waiting for him.

He smiled and said good morning, feeling more awkward than he ever had—for the second time, he was considering the possibility that leaving was the wrong thing to do, that there was a more important pull than the pull of the road. He wasn't sure, though, which pull to be true to, and he felt that he had to be on the road. He just didn't know why.

Lisa smiled back. "I just wanted to say good-bye," she said. "And thank you."

"No," Walker said, "I thank you."

"You know, if this had happened before, if someone would have left like this, I would have been very angry and resentful. I would have taken it personally, and I would have felt that one more person was abandoning me. But I know you have to leave, and there's nothing I can do about it, and that you're not abandoning me, but following your call, whatever that may be."

Walker was perplexed—he hadn't realized that Lisa's feelings ran so deep. Was this what was trying to hold him back, this feeling? "I'm glad to hear you say that," he said, not sure of what else to say. He suddenly remembered something, and he reached into his pack, way at the bottom, and pulled out a stone.

"This is for you," he said, handing it to Lisa. "A very wise man told me that it holds the story of the ages."

They stood silently for what seemed to Walker to be a very long time, though he knew he could have measured that time in seconds.

"Take care of yourself, Walker," Lisa said finally, and she stepped close to him and kissed him on the cheek. Then she turned and went into the house, and Walker knew it was time to go. He had already taken his leave of Timothy the night before, as Timothy said he didn't believe in saying good-bye and didn't want to see him off in the morning. They would see each other again, he said.

He started out slowly. He went in the direction that he had been going in before, except this time he had decided that he would take the train as far as he could in order to get out of the city quickly. Then he would walk.

He went to the train station just half an hour's walk from Timothy's house, and within two hours he was far out of the city, back in the country. He got out at a station in a small town whose name seemed very familiar to him, though he couldn't place it. The town itself reminded him of Gustav's village, though it was a bit larger and livelier. He started walking after he stopped for a cup of coffee and a roll at a bakery, and as he began traveling again and felt the familiar touch of the road beneath his feet once again, he felt the stress of the previous weeks start to fly from him. He felt the weight lifting from his heart as he went along.

Hours later, he felt much better—felt almost as he had so long before when he was alone with the road, before he had so many thoughts flying through his head and so many things to think of. He could see that harvest season was approaching, and he knew that he should be able to find work so that he wouldn't have to spend all of the money that Timothy had paid him.

The day was warm and peaceful, and he loved the sound of the birds singing freely once more and the sound of the breeze in his ears and the feel of the warm sun on his cheek. He loved the animals that played and worked all about him, and he even saw turtles, the like of which he hadn't seen since the day he had started out so long ago, walking slowly across the road. Chipmunks and squirrels scurried around here and there, their cheeks sometimes full of whatever food they were hiding away.

He lay down to sleep that night next to a stream, under the stars, and he was sure that when he woke up the next morning, the small bit of heaviness that lay on his heart, the feeling that he had some unfinished business, would be gone, wiped out by the sleep.

Chapter 26

Walker awoke in the middle of the night, somehow expecting someone to be there with him. There was nothing, though—nobody. The night was as dark as he had ever seen a night, and there was a strong chill in the air. Walker somehow had the feeling that something was going to change very quickly, and that there was nothing he could do about it. He tried to go back to sleep, but he couldn't; he ended up lying awake for several hours until the sun came up. As it began to light the world, he couldn't imagine a more peaceful, more beautiful scene to wake up to than that of the valley that lay before him.

But something wasn't right.

He started to walk, looking for the wonder he had always felt, but he began to feel that he was pushing something, that he wasn't admitting to himself something that he should admit, and his steps were slow and heavy. His confusion grew as he walked—what was holding him back?

Two hours later, he stopped in his tracks in amazement. There before him was a spot he recognized, a spot that he had seen before—the very spot where he had stepped out onto the road. He approached it slowly, carefully, unsurely. A very faint trail led into the bushes, and those bushes were so thick that he couldn't see what lay beyond them.

Was this what I've been looking for? he asked himself. If he followed this trail, he was sure, he might be able to unlock some secrets of his past, find out who he was, where he came from, how he had come to be on the road. Were there people somewhere who loved him, who missed him, who would stand by him when he needed them? Did he even have a past?

Turner had told him that there would come a time when he was ready to turn around, to seek out something from his past.

But what if the trail led nowhere? What if it led into the bushes, and past the bushes, he would find nothing but more bushes?

He sat down on the trail and closed his eyes, trying to calm the thoughts that were confusing him. He listened closely to his own breathing, trying to clear his mind of the many images and ideas that were running around in there. Soon he felt his body relaxing and his mind quieting, and peace started to emanate from the center of who he was. He felt a sense of love for that peace, and for his self.

And in the quiet and stillness, he suddenly knew what was right. He knew that while he might find out something interesting down the trail from which he might have come so long ago, anything he found there belonged to who he had been, not who he was now. And there was no use in spending his future days trying to recreate what might have been in his past.

He stood, and for the first time he turned his face towards where he had just come from. He stood there for several long moments, and then with one single step began the journey back towards where he thought he should be going. Turner had been right—there was a time to seek something from the past. And though he had no idea how Lisa might react to his return, he knew that he never would find out unless he actually went back.

www.ingramcontent.com/pod-product-compliance
Lightning Source LLC
Chambersburg PA
CBHW052134170626
46812CB00004B/1409